THE EMPEROR'S BARBER

About the Author

Graham Wade, writer and musician, living on the East Yorkshire coast, studied English at Cambridge University, is a Fellow of Trinity College of Music, London, and was elected a Fellow of the Royal Society of Arts in 1982. He has published over thirty books among them his critically acclaimed biographical studies of the great Spanish composer. Joaquín Rodrigo, and of the guitarists, Andrés Segovia and Julian Bream, as well as works on musical history, and several slim volumes of poems.

In 2002 he was awarded the Schotts Gold Medal for his contribution to Rodrigo studies and in 2010 won the David St John Thomas Prize for his first novel *The Fibonacci Confessions*. Graham Wade has written for many newspapers and periodicals including *The Times*, *The Independent*, and *The Guardian* and is an Advisory Editor and contributor to both the British and American *New Grove Dictionary of Music and Musicians*. In 1999 he was appointed General Editor for a series of paperbacks for the leading American music publisher, Mel Bay Inc., of Missouri.

The Emperor's Barber presents the memoirs of Kutaissov, the Turkish barber who became a trusted adviser to Emperor Paul I of Russia. As Kutaissov relates his intimate memoirs the many facets of his nature are revealed, as well as the development of a perilous relationship with a tsar usually considered as either mentally unstable or (at his worst) totally deranged.

The Emperor's Barber

GRAHAM WADE

The Choir Press

THE EMPEROR'S BARBER

Published in 2017
by THE CHOIR PRESS
132 Bristol Road, Gloucester GL1 5SR

ISBN   978-1-911589-13-6

Cover images by kind permission of
The State Hermitage Museum, St. Petersburg
Photograph © The State Hermitage Museum.
Photo by Natalia Antonova, Inna Regentova

Cover design by Chandler Design Associates Ltd

Typeset in 11 on 14pt Bembo
by Abstract Graphics

for Sue

Contents

...I will thrive some way: blackbirds fatten best in hard weather; why not I in these dog-days?

ACT I, SCENE I, *The Duchess of Malfi*,
JOHN WEBSTER

Historical Note

The strange career of Ivan Kutaissov could perhaps only have been possible in Russia. In the 18TH century the Tsar's court was richly cosmopolitan with various nationalities prominent in the public life of the country.

Kutaissov came originally from Turkey but rose to become the *confidant* of Emperor Paul I. His ostensible role was to act as Paul's valet, barber, fixer, gentleman of the bedchamber, and master of the robes.

In the history books he appears as a mysterious figure, deeply corrupt, somewhat sinister, and on an upward social trajectory which ultimately resulted in promotion to the rank of Count.

That Paul I's character was a combination of eccentricity and insanity may have aided Kutaissov's relationship with the emperor. Kutaissov was not interested in meddling in politics or policies, and this assisted his progress. He seemed more capable of making friends than enemies, though he met some opposition from aristocrats and army officers around the court. But Paul I's patronage carried him along on the crest of the wave.

The Emperor's Barber permits Kutaissov to relate his own story. The many facets of his nature are revealed. If he is impossible to love, he is certainly difficult to loathe. The impudent intelligence and charisma of the man enabled him to make his way from lowly origins into high society. Kutaissov was obviously very accomplished in the art of looking after himself in the labyrinth of royal and political figures who were part of his daily living.

But Kutaissov's relationship with Paul is the mainspring of the novel. Once Paul becomes emperor, Kutaissov's glorious period begins. When the emperor is murdered, the barber's usefulness to the state comes to an end.

The dynamics of this relationship are fascinating. It seems unlikely Kutaissov ever kept a diary. *The Emperor's Barber* is intended to reveal some of that which has been lost.

Perhaps the historian's usual judgement on Kutaissov that he was shifty and devious is factual. Yet for a confused emperor of feeble mind, Kutaissov provided some kind of friendship and devotion. In the harsh realities of courtly and political life such a relationship was extremely rare.

The character of Kutaissov has intrigued this writer for two decades. The questions he raises seem absolutely relevant in our modern world. In particular, what happens when a country is ruled by an evil man with a twisted mind?

There are a number of contemporary rulers in the 21ˢᵗ century with apparently dysfunctional personalities, let alone the many appropriate examples from previous eras. The erratic tendencies of Emperor Paul I continue to be re-enacted, one way or another, throughout the world, a constant, regrettable, and fascinating element of human experience.

GRAHAM WADE

Principal Characters

Kutaissa/Kutaissov, count, Paul's barber, fixer, gentleman of the
  bedchamber, master of the robes, nicknamed 'Figaro'
Abdullah, his friend
Mehmet, Abdullah's father
Leyla and Melis, Mehmet's daughters
Carpenter
Carpenter's wife
Sergeant Ahmed. In the Turkish army
Petrov, a friend of Kutaissov in the army
Surgeon
The General, Kutaissov's first Russian employer
Antonina, Russian girl
Grand Duke Paul, later Emperor Paul I of Russia, son of
  Peter III and Catherine
Colonel Steinwehr, deputy commander of Gatchina
The Grand Duchess, Maria Feodorovna (née Princess Sophia
  Dorothea of Hesse-Darmstadt), Paul's second wife
Father Nikolai, priest of the Russian Orthodox Church
Natasha, second wife of Kutaissov
Boris and Tatyana, Natasha's children from her first marriage
Count Alexi Arakcheev, commander of Gatchina, inspector-
  general of artillery, war minister, count
Feodor Rostopchin, count, adjutant-general, president of
  Foreign Collegium, postmaster
Alexander, grand duke and later tsar
Catherine Nelidowa, Paul's mistress, lady in waiting to
  grand duchess

Count Platon Zubov, Catherine the Great's former lover
Catherine II the Great, widow of Peter III
Princess Dashkova, close friend of Catherine the Great
Galina, a serving girl
Private Smirnov, Galina's lover
Orlov, governor of Moscow
Anna Lopukhina, later Princess Gagarina, Paul's mistress
Prince Lopukhin, Anna's father
Alexander Bezborodko, chancellor, prince
Iryma, lady in waiting to the empress
Prince Gagarin, later husband to Anna Lopukhina
Nikita Panin, vice-chancellor, nephew of Catherine the
    Great's minister
Peter von der Pahlen, governor of St Petersburg
Madame Chevalier, French actress
General Bennigsen
Olga Zherebtsova, sister of the Zubov brothers
Nicholai Zubov, brother to Platon Zubov
Valerian Zubov
Colonel Sablukov, commander of the Imperial Horse Guards
General Kutuzov
General Talytzin, a conspirator
Argamov, a junior adjutant and conspirator
Peter Obolyaninov, procurator-general, head of the
    secret committee

PART ONE

THE AWAKENING

Life is not a walk across a field.

RUSSIAN PROVERB

M Y NAME USED to be Kutaissa (pronounced *Koo-tie-sar*). But *he*, against my will, baptised me.

I was born again, with a new name, new religion, new wife, emerging like a newly-hatched snake as Ivan Pavlovich Kutaissov...That name, it was decided, suits me better...

Then, as a kind of jest he called me 'Figaro', the eternal barber, to remind me of what I used to be.

Who is that *he* to whom I refer with such awe and contempt, even though *he* is now stone dead, murdered, a nasty business, never to be forgotten? A necessary murder, I suppose. Did I have anything to do with his death?

Well, there are ways of being involved. *Not* doing can be as guilty as wielding the knife...In a manner of speaking I might be blamed for not seeing it coming.

Forgive me. My thoughts are confused. My life is divided into three parts – before I met him, afterwards, and since his assassination. Occasionally the three main arteries of my existence become intertwined, especially in dreams...

P AUL I, AT first grand duke and later emperor of Russia, son of Peter III and the illustrious Catherine the Great, a woman able to strike fear into the heart of Nero, Caligula, or Genghis Khan, should they have had the misfortune to be born at the same time as her...Paul was my lord and master.

I was his slave, his creature, interpreting his every mood, and adjusting my behaviour accordingly...To fawn, to flatter, to wheedle, to persuade, to advise...What a progression of weasel motivations...But that's how you deal with the great and powerful when, low-born as a mongrel, you rise to become the emperor's barber, his right hand man, his nanny, his *confidant*, his sycophant, almost (but not quite) his friend....

H E WAS, IN a manner of speaking, an evil man. But this is philosophical rather than moral. How can a man be blamed for the evil he commits if he is mad, his mind diseased as a rotten apple?

I'll take an example. When I was a boy in Turkey, ten or eleven years old, I witnessed the execution of a murderer, a wretch who did unspeakable things to destitute girls before he killed them by the cruellest, slowest means. (I'll spare you the details but such matters were gossiped about endlessly in bazaars and barber shops.)

On the scaffold it was obvious that the man was a half-wit. His behaviour was, one might suggest, 'abnormal' for a man in his circumstances. He joked with the executioners, taunted women in the crowd.

That is to say – he had no perception he was any moment due for death (though he soon found out). I must add that any 'abnormality' increased the crowd's enjoyment for the screams and antics of a maniac appear more entertaining than those of any of our usual criminals.

But what if a person such as our murderer (God rest his soul!) had become emperor of Russia?

For Paul the First was not only mad but, being of noble lineage, was treated, for most of the time, as sane. His madness was (in the end) the death of him.

But that's not the point. The question is how far a man is accountable for the evil he commits by reason of his insanity…

When you get to know me better you will understand the dilemmas this situation is apt to throw up. (Have no fear – I will let you into every secret.) Whatever repulsion may be felt at Paul's condition and actions he eventually paid for it with his life…

So between him and the murderer on the scaffold there was not much difference at their dying. Except that one was hanged with a rope and the other strangled.

I NEVER KNEW MY mother. Thus it follows I did not know my father either. My conception was a casual casting of seed. According to hearsay (from those acquainted with my mother) their coupling took place under an apple tree in full blossom in April, a touch of colour in an otherwise meaningless mingling of kisses and bodily parts.

I do not mean to imply he forced her. Spring is a wicked time for plants and animals and desire flows through the veins of women in that season as sap through a tree.

I was born at the appointed hour. My mother duly died from the experience. My father, a soldier in the service of the state, was killed in some scrimmage shortly after.

What then of the offspring?

Truth to tell (and sometimes I speak the truth despite the rumours about me that circulate in court) I was (not for the last time) lucky. A childless couple took me in, partly out of the goodness of their hearts and partly to fill a gap in their lives that needed filling.

Naturally their methods of rearing were Turkish. More than that, they were of peasant stock. That is to say their idea of bringing up a child was physical rather than cultural. They ploughed fields, attended to oxen and horses, grafted from cock crow till dusk for hard taskmasters – this they understood... In their turn they made sure I knew the ways of this world and how that understanding was best transmitted through the soles of the feet, or onto the thin but adequate flesh of the buttocks, the cheeks of the face, or the tender white palms of young hands.

In return for this I was rarely hungry, thick soup was usually available with mugs of goat's milk, cheese and bread to be thrust down my gullet. Sometimes we ate capons or slices of salt beef, as well as occasional sweetmeats.

IT TOOK A few years to appreciate I was more intelligent than the couple I had been billeted with. This may strike you as ingratitude from a boy who owed them the bread he ate and the bed in which he slept.

But certain things should be said and I intend to say them.

'Intelligence' is a means of discerning there is more than one way of skinning a cat. In other words, an 'intelligent' boy begins to appreciate that problems can be solved in diverse manners.

My adoptive parents, on the other hand, always acted like a bull at a gate – no subtlety of approach and certainly no guile (that indispensable tool in the armoury of any who would make their way in the world).

As it happened I had a good teacher in the school of guile, my friend, Abdullah! Though I cannot say I was ever fond of Abdullah. It's just that he lived nearby and thrust friendship upon me.

As he was certainly older and stronger than me, I found his attentions impossible to resist. He protected me from the rough boys of the village who formed themselves into tight gangs, picking on any sign of weakness.

But nobody picked on Abdullah. His nature was callous and hard indicating he would stop at nothing to achieve his will. This could be accompanied by smiles and charms, as well as by blows and arm twisting.

Sometimes Abdullah would hit me, but, believe it or not, this was a kind of special favour as I was his friend. A punch on the arm or in the small of the back, even a sound smack on the face, could be a sign he had just been punished by his father and was now giving me a taste of the same medicine. There was not an iota of malice in it — just a reminder that he was strong and I was weak.

Abdullah liked to wrestle, knowing he would win. I put up with the humiliation of defeat out of the respect I had for him. Despite my lack of experience I knew this was the best of all options. If I lost Abdullah I would lose everything.

It was a kind of love, a love devoid of affection, similar to how a beast of burden (if it could talk) might feel about a master who continually abused the animal but also gave it an occasional smile or pat.

Strange how such a relationship would prove a fine apprenticeship for my years in the royal palaces with Paul!

EHMET, ABDULLAH'S FATHER, a widower, was of a higher social status than my parents. His occupation was that of village barber, a profession which involved not only trimming the beards of local gentry but also extracting teeth, blood-letting, the setting of broken bones, and attending to ailments.

Our village was far from a town and no other persons skilled in medicine were to be found for leagues around.

At first, when visiting Abdullah's abode, I was on the periphery of events, especially when we were very young together. We saw the customers waiting for his father's services. They were then invited into a back room where they disappeared from our view.

Occasionally we heard cries of anguish as teeth were extracted or a broken arm laid into alignment. But we took no more notice of this than we would of a beggar in the street or a peasant herding cattle.

One day Mehmet appeared at the door, his apron besmirched with the gore of his trade, a look on his face of either frustration or anger:

'Abdullah', he shouted, 'Come and give me a hand, *now!*'

My friend winked wickedly and whispered, 'Come on – this could be interesting!'

I was reluctant but Abdullah gave my shin an almighty kick to hurry me on my way. Thus, as if I were a mere shadow, I stumbled in through the door expecting any moment to be ordered out.

Mehmet had his back towards us. In front of him was a waist-high table, set up with blankets and pillows. On this divan lay the village butcher, face downwards, his breeches round his ankles.

It was a shocking sight. From his posterior a wound gushed out blood which ran onto the blankets, spattering down the leg of the table till it gathered in small puddles on the floor. From his throat came low groaning, as if from a man too weak to make louder expression.

In the course of his duties the butcher had been attacked by a bull. As he turned to run the bull impaled him with its right horn. The lunge threw him over the stockade fence, leaving a wide gouge on his backside. A soldier receiving a similar injury would have been awarded a medal.

Mehmet turned to Abdullah and saw me gawping at the unfortunate victim. The formidable barber merely beckoned me to move closer to the table, barking suddenly, 'Abdullah will show you what to do!'

Our task was to hold down the patient. Mehmet cleansed the wound, analysed the damage, and stitched up the gaps in the flesh.

Abdullah pressed the butcher's face into the pillow on which he lay, though allowing the man's mouth to extend beneath the cushion to be able to breathe. With his left hand Abdullah exerted a wrestler's grip against the man's shoulder so that he could not move – I recognised the hold from the wrestling sessions I had frequently endured. Such a grip (did I but know it) proved the triumph of guile over strength. Abdullah was younger, lighter, weaker, than the injured man, but subtle expertise enabled him to exert his will, quadrupling the power in his hands and arms by means of torsion and anatomical logic.

'Hold him! As best you can!' exhorted Abdullah.

I was in no position to emulate my friend by trying a similar grip. So I pressed down onto the butcher's back and shoulders, levering my slim weight on top to render him motionless.

I observed Mehmet looking at me prior to beginning his work:

'Good boy, Kutaissa,' he said. (He had never addressed me by name before.)

Our butcher was still groaning but our firm grip on his torso seemed to give comfort.

Mehmet turned to his main task, saturating the wound with water which mingled with the blood and flooded the floor. As Mehmet splashed water into the wound the more the blood seemed to flow. But with the application of colourless liquid from a tumbler (causing the victim to scream, but move he could not), followed by special powder, the flood began to abate.

Mehmet thrust padding into the wound, tossing blood soaked rags to the floor in an ascending molehill of red, messy cloth. When satisfied he proceeded to the next phase.

'Hold tight, Abdullah,' said Mehmet. 'You too, Kutaissa, you're doing well.'

With that he took up needle and thread and, having inspected the wound a further time, drew the edges of the flesh together. Like an old washerwoman or sailmaker he stitched together the jagged edges.

Naturally this provoked much writhing from the butcher, the pain of the encounter now beyond forbearance. But Abdullah's handling, and my added efforts, succeeded in keeping the patient still enough to allow the operation to be completed.

Having applied a mass of bandage to the area, skilfully fastened and knotted (I knew not how at the time), Mehmet gave the command, 'Let him go, turn him over.' At this point we saw the gentleman's face, quivering with pain.

Of course I knew the butcher. In our village everybody knew everybody. It might seem such an eminent person as the butcher would not take kindly to having his rear end seen by young boys. But the man nodded and muttered, 'Thank you, thank you', first to Abdullah and then to myself as if we had distinguished ourselves by the services offered.

The three of us lifted the butcher to his feet. Mehmet pulled up the man's undergarments and trousers and fastened them with a firm belt round the waist. Such indignity did not now matter to the butcher, pleased as he was that his bottom had been patched and stitched.

'You will find it difficult to sit down for a while,' said Mehmet. 'Fortunately the wound was lighter than similar cases I have treated.'

The butcher paid Mehmet with a small gold coin and hobbled out of the door, sore but repaired.

Abdullah's father turned to me with something of a smile:

'Kutaissa, I didn't know you had it in you. You could be useful.'

'Thank you, sir!'

'You didn't faint at the sight of blood,' he replied.

'Oh no, sir,' I said. 'I don't mind blood.'

'Good. Perhaps you are suited for this profession. There is always a need for a good barber.'

I blushed at this compliment. The job of barber had never occurred to me. I thought I would follow my adoptive parents into labouring tasks of the field.

'I would like to do that, sir,' I replied. 'But I need my father's permission'.

'Leave it to me,' said Mehmet. 'Your father owes a favour for a tooth pulled last year. He couldn't afford to pay my fee. Barbers often take credit for granted, being paid later in various ways.'

'Thank you, sir,' I said. 'That is kind.'

—

Abdullah was standing at the head of the operating table, a broad grin on his face. He seemed delighted. To show his pleasure he struck me on the bicep with the side of his hand.

'We shall be apprentices together,' he said.

'When do we begin?' I asked.

Mehmet smiled again:

'Kutaissa – you have already begun. You passed the test. Come tomorrow and we'll work, all three of us. After five years you will complete your learning.'

Inwardly I quavered. In my mind's eye was the image of my father, his plans for a life of helping him in the fields thwarted. I need not have worried. Mehmet's will was strong, his manner persuasive.

As I found out that day, and the next day – there is indeed more than one way of catching a hare. The path of life is twisted and guileful beyond anything a simple peasant can envisage.

Mehmet had already seen in me something of value. He was not the kind of man to pass over an opportunity.

THAT EVENING MEHMET came to my parent's poor hovel, took my father for a walk to discuss business, and returned an hour later. Papa looked harassed, defeated and forlorn.

The barber had explained the excellent prospects in his service and how I would earn rewards beyond that of a humble peasant, possessing a skill beyond the price of rubies, acceptable among all nations.

'Besides,' he said slyly, 'Kutaissa is not suited to hard labour. He is not your own son. Who knows what his lineage is? He has not been bred to life on the land. Wasn't his father a soldier?

Kutaissa is intelligent. He needs to open his wings that he may fly. But his limbs are small and unformed. He'll never make his way labouring from dawn to dusk. With me he will be apprenticed for one of the universal skills.'

Against such utterances what was my poor father to do? Despite his innermost desires and my dear adoptive mother's wishes he agreed to put his mark on indentures of apprenticeship. That evening I left my parents and moved in with Mehmet and his family.

The rapidity of the alteration was to my liking. Mehmet's home was four or five times more spacious than the three simple rooms I had been accustomed to. It was not that I disregarded the parental tenderness of my parents. Quite the contrary. Such thoughts just did not enter my head. Years later it occurred to me what treacherous ingratitude was perpetrated that evening. For years I had been with them. Now in a few hours I departed.

I packed my few belongings and left with Mehmet. The faces of my parents were too numb with sadness to permit any tears.

I felt no emotions, just elation at the thought of adventures ahead. A new life dawned. I felt nothing for anyone beyond my own needs. Of course, the move to stay with Mehmet was not far from my parental home. But its distance for mama and papa was infinitesimal, further than from the earth to the moon or from the moon to the nearest star.

Since that day I have loaded so many other sins on my conscience that such nostalgic regrets do not add up to much. Besides, we cannot expect the young to assume the responsibilities of their seniors.

Perhaps I blame myself too much for too little.

PART TWO

THE APPRENTICESHIP

My soul is full of sadness. Ah, Happiness
Do not come!
In one home you cannot welcome one guest
After another.

RÂSIH BEY (d. 1731)

SAID MEHMET'S HOUSE had more space than my first home. At first it seemed a dozen times bigger.

The next morning I was summoned at dawn, provided with bread and a cup of goat's milk, and told to scrub out various rooms.

After I had been doing this for an hour or two Mehmet came to inspect. He was not happy with the results. Several areas had to be re-scrubbed and re-polished, with Mehmet standing over me to make sure I did the job properly.

Abdullah was elsewhere doing *his* cleaning chores. His two sisters peered round the door from time to time to giggle and mock.

I soon understood my feeding arrangements were not to be the same as the rest of the family. My portion of food was distinctly smaller than theirs (not that I realised this at the time) and I had to eat whatever I was given in my tiny room by myself.

When I grew weary of hard labour and poor food and suggested to Mehmet I was not suited for this work and wished to return home to my parents, he became angry. He waved the apprenticeship papers in my face and shouted that the penalty of forfeiting such valuable training was a legal flogging with prison to follow.

As I could not read at the time I was forced to remain where I was, not wishing to be beaten or locked away.

SOMETIMES, WHEN WE had finished our toil, Abdullah and I went swimming in the river. In summer it was just a dribble of water, at some other times a treacherous torrent. Usually it was half and half, gentle water and not too deep.

He could swim very well and delighted in holding my head under the water while I struggled for air and kicked against him. Now that he could bully me for most of the day every day our relationship had changed (and not for the better).

To Abdullah and his father I became a skivvy, higher than a goat but lower than a horse in their estimation. But for every rat caught in a trap there may be a way out. I applied my mind to the situation but immediate escape was out of the question..

So for three or four years I endured this misery, suffering blows and insults from most of the household in the same manner as a mule or donkey is castigated, a constant reminder to the animal of its obligations and its place in the hierarchy of creation.

Abdullah grew into a strapping youth. Eating less food than the rest of them I was gaunt and scrawny, wiry but always thin. Abdullah and his sisters teased me for my lean appearance.

'It's a scarecrow!' said Leyla, the eldest of the trio.

'No, it's a ghost!' replied Melis, who was two years younger than her sister.

'It's neither,' joined in Abdullah, 'it's a bogeyman sent to frighten us.'

This jesting was often accompanied by prodding and pushing, especially in the direction of my unfleshed ribs.

If during these games I fell to the floor the real kicking started, beginning with taps on shin and hip but escalating to unpleasant punishment round the stomach and back.

Fortunately not one of the three stuck at anything for long.

Growing bored they would slope off, having administered their final *coup de grace* with a blow followed by a kick. Bitter tears filled my eyes because of the humiliation rather than the pain.

After they left I would lie there on the floor in a curled position never uttering a word or letting out a cry. My silence always astonished them but I was determined not to add to their enjoyment.

One day as I lay thus, prone in the mud-strewn yard following a vigorous session, Mehmet appeared out of nowhere. He must have known how his offspring behaved. This time he seemed thoughtful:

'Kutaissa,' he shouted, 'what *are* you doing?'

'I was knocked down,' I said. 'I'm hurt.'

'Come into the barber shop. I'll take a look at you.'

In the operating room he took the shirt from my back and twirled me round a couple of times. A mass of yellow and blue bruises spread like a disease across my chest. My back was red and chastised.

Mehmet applied cold water to my wounds with a clean cloth and rubbed on a kind of ointment which at first stung the skin like bees but after a few minutes was soothing.

'Stretch out your arms,' he commanded. I did so.

'Nothing broken!' he commented in his professional voice.

'We must do something about this,' he said. I lowered my eyes for I did not like to meet his gaze. 'Go to the kitchen and get yourself some food and drink. Tomorrow you need not work.'

'Thank you, master,' I whispered. 'That's very kind.'

When Abdullah and the girls came back from where they had been, probably in the woods making mischief, I heard Mehmet shouting at them.

From inside the house came sounds of beating and cries of anguish, first from Abdullah, then from the sisters. Suddenly Mehmet called my name:

'Kutaissa – come in here!'

I had no option but to obey. Entering the house I saw the three miscreants standing against the wall, their eyes red with weeping and hurt, their arms folded as if to mitigate the agony.

'Kutaissa,' said Mehmet, 'they will apologise to you or be beaten again.'

'I am sorry,' said Abdullah and Leyla and Melis, whining and cringing together, their silly voices rising in chorus, terrified of further punishment from their father.

As I have learned many times since, silence is the best medicine on these occasions. This was one such moment.

I looked into their faces with contempt in my soul, vowing my own hideous vengeance on my tormentors. Seeing the hatred like burning coals in my eyes Abdullah began to whimper again. His evil sisters seemed to recoil as if from a snake.

'We're sorry, we're sorry,' they exclaimed in pitiful unison. I looked at Mehmet for permission to take my leave. He nodded gravely.

I went out, my anger like boiling water in my blood.

ABDULLAH NEVER HIT me again. I bided my time.

A year or two passed and I was around sixteen years old. Abdullah (now nearing the end of his apprenticeship) was at least seventeen though one could never be sure of these things.

It was a peculiar summer. First it was intensely hot as if the sun had drawn nearer the earth and threatened to consume it. Then it rained and continued to rain in perpetual downpour for days and days. The beating of the rain on the roof was like the hooves of horses drumming in the brain. Yet despite the deluge, the house seemed hotter than hell itself, the worst of all worlds.

When the inundation eventually came to an end Abdullah suggested we should take a walk to see the river in flood. We set off amicably enough. But somehow as we walked to the river we quarrelled.

I can hardly remember the nature of the dispute. But the heat and the wet had made everybody irritable.

Arrival at the swollen river was dramatic. The water was foaming like a lunatic, spinning boulders before it, frightening to behold. Abdullah and I stood on the bank watching the spectacle, never having seen anything to equal such a colossal torrent of water.

Then it happened. In some manner Abdullah was in front of me gazing as if hypnotised by the flood, his back towards me. He advanced to the edge of the flood, so close I almost called him back. Suddenly, for no obvious reason, losing his balance he plunged forward, in the blink of an eye toppling into the maelstrom.

I recall a sensation of delight as I saw him fall.

He let out a cry as he entered the furious embrace of the torrent, waving as if imploring my help. He was in the stream, I was on the hard edge of the bank.

With a shrill screaming he was thrust along at speed, drift-wood in the flow, twisting and turning in the manner of a large fish.

I ran along the bank in the direction of the current. He was disappearing beneath the water and all his swimming prowess was not sufficient to buoy him up.

He must have known he was gone. One minute a fierce youth, the next a lifeless drowned nothing. Death by drowning. A horrible fate.

How was I to explain this to his family? Who would be blamed? I felt no guilt then or now. Was I responsible? I cannot remember.

All I know is that I ran back to the barber. On entering the house I was engulfed in frantic tears through which I attempted to tell them what I believed had happened.

LIFE IS FULL of surprises. When you expect the worst, you might get something better. Such it was.

No funeral ever took place as the body was never recovered. Wretched, impetuous Abdullah, swept downstream, was, I suppose, dragged beneath the surface for leagues away from where he plunged into the river.

Thus the family received no mourning round the graveside, no black garments paraded, no coffin, no burial, no headstone. Instead an empty death, hardly explained, a tragic occurrence, their son removed from them in a single mad moment.

For months I appeared as inconsolable, my shoulders drooping, my voice penitent and trembling.

And do you know what? Far from casting me into the pit of resentment Abdullah's relatives took me to their bosom, spoiling me with food and kindness, changing from their previous unkindness into guardians of my well-being.

In a manner of speaking I *became* Abdullah, a substitute son, a living monument to the youth who had died. They seemed to attribute no blame. Quite the opposite.

I assumed the mantle of a kind of living martyr, someone who was there when it happened. Like a soldier who had suffered a battle but survived, my presence became something to cling to.

I was a holy relic of someone gone forever, a daily reminder of Abdullah's previous existence.

THE BIGGEST CHANGE was in Mehmet. I became his apprentice and true heir in the art of barbering. He taught me everything he knew and all that I needed. From shaving heads, faces and chins, to letting blood, to setting broken limbs or binding up wounds, to prescribing herbal lotions and medicinal remedies, to helping women give birth, to dealing with the bodies of individuals who died during treatment − there was nothing he omitted.

He even taught me how to read and write. After Abdullah's death I received a splendid education.

Leyla and Melis vied for my affection in open contest, each trying to outdo the other in what they could do for me. It was embarrassing at first. But I got accustomed to their new ways once I appreciated this was a permanent change in their behaviour.

Before they had represented a common enemy, bonded with Abdullah against me. Now they became my sisters. Except they were *not* my sisters.

They became casual in their dress when I was around, sometimes appearing in their undergarments as if on the way to the privy. As little more than a boy, though possessed with instincts and passions, I hardly knew what was going on.

Melis's white skin and sly smile attracted me more than Leyla's melancholy nature. But there is much temptation in a sultry character, secret like the darkness of a deep forest.

In awe of Memhet's patriarchal authority I let things ride at first, not wishing to be caught out in some misbehaviour.

But Mehmet himself began making remarks, leading in a single direction. 'Kutaissa', he said one evening, 'soon you will have to take a wife. Have you thought about that?'

'No master,' I said. 'I have no money for such an undertaking.'

'That need not matter', he replied quietly.

'I wish to complete my apprenticeship,' I said. 'Then I will be a proper man, able to manage my affairs.'

'Hmm,' he mused, and went silent for some minutes. 'But you have almost finished your term as an apprentice.'

I said nothing, waiting for the outcome.

Mehmet, however, clearing his throat as if embarrassed, stalked off to the kitchen where his daughters were clattering pots and pans in preparation for the evening meal.

APPRENTICESHIPS ARE NOT necessarily bound according to fixed terms. The system is such that the master sets the details of any agreement. More often there is no formal legal basis, just an understanding. But as we all know, 'an understanding' can soon lead to 'a misunderstanding'.

First and foremost an apprenticeship is an arrangement whereby a master obtains cheap labour for offering experience of a trade. Everyone knows that. In Turkey the system has been running for centuries, allowing all manner of abuses to creep in.

Officially there are three levels at which the pupil finds himself. The first is the lowest or beginner, called *çirak* in our language.

On these underlings many burdens are loaded, sometimes of a most unpleasant kind if the master has a mind to exercise his rights.

The next step is *kalfa*, when a goodly degree of required knowledge has been absorbed. Finally one might be promoted to the senior rank of *usta*, at which point such an individual may well be entrusted with a few young *çirak* lads to abuse and humiliate, as well as to teach.

Mehmet did not use these terms to measure which stage of development I had reached. I was at that time too ignorant of the ways of the world so did not trouble my head too much with labels and categories. Sufficient to say that Mehmet taught me what he knew as far as he could.

As you may realize I am *not* an idealist. I take the world as it is and for what it is. Changing the world is best left to those who think themselves best at it. I have long learned to look out simply for my own welfare. Unless you are born blessed, with a wealthy family and opportunities, it is necessary to do just that.

For all the changes in my position in the household since the death of Abdullah, Mehmet was still his old guileful self. Simple peasant that he was at heart, the man was as devious as a snake. To learn the rules of whatever game he was playing at any particular moment was almost impossible. Not even his daughters had thoroughly mastered all the ins and outs.

Thus he returned to the subject of a wife late one afternoon when we had finished our work:

'Kutaissa,' he began, 'I have been thinking about your

apprenticeship, which is now drawing to a close.'

'Thank you, master,' I murmured, wondering if he was about to seal our deal and offer me the full status of master barber. It would happen one day.

'Well,' he continued, plucking with his right hand at his beard, 'these matters are complicated.'

I said nothing.

'I presume you will, when granted the indentures, carry on working here in the village for me.'

'I have nowhere else to go,' I replied. 'What do I know of the world beyond this village?'

'Exactly. That is precisely what I mean'.

He was speaking in riddles. I stayed quiet.

'I am thinking of your future, Kutaissa.'

'That's very kind of you, master,' I said.

'Hmm…You understand I cannot afford to pay high wages.'

'Of course,' I said. 'But my needs are simple.'

'Good. I'm glad you see things the same way as I do.'

We waited. None of this was making sense. To solve a puzzle one must have a clue to unlock the mystery.

After some moments Mehmet spoke again:

'Well…if…if you are staying with me to work after you become a master barber, then…perhaps…you should have a wife to help you.'

'I shall take your advice,' I said.

'Good,' he replied, 'I believe you will.'

I remained in the dark. Then the light came up over the horizon, illuminating all:

'I have a daughter,' he said, as if merely stating a fact.

'Leyla *and* Melis,' I simpered.

'I was thinking of Leyla,' he said. 'She is older than Melis, and should be married first.'

I felt my heart beating in chest and temples. One of those moments where the die is cast.

'Perhaps she should,' I replied

'Should what?' he said, a little sharply.

'Be married first!'

'Of course. I agree with you.'

He was becoming confused with his own discourse, such was the weight on his mind.

'Well?' he asked.

Well *what*, master?' I said.

'How about Leyla? Getting married!'

'Very good,' I answered. 'I think she should.'

'Hmm…well, that seems to be agreed then.'

'Master, I do agree. But how does Leyla's marriage concern me?'

'The boy's an idiot!' he said. 'All my efforts to help him and he still doesn't understand.'

'I am very stupid, master,' I whispered. 'I appreciate you asked my advice on a family matter. It is an honour to be consulted. But I am not sure beyond that.'

He turned on me in an instant:

'You ungrateful fool, Kutaissa. Here am I offering you the hand of my daughter in marriage and all you do is pretend to be indifferent.'

I was struck dumb. Marrying one of the daughters had never entered my thoughts. If given a choice I preferred Melis. She was prettier, more intelligent.

Leyla was like her father in temperament. Not an ideal recipe for a marriage. But I had to restore his mood, that is – to speak:

'Master,' I said, 'forgive me. I had no idea you would bestow such an honour upon me.'

He smiled benignly. 'Well, I take it you accept my daughter's hand. When you marry her I shall grant you the rank of master barber with signed agreement.'

I bit my lower lip so hard it bled. Whatever random thoughts might ever have occurred to me about the future, Leyla had not been among them.

FROM THAT MOMENT on I looked at Leyla from an altered perspective. Her hips, her hair, her eyes, her legs, her hands, her arms – this was to be my new domain. A tinge of excitement swelled through me.

Melis, like a clever child catching a ball, saw my glance of admiration towards her sister:

'Kutaissa, what is it?' she said.

Leyla turned from the soup she was stirring to look me in the face. 'Ah, Kutaissa. What's going on?'

'He has finished his apprenticeship,' said Mehmet. 'He is henceforth to be deemed a master.'

It was Melis who approached first, winding her slender arms round my neck in congratulation, kissing me slyly on the cheek.

'Thank you, Melis', I said.

'Well done,' said Leyla. After wiping her hands on a cloth she patted me on the back in the same way as a child might touch a pet goat.

'What's for dinner?' asked Mehmet, breaking the tension.

'Just the usual,' said Melis. 'You didn't tell us this was a special evening.'

We ate supper that night in a strange mood of felicity and interrogation. Mehmet was expansive and jovial, Melis slightly restrained, Leyla returned my frequent glances with looks of surprise.

'This soup is delicious,' said Mehmet, not usually given to praising his daughters' cooking. Melis blushed slightly at this compliment even though it was Leyla who had prepared the dish.

'Kutaissa,' said Melis, out of the blue, 'will you be staying with us now that your apprentice days are over?'

'Of course,' said Mehmet. 'Where else would he go? This is his home now.'

'Oh, good!' exclaimed Melis in true delight. 'I would hate to lose you, Kutaissa.'

'There are many places he could go,' said Leyla. 'A master barber is welcome everywhere.'

'I don't want him to go,' pleaded Melis, looking momentarily tearful.

'Well, he isn't going anywhere!' interrupted Mehmet. 'So can we stop all this chatter? I've trained the boy, and here he will remain.'

After eating our fill Mehmet took me outside for a walk.

'Kutaissa, I've been thinking about things. It might be better if you asked Leyla yourself. I could have mentioned it to her. But you should go to her directly. Under the circumstances.'

'What if I took Melis instead?' I ventured. 'I think she likes me.'

'I won't hear of it,' said Mehmet, irritation in his voice. 'The older daughter has to be married first. She likes you well enough. You're exactly the right man for her.'

'When should I ask her?' I replied. 'Tomorrow? Next week?'

'Ask her now. I'll call her out of the house, then leave you alone together. That should do it.'

Within five minutes I found myself walking with Leyla in the twilight down the long lane which stretched from the house.

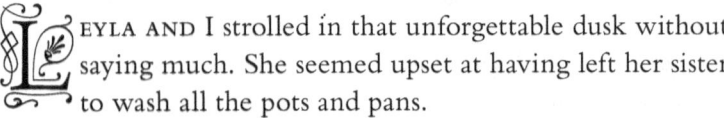

EYLA AND I strolled in that unforgettable dusk without saying much. She seemed upset at having left her sister to wash all the pots and pans.

Certainly Mehmet's peremptory comment that she 'should keep company with Kutaissa for half an hour' was entirely unprecedented.

Accustomed to obeying her father's slightest whim she accepted this imposition as yet another duty. Men were unpredictable creatures and among the whole race of men her father doubly so.

For my part, I was content to amble in silence, secretly rehearsing my words and then finding what I thought to be adequate was not in the least sufficient.

'You're very quiet this evening, Kutaissa,' she said. 'Is it the shock of ending your apprenticeship?'

'Partly,' I replied, 'but not entirely'.

Walking by her side, our hands sometimes almost touching, her long hair swinging freely, I was beginning to have amorous thoughts.

I kept looking sideways at her and she pretended not to notice. But eventually even Leyla appreciated that something was in the wind.

'Why do you keeping looking at me like that?' she said irritably.

'Like what?' I teased. 'I wasn't aware I was looking at you.'

'You kept looking at me during supper. I saw you.'

'Can I kiss you?' I said, taking courage in both hands.

'Why should you want to? You're like a brother aren't you? What have we to do with kissing?'

'You're a woman. I'm a man. Why shouldn't we?'

'Why not try Melis? I'm sure she likes you a lot more than I do.'

'Because, Leyla, I have chosen you.'

At this she turned up her little nose in a gesture of pure contempt.

'When did you choose me, Kutaissa?'

'Yesterday!' I said, in an unaccustomed moment of honesty.

'Why yesterday?'

'Because that was when your father offered to complete my apprenticeship. He also said he wants me to marry you. I have agreed.'

She said nothing for a few seconds, proof I think that she knew nothing of her father's intentions till now.

'So I'm like a sheep in the market am I? Up for the highest bidder?'

'There is only one bid on the table – that's mine. And it's a good offer.'

Leyla paused to think some more, taken aback by this sudden proposal. To ease her mind I spoke again.

'If you marry me, I'll try to be a good husband. I don't know much about these things.'

At this she smiled slightly as if pitying the poor dolt beside her.

'Are you doing this for my father?' she enquired.

'In a way, yes. But also for myself. I have thought about it.

—

Things could be worse.'

'I suppose they could.'

'It is difficult for both of us,' I said in a soft, persuasive voice.

'Yes, for you and for me.'

I paused for half a minute. As yet nothing was decided. If I went against Mehmet's wishes the devil knew what would happen.

I turned towards her, took her gently by the shoulders, and kissed her firmly on her warm nubile cheek. It tasted of sun and apples in my mouth.

I had never kissed a woman before and the memory of it will always remain exquisite among the good things that happened in my wretched life.

She did not pull away. I eased into a position where I could kiss her mouth. She moved her head just slightly as if shy, causing me to kiss the area of face adjacent to her lips, namely the side of her chin.

'We will leave all that till the wedding night,' she said coyly but definitely.

Thus the matter was agreed.

I INFORMED MEHMET THE next morning that it was a done deal. I would marry his daughter on condition of receiving my new status of master barber.

'Splendid, my boy,' he chuckled. I had never seen him so happy.

A man unaccustomed to giving or receiving affection he even took Leyla in his arms as he passed through the kitchen and hugged her for at least a minute. I noticed her eyes were slightly red as if with weeping.

Even more obvious was Melis's mood of dark melancholy. Melis glared at me with undisguised anger.

'Oh, here's the lover boy,' she whispered when both her father and Leyla were out of earshot.

'Did Leyla tell you about it?' I said.

'Of course, every detail.'

'I'm sorry.'

'So you should be.'

'I tried to persuade your father to let me marry you. He wouldn't hear of it.'

'Perhaps you didn't try hard enough.'

'Believe me, it was impossible.'

'Do you love me?'

'Perhaps.'

'Do you love Leyla?'

'I shall learn to do so.'

'In that case, there's no more to be said.'

She rushed from the room with furious tears, making a sound painful to listen to, a kind of groaning as if in deep pain.

As for me I applied my mind to the task in hand, the wedding to Leyla, a prospect I began to relish quite beyond my original expectations.

MY RESPONSIBILITIES AS a barber now increased a dozen fold. Mehmet allowed me to work on my own with bloodletting as well as with various individuals whose chronic ailments usually took up most of his time.

I also dealt with hair cutting, beard trimming, the extraction of teeth, and the soothing and binding up of scratches, gashes, and sprains incurred during daily labour.

The wedding when it came a month or two later was a simple affair, sparing the cost and yet for all that a happy occasion.

Melis had almost stopped speaking to me, a development that angered her father. But otherwise she kept her jealousy under control sufficiently to act as unofficial bridesmaid in attendance on her sister's needs for the day.

After the ceremony was completed Leyla and I went off to a small dwelling on the edge of the village. Mehmet had rented the place for us at a reasonable price in return for some medical favours to a local landowner.

Mehmet in his wisdom had collected a sufficient hoard of furniture and linen to provide for our needs. For the first time I was lord of my own tiny manor. I liked that feeling.

After the wedding celebrations the bridegroom and his lady arrived at the new dwelling in a horse-drawn carriage, rented from the same landowner who had supplied the cottage.

It is a peculiar moment when two youngsters find themselves alone in a strange home, permitted to do those very things which previously were forbidden almost on pain of death.

The secret of this activity, I had concluded, was to take things slowly and easily, not rushing the pace, not dawdling either.

On those occasions when I indulged in fantasies of the female who might become my wife, Leyla was not such an image. But within my soul and body was a healthy residue of lust which on this particular evening burned with energy as I contemplated the night ahead.

Leyla could never be the most attractive woman in the

world. But she had done her best in the guise of a bride to appeal to the basic instincts and raise in me strange emotions.

The result was that I threw aside the previous plan to move with caution. I became what you might call 'impatient' to try out whatever husbandly skills I was about to learn. The upshot was the game became more vigorous than anticipated.

On her entrance to our bedroom I disrobed her with singular speed, casting her upon the bed in her undergarments to thrust myself upon her. On discovering the delights of her limbs, her breasts, and her secret parts, shielded at first from view by a modest covering of soft down, my ardour renewed itself a thousand fold.

Before long I found myself rutting like an animal in the tenderest cavern in the universe, penetrating depths beyond the imaginings of mere boys and youths.

After initial pain and some squealing and protestation, Leyla's struggle against me transformed itself into a grasping and clasping of me to her, her nails grooving scratches and gouges in my back.

This outcome I had not anticipated. I gave no thought prior to the deed that women might enjoy coupling as much as the male. All the animals I ever saw copulating involved no ecstasy on behalf of the female, the mare seemingly indifferent to the mounting stallion, both parties going about their business with casual indolence.

By the morning, I believed I had begun to love Leyla. Was it not wonderful, that I, Kutaissa, was changed that night into a passionate angel, all by the power of affection?

Alas, that such youthful goodness and joyfulness are not destined to endure on this sinful, harmful earth.

WHAT SOON CHANGED everything was the act of pro-creation, nature's snare. All this pushing and pulling, kissing and canoodling, ecstasy and release, is but the prelude to breeding.

Not that I have anything against breeding. I was as willing as anyone to give Mehmet a grandchild and become a proud father. It was just, as with so many things, I had not anticipated this development so soon.

Within a matter of weeks dear Leyla was indeed 'with child'. Her body became puffy and uncomfortable for her, all physical contact, even a kiss, was distasteful to her. She just could not bear my touch, through no fault of her own.

Such was my passion for her that I heeded this not a jot. I had become enamoured and, given this, I delighted in all that she did as long she was by my side.

She could throw upon me any mood she wished, whether pleasant or unpleasant, sweet or sour, I would accept it. If I was the slightest bit irritated I would bite my tongue, as it were, and keep silent.

Just before her time was due Mehmet sent me on an errand to a village located at one day's riding distance. The message arrived that a carpenter had broken his right arm falling down-stairs. My father-in-law considered I was now capable of dealing with such a calamity in a competent manner.

The man I treated turned out to be a cowardly creature, unable to withstand pain without a quantity of childish blub-bing and squawking.

With considerable difficulty I secured his arm firmly in its splints and promised to return in two weeks or so to take him to the next stage of recovery.

I could not guarantee the future use of his arm in the

manner of his past endeavours, but I hoped for the best and did all that was possible.

I sedated him with a potion or two of opiate till he snored like a hog and returned to the living room where his wife was waiting. I was to stay the night on account of the journey's distance. Besides my horse was tired and possibly lame.

His wife, I observed, was a most attractive creature, quick of eye and full of smiles and giggles. She cooked me a fine meal which we ate together, our conversation punctuated by loud grunts and snuffles from the patient elsewhere in the dwelling.

Not having enjoyed a woman's touch for several months I was becoming keener by the minute on this delightful young thing. I made many jokes, causing her to laugh. Some of the jesting from her aimed at the husband's inability to muffle his voice when subjected to mild agony, a subject which caused her to guffaw ever more loudly.

When I feared our merriment might awaken the sleeping prince I went to the poor man and administered a further sedative, enough to keep him subdued for hours to come.

The girl decided to lay my bed in the barn, providing an abundance of bedding, pillows, and coverings. Ignoring my obvious dislike of being billeted outside among the animals she muttered a curt goodnight and hurried away.

Unable to sleep at first, my imaginings were a blend of the events of the journey, confused with images of the carpenter, and fantasies about the carpenter's wife.

The scuffling of the cattle in their byre and the shiftiness of the horses did not aid my slumbers. Eventually I slipped into dream worn out by the exertions of the day.

Imagine my surprise to be awoken by the creaking of the barn door and the shuffling of soft feet over the straw. The carpenter's wife crept in beside me, scantily clad.

'He's sleeping like a baby!' she cooed into my ear.

'He should be,' I said. 'I gave him three doses.'

Her lips met mine in an irresistible seduction. I clawed off her clothing in a trice.

Her passion was like an enormous wave from far out at sea, bearing us down below the waters of reason, binding us in desire. Her body was exquisite, soft to the touch beyond words, her movements practised and purposeful, intended for pleasure, skilled in its pursuit.

At the culmination of all this I lay spent like a discarded shell on a beach. She kissed me firmly, put on her clothes, and departed, leaving a warm space where her body had been.

The next morning I told her I should remain in the house a further day to ensure the carpenter's treatment was satisfactory.

'I'm sure Mehmet would do the same,' I said.

She winked and smiled, muttering, 'Of course, of course.'

When the carpenter was roused from his deep repose I assured him of my utmost care and advised he should retain my services a little longer in order to care for his broken arm.

At this the poor man was overjoyed, and thanked me pathetically, patting my arm like a sick child and promising to double my fee.

In the evening I once more applied my sedatives to the man, giving him another extra measure or so to ensure the benefit of the doubt.

Comfortable in the barn I again entertained my visitor of the night who this time appeared even more passionate, aware perhaps our fun and games would soon be coming to a conclusion.

'He's a useless fellow,' she confided when our rompings

and fondlings reached a pause. 'I only married him to please my father.'

'Women have to do these things,' I said. 'It's a hard world.'

At this her efforts to catch time on the wing grew yet more intense. But our groping and cuddling became tinged with sadness that such mingling was only a temporary halt in life's onward flow.

'I think I love you,' she whispered, as the last embrace kissed and slithered its way towards satisfaction.

'Hmm,' I hummed into her ear, feeling the same but not keen to express it in words.

She stayed throughout the night, leaving only when the dawn came up in a crimson blush of flowers and flame. I held her tightly to me, her breasts soaked with sweat and the wetness of my kisses.

'What a shame!' she murmured.

I knew what she meant.

WHAT SORROW THERE was in that departure! I looked in on the carpenter, still sleeping, his face calm in opiate bliss. At the doorway I hugged his wife, our lips meeting for the last time. She cooed into my ear like a turtledove, a declaration of desire without words.

With heavy heart I turned away. I heaved myself into the saddle and trotted away.

The journey was slow, both my horse and myself loathe to hurry. I felt pulled as if by a rope of silk back to the carpenter's wife, drowned in images of the night, lost in myself.

Nearing home my head cleared. I thought of Leyla, and

our forthcoming child.

As I came into the village, my horse going slightly lame, I saw Mehmet and Melis coming towards me. His broad shoulders drooped. Melis wore a black shawl. I leapt off the horse and ran towards them.

'What is it, master?' I said. 'Is everything all right?'

Melis burst into tears. Mehmet too was weeping.

'What kept you?' he said, accusation in his eyes.

'It was not straightforward,' I replied. 'A difficult case. Had to stay on.'

Mehmet was not listening. He sank to his knees, his head in his hands.

'My son, it's terrible. She's gone!'

Now they lamented together, Mehmet and Melis, Melis and Mehmet, as if competing, the sound of their mourning like the baying of cattle.

'Leyla?' I said.

'She lost the child. And her life. She's gone. She's gone.'

I could not weep with them. A dreadful blow, like an axe on a doomed tree, was laid at the root of my being. All expectation was altered in the twinkling of an eye.

I stumbled home leading my crippled horse, Mehmet and Melis followed.

We made our way to my dwelling and then to the family home.

LEYLA DIED ON the evening of the day I departed. They had expected me to return on the second day.

As is the custom, she was laid in the earth that afternoon.

THOUGH THEY HAD never blamed me for Abdullah's death the passing of Leyla was different.

The burden of their grief was duly loaded onto my shoulders as if I were entirely responsible for her passing. Such things were never said openly. But sullen looks, nudges, the side-long glance – all suggested a change in the weather.

I thought it would pass. After a month it was beginning to get tedious. My days were marked by silence broken only by Melis's weeping.

In the treatment room Mehmet dealt with me with courtesy to please our clients and give the appearance of normality.

Eventually I broke the ice and put the matter to him:

'Master,' I said, 'my situation here is not good.'

He did not answer for several moments, washing his hands in the basin.

'What is on your mind, Kutaissa?'

'Since my wife died, you have regarded me with disfavour.'

'Since my daughter died, I have been sad. Melis also.'

'I was her husband. I loved her.'

'What do you intend to do?'

'What do you suggest, master?' I said quietly.

'Perhaps it is time to leave,' replied Mehmet.

'What would Melis think?'

'She used to be fond of you. Now she might agree you ought to go.'

'Where would I go? This is my home. This is all I have.'

'Where you go is your affair.'

'Don't you need my services?'

'Perhaps. There are other considerations.'

'I thought I had become like a son to you?' I said.

'You nearly did,' he replied.'

With that he dried his hands on a towel and turned away.

I understood only part of what was happening. I was too young to disentangle the webs of grief and love.

I was not Mehmet's flesh and blood. Without family or relatives one learns that a man is a fleeting shadow on the earth's face, a tree without roots, a cuckoo in the nest.

We ate the evening's meal without a word. Before we retired to bed Melis approached and kissed me on the cheek.

Was it a kind of forgiveness? Or something else? I never found out.

Before dawn I gathered together my belongings and the money I had managed to save, took the best horse and saddle from the stable, and set out on the long journey without a backward glance.

PART THREE

THE ARMY

And there was mounting in hot haste: the steed,
The mustering squadron and the clattering car,
Went pouring forward with impetuous speed,
And swiftly forming in the ranks of war;
And the deep thunder peal on peal afar;
And near, the beat of the alarming drum
Roused up the soldier ere the morning star;
While thronged the citizens with terror dumb,
Or whispering with white lips —'The foe!
They come! They come!'

Childe Harold's Pilgrimage,
LORD BYRON

I KNEW NOTHING ABOUT maps, directions, or where it might be best to travel. The location of my own village relative to other places was a mystery. With this basis of ignorance as my guide I followed the sun.

After several weeks of sleeping in the open, scrounging from villagers, and keeping clear of undesirables who were also on the open road, I smelled the sea in my nostrils and arrived at the coast. My first view of the ocean was one of awe. Fierce waves were piling up on the shore in the teeth of a fresh gale.

After a meal of fish and rice my spirits revived. I was told of a city two days ride away following the contours of where land and sea met.

That night a band of strange men captured me, subjecting my tired body to beating round the abdomen and chest. Their intention was not to kill but to take away all I possessed (except my blood-stained clothes). They delivered me as a prisoner to that very town I was intending to visit.

I was taken, blindfolded, my hands bound behind my back, to the ancient crumbling garrison of Trabzon. Here I was provided with a stinking cell, a few crusts of stale bread, and a cup or two of foul water. A leather bucket in the corner was supplied for physical needs.

On the third day the guards seemed to remember I was still there.

They dragged me into an interrogation room and threw me onto the stone floor. They lined up against the back wall as if to thwart any misguided attempt at escape.

I almost laughed at the folly of their alertness as they stood like puppets, hands behind their backs.

Two officers in red uniforms with gold braid and elaborate headgear entered and the guards snapped to attention. I thought of scrambling to my feet but one barked out, 'Stay where you are!'

The officers seated themselves, gazing down with distaste. The right hand officer addressed me first:

'We understand you are a criminal, captured in the act of robbery.'

'No, sir,' I replied. 'I am a master barber on my way to Trabzon'.

'You have arrived in Trabzon', said the other. 'But perhaps not in the way you intended.'

'Certainly not, sir,' I answered.

'You realize we could try you for your crimes and punish you this very day.'

'Yes, sir, except I committed no crime. I was unlawfully captured.'

'Can you prove such allegations are false?'

'I have not yet been told of the charges against me.'

'Robbery, man, robbery. That's simple enough,' snapped the officer on the left.

'What did I steal?' I replied.

'Money, a horse, a saddle. We have the evidence.'

'From whom did I steal these things?'

'Why, from the very men who captured you.'

'They are liars, sir!' I said.

'Well, no matter,' answered the officer on the right. 'We have you now. We will absolve you of all charges on one condition.'

'What is that?'

'That you swear to serve your country faithfully.'

'I would rather be a master barber,' I said.

'We have no need of barbers, masters or otherwise,' said the officer to the left. 'But if you behave yourself, we'll see what we can do.'

Bereft of money, horse, saddle, and other items, I was in no position to bargain.

The first few months of my military service were severe and harsh. But through such servitude many a lesson was taken. As recruits in the Janissaries we were to become part of the greatest army of Europe since the days of the Romans (or so they told us).

Our master was our sergeant (or *cavusbasi*) who took a dislike to me on the first day and delighted in giving me the most degrading tasks. Latrines and the cleaning thereof became part of my daily existence.

My fellow recruits were of the basest kind. Some came from the surrounding areas of Trabzon. Others were foreigners including one who became a particular comrade, a youth from southern Russia, whose destiny was to die fighting his own countrymen. United in enmity against Sergeant Ahmed, Petrov and I formed an unbreakable bond. To this day I remember him with the utmost affection.

Through his patience I learned the elements of the Russian language, a knowledge which would quite soon save my life.

We marched and drilled day after day, cleaned filthy barracks, learned about weapons, and were regularly smacked round the pate by Sergeant Ahmed and his minions. In the meantime they paid each recruit each month a tiny sum, and we wore the distinctive uniform.

If you tell men the same things for long enough they will believe anything. Our perspectives of life became the same as each other. All that mattered was pleasing our superiors and keeping out of trouble.

When initial training ended and the recruits had become in appearance, speech, and demeanour as alike as peas in a pod or rats in a barrel, we were instructed in the possibilities which might lie ahead. Many would be proper fighting soldiers to be directed to the front line among the heat and fury of battle.

This option did not appeal to me. While I had no objections after this military education to ramming a sword through any enemy guts (especially if it happened to be someone like Ahmed) the prospect of close combat appalled me.

Fortunately, unlike some armies, the Janissaries had many support battalions. These included diggers of roads and trenches, the maintenance of camps, the cooking of meals, and baking of bread. More relevant to my own ambitions was the corps of surgeons and assistants who supervised the sick and wounded, evacuating officers and the like to hospitals far away from the fighting.

Of course, each recruit was not allowed to choose his own path. The particular need for any army is for fodder in the field of conflict. It was expected that Janissaries would wish to lay down their lives for the Sultan who had been good enough to accept them into the ranks. One's natural instinct of self-preservation was an attribute discouraged by the authorities for obvious reasons.

It was up to one's sergeant to recommend the direction of each trained soldier. With Sergeant Ahmed this could have been a problem. But a fortunate accident propelled me into his good favours, much against his will.

Just before our passing out parade, training intensified to the point of insanity. We were woken at dawn, slogged till breakfast on the cleansing of quarters, and for the rest of the day were subjected to chores, some of which involved simulated combat on various kinds of terrain.

One day our mission was to climb a cliff on the beach, having marched many leagues to reach the objective. I had no love of ropes and tackle to reach the dizzy heights of the obstacle, especially as there were men positioned at the top to dislodge us with sticks and stones.

I followed Sergeant Ahmed up a rope ladder rigged to the summit, on the basis that his journey upwards might be less hazardous.

In this I was mistaken. Only halfway up the cliff a stone from above struck Ahmed on the helmet causing him to lose his grip and crash to earth, nearly bringing me with him.

I clung to the ladder and saw him plummet to the rocky shore beneath.

With satisfaction I observed his prone body, annoyed that I was now exposed to any stray missiles hurled upon us.

To protect myself from any recurrence of the happening that had swept the sergeant from his perch I decided to abort the climb and go to ground level to see if Ahmed was dead or alive.

This involved pushing past some of those still ascending, bringing forth much cursing at my interference with their progress. But with determination I achieved my aim.

—

Sergeant Ahmed was stretched out, his left leg twisted beneath the right. His nose and mouth were oozing blood. I wondered if these were mere abrasions, his body having taken the force of the fall.

It was clear his left leg was broken. I found a strip of wood, flotsam on the beach, and straightened out his leg as gently as possible, binding the splint to the shattered limb.

The pain brought him round. Opening his eyes he began to swear at me. By now a few recruits, not wishing to risk their health on the ropes and ladders, joined me.

'What are you doing, Kutaissa?' said one.

'I have set his leg,' I replied. 'I need you and the others to improvise a stretcher for the sergeant. There's plenty of wood on the beach.'

They set to it with a will. A few minutes later we moved down the shore to where the officers waited. They carried the patient to the outside of the tent set up for casualties. A surgeon came out to meet us and I explained the situation:

'Sir, this is Sergeant Ahmed. He fell from the ladder. I have strapped up his broken leg in the manner in which I have been trained.'

He looked down at the stretcher.

'Bring him in. And you,' (pointing to me) 'you come too. I need assistance.'

The military exercises had only just started but even so there were some dozen injured men on beds round the tent.

The surgeon cut away Ahmed's clothes. I helped as best as I could, eager to make a good impression.

He removed the makeshift splint, complimenting me on my workmanship. When he examined the leg itself the surgeon appeared even more satisfied.

'I think you saved his leg,' he said, though I was not sure how he knew this.

While we worked Ahmed regained his senses once more, a current of foulness emerging from his mouth. The surgeon looked at him sharply, the sergeant realised where he was.

'Sergeant,' said the surgeon, 'you have this man to thank for saving your life as well as your leg.'

Ahmed might have preferred to curse both of us. But he thought better of it and went quiet.

'What is your name?' asked the surgeon, looking towards me.

'Private Kutaissa', I said, coming to attention as I spoke.

'Well, Kutaissa, we have need of men like you.'

Sergeant Ahmed, who on his previous record would have had me marked down for latrine digging and heavy labour, did his best to nod in agreement.

From that very day I was assigned to the surgeon, to serve him and learn what I could.

WHATEVER SKILLS I had received from the hands of Mehmet proved limited compared to the knowledge my new master now demonstrated. It became necessary to learn how to hack off limbs, gouge out a bullet from the flesh, deal with sword wounds, and carry the wounded from the battlefield.

It was not long before the unit moved to the scene of a real battle. This involved much work in the dismantling of tents, transportation of surgical instruments and operating tables, shifting of bunks and other items of furniture, and all the paraphernalia of logistics.

—

We had many wagons and horses but needed more strong labourers. But every available man was mustered to face the enemy. Even the entreaties of the surgeon himself could not induce the authorities to budge.

As a consequence I retired each night to bed with aching limbs. As the battle drew nearer the number of those on sick routine diminished, aided by periodic downgrading of all trivial physical conditions among patients from 'unable to attend duties' to 'fit for active service'.

We travelled for weeks on the long road to the war zone. As we approached we heard the noise of cannon and shot in the distance, a frightening sound. One of my companions instructed me that such a commotion merely indicated the fighting was some leagues away. We were (as yet) in no kind of danger.

As we advanced nearer the front we were overtaken by lines of men tramping towards glory and death, loaded with baggage, weapons, and supplies, feet trailing in the dust, their shoulders bent under the burden. Occasionally a cavalry regiment swept past, the plumes of the helmets waving proudly, a bright sun reflecting on breastplates and swords.

Eventually our surgeon decided we had come forward enough. Then began the setting up of camp, digging defecation trenches, unloading goods, and preparing to take in the mangled torsos of those who an hour or so before had been lusty and able bodied.

The hours before battle presented a warm night full of stars. A golden moon shone its ghostly light over our silent world. A league or two from us thousands of fighting men slept uneasily or not at all.

Here our unit waited with different expectations.

A T DAWN THE guns and shouting began promptly. Either we had attacked the enemy or they were attacking us. Somewhere in the wooded hills ahead a great noise erupted, its tumult like a storm pouring its blood-stained lava over the face of the earth. A sound like nothing heard before — shouts, shrieks, drumming hooves, explosions.

A stream of stretchers, limping men, frightened horses, could be seen coming towards us. The bearers of their sad cargoes advanced doggedly into our camp.

We had procedures, well drummed into us. Hopeless cases were set to one side, potential amputees were sorted by orderlies. Officers not seriously injured were allowed priority, flesh wounds were bandaged by poorly trained underlings.

My task was to assist the surgeon. The first patient was placed like meat on the table, his garments stripped from him, a diagnosis speedily made and treatment administered. Half the skill was in holding down these young fellows, their dignity taken from them the instant the bullet or sword struck, changed from men into slobbering children.

Hour after hour we worked, the pile of amputated limbs growing, each man in attendance sweating and silent. We lost many warriors that day on the table, each dying in his own manner, some with a curse or prayer, others screaming and yelling.

The floor, our clothes and hands, the walls of the tent, were crimson with gore. The smell from bodies blown open became our memorable companion, seeping into our garments, marking us with battle.

Most pitiable of all were the boys, some not more than twelve or fifteen years old. They yelled for their mothers in

—

delirium. There was little that could be done for them. I longed to stab a dagger in their hearts or slit their throats to still the cries that poured from them, their smooth, small bodies rent with cuts and fissures.

The battle continued most of the day. The enemy were Russians, stubborn and courageous, outnumbered but equipped with guns and leaders superior to ours.

In the early afternoon we became aware that dreadful things were happening. For one thing the tide of wounded became a deluge overwhelming our poor facilities. Newly wounded men were placed in rows round our tent. Yet more and more still came for our help, broken, groaning and pathetic.

Past our encampment came running soldiers, no weapons in hand, having thrown them away to aid their flight. Riderless horses and fleeing cavalry raced by, hell-for-leather in twos and threes.

But this trickle changed to a horde, a mighty host of former fighters, running for their lives. Some on foot were trampled by the cavalry who appeared now in greater number. One or two high ranking officers also rampaged past.

Our surgeon looked up at me as he bent over his three hundredth patient that day:

'Kutaissa, the retreat has begun. We wait here whatever happens.'

'Yes, sir,' I replied.

I had expected our troops to be victorious. The mettle of the enemy was unknown. New fears entered our hearts. It was a complete rout of the Turkish army.

After an hour or two the avalanche of men passing the tent diminished. A strange quietness came over us. The prone squads of wounded seemed to hold their breath as if listening for what might happen next.

We worked on. One of our colonels appeared in the doorway, blood pouring from his head from a sword wound.

'You can all leave now,' he shouted. 'The enemy is coming. You have ten minutes at the most.'

The surgeon took no notice. The colonel saw that not a single man moved, such was our stupor. It was less our obedience to duty than tired apathy, a numbing of the senses.

Half any hour later any questions about the incoming foe were answered. The vanguard of their force advanced on our tent with wrath, fired up by the slaughter they had already enjoyed.

We heard the slicing and the chopping of their weapons as they gorged themselves on the wounded laid round our perimeter. The screams of the dying were terrible as were the yells of the victors.

'Stand fast!' said the surgeon.

At that moment Russian hooligans burst in through the opening of the tent their swords red and dripping. But entering this arena of blood was enough to give even such villains pause for a moment as they stared at our own frightful mess.

Not for long. One of them ran the surgeon through and killed the man on the table with a quick thrust. An orderly was slashed through the arm to the bone. Others fell to the ground as more assailants rushed in, hot on the chase.

I had gone to the back of the tent to collect more bandages so was furthest from the entrance. By the time the Russians reached me they had killed a few more and the impetus of their movement was blunted.

I put my back against the tent. In such moments is one's destiny sealed. I raised my arms, and in a trembling voice spoke to them in the Russian language in words I had learned from Petrov during the months of training:

'Good soldiers, I am your prisoner, I am your prisoner.'

A huge man with blood smeared on his face advanced towards me and knocked me round the head with his fist.

As I fell to the ground one of the Russian officers appeared in the doorway. A single word of command saved my life, though I was seized and trussed up like a turkey with my hands behind my back, and forced to my knees. My head reeling, I remembered another word or two:

'Thank you, thank you,' I said to the officer.

Things were calming down even though the danger was not quite past. The officer came to me as I knelt like a penitent before him:

'You speak Russian?'

'Yes, sir, yes, sir!'

'Take him outside,' he shouted.

I was half carried, half pushed, past the bodies of my companions. Outside lay butchered men. Those who escorted me slapped my face and obliged with a kick or two. I dragged my feet causing them to grunt and mutter but I did not wish to lose sight or contact with the officer.

Fortunately the latter had no desire to stay in the stench of the treatment tent and emerged looking disarranged as if offended by the savagery of his minions.

'That wasn't necessary!' he said to himself.

Coming to me, I saw that indeed he looked crestfallen.

'What is your name?' he asked.

'Kutaissa, sir,' I said, lowering my eyes from his gaze.

'What is your rank, Kutaissa?' he said.

'Orderly first-class, sir.'

'And what were you before you joined the army?'

'A master barber, sir.'

'Well, Kutaissa, will you promise not to escape if we untie you?'

'I do, sir.'

'Very good.'

'Yes, sir. Thank you, sir.'

The interrogation ended. My hands were untied. I was taken deep into the Russian lines.

THE CARNAGE ALONG the lines of battle was horrendous. Our army had been decimated. It would take days to clear the fields of their debris.

I joined my fellow prisoners, though few in number. They set us to work digging pits for the dead and carrying corpses to be disposed of. In this way, by sad chance, I found the remains of Petrov, his face anguished in death, chest and legs cut to pieces.

I rolled him into the great pit where soldiers are dispatched by the hundreds every time armies collide.

Whatever we had to do, we did. We wrapped dirty cloths round our faces to lessen the smell. Some prisoners were full of loathing against the brutal enemy.

As far as I was concerned it seemed I had passed over the bridge of Death and returned. I was a man who had dug his own grave and yet found he was still living.

Inwardly I laughed at the antics of the Russians urging us on in the burying of the dead, as if hurrying this way and that made any difference.

T HE NEXT MORNING, after a shallow sleep, I was summoned from our group of prisoners to attend a patient. The man in question was a general whose stomach was subject to spasms and exceptional bouts of pain. He was lying on a chaise longue in a spacious tent, surrounded by servants.

The general's valet had been killed by a bullet in the thick of battle. Why were no Russian physicians available to attend? But this was not the point. The general required relief. By chance I was on hand to minister to him. Not that, in my ignorance, I could do much.

I prescribed a mixture of honey and milk, adding a small preparation of laudanum.

Within an hour the general's discomfort settled. He was up on his feet, his face bright with content. Ordering me to be brought into his presence, he slapped me on the back, guffawed, and appointed me as his own barber, helpmate and companion.

Well, perhaps I exaggerate a little. But the transition from sickness to health would make any man sing like a bird or confuse his wits. Forthwith, the general's underlings attired me in appropriate livery, though by their faces one or two resented my promotion.

N THESE NEW circumstances I discovered my birth and origins provided me with a number of advantages over more privileged aspirants. Having nothing to lose I could afford to be honest with my new employer. Within a few weeks I was able to whisper in the general's ear about shortcomings of certain members of his entourage, their laziness, incompetence, and fawning falseness.

The poison of truth was gradually introduced into our private discourse, perhaps as I dressed him in the morning, brushing the slightest touch of dross or dusting off the gleaming uniform with light caressing fingers.

At first caution was essential. I was not sure in those early days whether a general wished to hear of certain observations from a mere dresser. But all men of great rank and authority are in love with snippets of trivial gossip, mild slander, and the gist of private conversations secretly eavesdropped.

'Ah, that's the way the wind blows!' sighed the general, as I mentioned to him (quite casually) how one of his officers had mildly criticised his treatment of another member of his staff. The officer in question, from that day onwards, became noticeable by his absence, having been transferred to one of the more dangerous battle areas of the Russian empire.

Having tasted a little sup of the heady potion of such power, I went out of my way to find out more about everything. As my knowledge of the Russian language increased daily I was not averse to hiding behind doorways or curtains to overhear fragments of useful material.

Sometimes I made up a few stories to see if my fish would take the bait. To my amazement, the more outrageous the tale, the more my general swallowed it whole.

The exercise hinged on a simple fact. The general trusted his valet who shaved him, washed him, dressed him, cared for him, etc., far more than any in the circle of sycophants who gave him military advice. Of his immediate companions the general was dismissive and suspicious.

After all was there a single one of them who was not after his job, one way or another? If they hitched their wagon to his star there was a field-marshal's baton in the offing perhaps. But the humble, low-born, obsequious, soft spoken, Turkish valet – there was a friend in disguise to be trusted and listened to. For, having achieved, without expectation, the zenith of his elevation, what had this small, insignificant foreigner to gain further?

Moreover, the general actually liked me. In my presence he became infinitely gullible, like a little child, open to every malicious lie or half-truth the mind could engender. I had stumbled across an inalienable truth forgotten by a world blinded by an individual's overweening rank and status.

This truth was as follows. My general was not a clever man. In effect he was a simple man. Far less complex than say, Mehmet the master barber, that paragon of duplicity and scheming. The beauty of the situation was that my general incarnated the simplicity of a kind of genius. Such a man has little problem in making up his mind one way or the other. Such a man believes in his very bones that all his decisions are rational and straightforward. Excessive thought merely confuses a man of action. Better to go straight to the point every time.

The inferior mind is handicapped by complexity. In strategy meetings, which from time to time I attended, standing at the back of the room hands clasped behind my back, the pathetic minions advanced all kinds of theories, spun like a spider's web with weak but plausible links.

The general usually swept every iota of this high spun balderdash aside with a single phrase. The stupid officers capitulated without a struggle.

In battles, it became clear, as in life, a simple approach trumps the complex. A general must think clearly, moving from A to B and from B to C without digressing into the superfluous. That, for the most part, is how soldiers attain the glory of becoming a general. Such thinking is the product not so much of a military education but of natural propensity.

I have never since met a successful general who was not at heart a simple man, with simple pleasures, and a simple understanding. That is the way to win wars, to see the outline of things uncluttered by extraneous matter, to make up one's mind in minutes, and then to be able to push the plan further forward as events unfold for better or for worse.

Such was my general − clear thinking, simple, brilliant, successful, a winner, and, as a consequence of his strengths, easily fooled by those who knew what they were up to. To get close to this kind of man is not easy or usually possible. The mere sight of another uniform with much gold braid and ribbons would put the general on his sharpest behaviour.

Only a valet with a silver tongue could outflank him and lay an ambush from the most unexpected directions.

My persuasiveness was steadily built up, brick by brick, day by day, month by month. I would try a trick or two and see if it worked. Usually, if planned in advance in detail the system operated like a dream. I made sure that those who spoke or acted against me, by small deeds, irritable faces and gestures, were punished for their folly.

In the same way a polite whisper in the general's ear could

alert him into promoting some officer or other who had treated me in the way I believed I deserved.

Naturally, my endeavours remained subtle. The dividing line between achieving one's aims and failing to do so is, in the case of a valet, a true art. To succeed everything had to be perfect.

Thus my laying out of his clothes, my organisation of his wardrobe, my remedies for his health, the smoothness of coiffure and shaving, the immaculate quality of his uniform (and boots), the sense of ease that he felt in my company – every single thing needed to be better than could possibly be imagined.

I felt as if a single speck of dust on newly polished boots, or a tiny touch of corrosion on a brass button or belt, or the selection of an incorrect uniform on just one occasion, would be enough for a loss of confidence. Any sloppiness due to human frailty was avoided like the plague.

The faith my general placed in me soon became noticed in his entourage like a stone gently cast into a pond arousing slight ripples on the surface. Thus a reciprocal effect came about, quite surprising at first, but logical in its place. In other words the general's officers, at first slyly, and later more openly, began to feed me nuggets of information they wished to communicate to the general privately, perhaps even anonymously.

Some began asking questions, initially of an innocent kind such as, 'How is the General today, Kutaissa?' to which I invariably replied, 'In absolutely splendid spirit, sir!'

Later the same individuals would venture further such as 'Is the General available for a few moments later in the morning?' This suggested that they needed to confer with him, perhaps on a personal matter, or merely to draw attention to themselves.

The upshot of such requests was that soon after, when I was

at the general's feet giving his magnificent boots a final flourish with a duster before he went about his duties, I would whisper:

'By the way, sir, I believe Major Fedorov would like a word with you later.'

This was followed by a moment's silence and then, always:

'I wonder what *he* wants.'

If I knew the answer, I might occasionally supply it. But better to bite one's tongue and say nothing, for to know a fact and not let on is in itself a source of power.

After the meeting was accomplished the general often told me what it was the officer had on his mind. It could be a request for compassionate leave, to get married or visit a sick relative, or possibly a fussy detail that Fedorov, or whoever it was, thought the general should know about.

Occasionally the officer in question would thank me for arranging the meeting. If that happened it were best no eavesdropping ears were present. (Enemies could be made that way.)

THE POST OF valet eventually involved travelling to various territories, as well as visits to St Petersburg for several weeks at a time, for the general to confer with his peers and superiors.

It was in this charming city that a somewhat embarrassing event brought the general and his servant into closer partnership and intimacy. The general was a widower and, as such, when opportunity arose, susceptible to the charms of women. At a state ball one evening the general's eye fell on a young maiden of outstanding beauty.

By reason of his rank the general managed to outmanoeuvre

the young bucks who vied to dance with her. From my observation post in the gallery near to the orchestra I saw how the cunning man remained by her side throughout the evening, ignoring all protocol and dancing etiquette, resolutely fending off any usurpers who might loiter on the periphery waiting for their turn to court the pretty thing.

Distant though I was from the action, I surmised that the general's attentions were not entirely welcome to the beautiful creature. Whenever she tried to break off the engagement he would sweep her into the next dance, pulling her closer to him as steadily he drank more vodka, oblivious to the resistance in her demeanour.

As a valet's occupation involves being informed about such things I took care to infiltrate the company down below, using the excuse that I needed to convey an urgent message to my general.

By these means and discreet questions here and there I discovered that the lady in question was the orphan of a military family, in the guardianship of her uncle, a middle ranking officer of some distinction in the service.

(For reasons of discretion, let us assume her name was Antonina, for she later married a wealthy courtier who should not, even years later, have cognisance of this unfortunate affair.)

The general, in his infatuated folly, decided to invite Antonina to tea one afternoon, a request which he imagined could scarcely be denied by her guardian in view of their respective positions in the military hierarchy.

'Did you see her, Kutaissa?' said the general, excited beyond belief. 'I have never seen such a lovely woman!'

I apologised that my own vantage point throughout the evening was that of a distant observer. This therefore rendered me incompetent to put forward an opinion.

The general, just for once, was not listening to me, caught up in the flood of emotions that quite unbalanced his usual poise:

'I want you to deliver this invitation, Kutaissa. Take my carriage, invite her for Monday afternoon, and make sure she comes.'

If the general had asked my advice I might have advised against this. The girl was too young to be fooled with in this way. I could see potential hazards. Nevertheless the general's whim was my command. Thus I was taken in his private coach to the lady's home.

By some extraordinary chance Mademoiselle Antonina answered the door herself, the maidservant being indisposed that day and the guardian out of town on battalion business.

I tipped my cap and put on the charm. She was certainly exquisitely tasteful, a peach waiting to be plucked. Apart from her physical beauty there was a becoming innocence in her voice liable to inflame the senses.

'Mademoiselle, I have a message from the General.'

'The General himself?' she whispered, partly in awe but also in apprehension.

'Yes. He is a busy man. But he would like to arrange for you to attend at his invitation for tea tomorrow afternoon.'

She paused, her long eyelashes lowering in modesty, her bright blue eyes however not too coy to gaze into mine.

'But my guardian is away this week. I would have to ask his permission.'

It was time to dissemble. I had my clear instructions.

'No matter, mademoiselle. I believe the General has already put the matter in hand.'

'Oh! Do you mean I already have permission?'

I bowed to her, as a servant should.

'Well, the General has asked me to invite you. He is fully aware of all that is involved. And he *is* a very honourable man.'

Across her peerless features I observed the elements of confusion flitted briefly. The tight compression of the eyebrows, the top lip pursed downwards, the delicate biting of the lower lip. I felt myself stirring to her perfection. I knew now what the general saw in her.

'You will of course be fetched in the General's own coach,' I added, as if this was a further inducement sufficient to conclude the deal.

She was thus caught in the trap, unable to turn to her guardian and not wishing to appear rude to the general's servant.

I handed her the general's invitation, written on a small piece of card in his neat, soldierly handwriting. Antonina glanced down at the brief note, flustered, out of her depth, vulnerable.

'Well...thank you,' she said.

'Tomorrow it is then, mademoiselle,' I replied, bowing once more.

'Well, I suppose it is,' she said in a voice both tremulous and uncertain.

'Good. I will be here with the coach at three.'

'Thank you.'

She closed the door. I caught a scent of her fragrant perfume and my heart beat a little faster. When I got back in the coach I mopped my brow with a handkerchief, having caught some of the Antonina fever.

I returned in triumph to the general and told him the good news.

'Did you see her guardian?' he asked.

'He was absent, sir,' I said. 'But she seemed delighted to be invited.'

'Really?' he replied, a slight gloating appearing in his face. 'Kutaissa, what would I do without you? You make everything easy for me.'

'It is my duty, sir. And, of course, my pleasure, sir.' I bowed courteously.

He beamed at me like a man about to make a conquest.

THE NEXT AFTERNOON I was thrilled to see Antonina again. But such feelings were well masked behind my servant-like composure. By the time I arrived at her house at a discreet ten or twelve minutes past the appointed hour, she was ready to step into the coach. It was a warm summer day and she had placed a light shawl round her shoulders to cover her *décolletage*, fashionable at the time.

As is customary I took my perch next to the coachman, allowing Antonina the required privacy for the short journey to my general's home.

The coachman was a taciturn man, neutral in appearance, a mere cipher on the landscape, without opinions or conversation, whose function was to look after the horses and drive the coach, work he did very well. (I admire these attributes in a servant more than I can say.)

At the general's abode I opened the door for the girl, helping her with a gentle hand down the step. Her smile was a ray of sunshine from heaven. My heart melted with desire for her but I merely bowed my head and directed her through to the salon.

'The General will be with you in a few minutes,' I said,

as she alighted like a glorious bird of paradise onto the silk cushions of the chaise longue.

The general, in his best uniform, was loitering in the dressing room.

'Mademoiselle is in the salon, sir,' I said, inclining respectfully towards him.

'Well done, Kutaissa! How do I look?'

'Excellent, sir,' I replied, deftly brushing round his shoulders to remove a speck of hair which had come from his mature bald head like an intruder. 'Excellent, indeed.'

After a brief, proud glance in the full-length mirror our warrior wheeled round and departed towards the field of battle.

WHAT PERHAPS THE general did not know was that high up behind the salon was a tiny, forgotten corridor I had discovered quite by accident when ferreting about in a quest to chart every room and cranny in the building. From this cubby hole I could, by means of a discreet spy hole set in a picture, listen to and watch all that transpired in the room beneath.

I spent many a happy hour eavesdropping not only on the general himself but also on his visitors as they spoke among themselves. Gossipy morsels such as that can be very useful in a number of ways.

I was curious to see how the general might behave on this special day. He presented himself to his guest with a mild flourish, and sat down in the armchair opposite the chaise longue like a polite suitor. The conversation featured the usual opening gambits with chit chat about the weather, the ball the previous week, the busy life of a general, and an enquiry about the health of her guardian, whom the general understood to be out of town.

The recipient of these jewels of discourse seemed somewhat nervous, as well she might, but her magical voice still resonated in my soul whatever banalities might be exchanged. The effect on the general himself in a state of love sickness was even more intoxicating.

A manservant knocked at the door and entered with trays of cakes and a samovar. The formalities of pouring and choosing were enacted. After such ceremony, lasting for half an hour, the manservant returned and removed the impedimenta with quiet dignity, closing the door behind him as he left.

Antonina gestured as if to leave but the general insisted she should not depart yet for the afternoon was still fresh and bright. He expressed a desire to show her some miniature paintings of scenes of war. She answered in terms of the warmest appreciation of seeing these little works of art.

Emboldened by her apparent eagerness the general advanced with two such miniatures in his hand, and sat next to her on the chaise longue to point out the precise details that distinguished the paintings. As she bent her lovely head to look, her long hair trailing down like a horse's mane, I noticed how the general moved closer to her.

They whispered a little more about the paintings though by now the subject had run its course. He took the miniatures from her and placed them on a table behind the chaise longue. Turning to more important matters the general slipped his arm round the girl and pulled her towards him.

She became alarmed.

'Oh, sir!' she said, almost in a parody of modesty. But it was genuine enough as far as I could make out.

The general kissed her firmly on the side of her face and then attempted to move to kiss her squarely on the lips.

In the slight melee this action provoked the girl appeared to slip off the chaise longue onto the floor. Nothing daunted, my brave general pursued her to the floor, pushing her flat to the rich pile pattern of the Persian carpet, clasping her strongly and pressing his lips onto hers.

She twisted like an eel but the corpulence of the general was sufficient to pin her where she lay. She squealed a bit when managing to turn sideways to escape his immediate kisses. But he covered her mouth with his left hand, making sure she could not move away or make any sound.

With his right hand he plunged beneath her dress, tearing down the petticoats and undergarments, opening her up to his frontal attack with cannon and cavalry. In a trice he had thrust off his breeches and commenced the deed, his left hand shifting from her mouth to her breasts which he groped and pummelled with fierce intent.

The scream she let out was truly terrifying, the cry of a betrayed soul lost in a drowning world. As he found relief, the general too uttered deep groans and sighs of satisfaction, thrusting mightily till completion was nigh and he was drained of all passion.

Antonina lay back on the carpet, silently weeping. The general moved off her recumbent body, pulling her dress down as if to preserve her modesty.

After what seemed ages they both rose to their feet, each in a particular way attempting to restore their clothing. He pulled up his trousers, she tearfully put back together her female attire.

The general relapsed into the armchair. Antonina sat shivering where she had been before on the fatal chaise longue, her body shaking as if with convulsions.

I SPEEDILY EVACUATED MY point of vantage, brushing any stray dust from my face and livery. Hurrying to the salon, I knocked on the door. Though no answer came I entered the room without permission. The general seemed pleased to see me.

'Ah, Kutaissa,' he said, like a man at the end of his tether. 'I am glad you are here.'

Antonina appeared bereft and no wonder. She was no peasant girl used to being taken by any passing labourer. She was a woman of sensibility and beauty. Now, like a precious vase, she seemed to have been broken and ruined.

Antonina, looking up at me, in a pleading tone, asked, as a child asks for a doll, 'Would you take me home, please?'

'Certainly, mademoiselle. Let me escort you.'

She rose from the chaise longue. Leaning on my arm she limped along out of the salon and along the hallway. The coachman was waiting, his horses sweating in the heat of the afternoon.

I helped her into the coach and went in with her, sitting next to her. We set off at a gentle trot to her dwelling.

'I gather,' I said quietly, 'the General was indiscreet.'

She said nothing, her face red with weeping and shame.

I waited for a moment or two.

'What do you intend to do?' I asked, speaking gently as if to a frightened mare.

'Nothing,' she said, 'nothing at all.'

'Good,' I replied. 'The General is a great man, a friend of royalty, a hero of the nation. He should not be subject to scandal.'

'Of course not,' she said, wiping a tear from her face.

'Besides,' I added, 'none of us is without sin.'

She cast me a curious look.

'What do you mean by that?'

I smiled slightly.

'Only what I said. We are all sinners.'

'Does that help?'

'It might.'

She lapsed into silence. She knew what I meant. In the previous few days I had made enquiries in the right places.

Yes, there were whispers that her guardian had already sampled the golden fruit. God knows how such things emerge. But servants, especially maidservants, know everything about lords and masters and mistresses.

Money opens mouths and from greased lips much is whispered, salacious, malicious, partly true and partly exaggerated. It is that which is more or less true that interests a person in my position. This time I felt secure in the information gleaned. Such knowledge, gained by gossip, can also be used for purposes of security.

By the time we reached her guardian's house her silence and mine implied agreement that her secrets and those of my general would remain dormant.

WHEN I RETURNED to the general he appeared in a state of despair. He paced up and down, his polished boots thudding like drum beats. 'Things got out of hand, Kutaissa,' he said. 'I did something I shouldn't have done. If this ever gets out, I'm finished.'

'Such things happen, sir,'

'I don't know how it came about. Something got the better of me.'

'It's understandable, sir,' I replied. 'She is a beautiful woman.'

'Am I an evil man, Kutaissa?' he said, almost breaking down in tears.

'You have no need to concern yourself, sir. I have settled the matter.'

'How, Kutaissa, how?'

'Not without difficulty, sir. But the problem is resolved.'

He sat down on a chair, holding his head in his hands.

'If this ever gets out...my career is over. I shall become a leper in society.'

'It will not, sir. On all I hold sacred, I promise you, sir. It is over.'

'How, Kutaissa. What have you done?'

I waited a moment or two before replying.

'Let us say, sir, that the lady herself is not entirely beyond reproach. I have information to that end.'

'How do you know such things, Kutaissa? What are you? A devil in disguise? Or a ministering angel?'

I laughed aloud.

'Neither devil nor angel, sir. Just a man. But I am your servant. It is my duty to protect you where I can.'

'Thank God for you, Kutaissa,' he said. 'I've never met anyone like you. I am in your debt.'

—

'Not all, sir,' I replied. 'Rather it is that I owe everything to you. And will continue to do so.'

With that he clapped me on the shoulder. For the rest of the evening we drank wine together as if we were brothers.

SUCH WAS THE general's relief at avoiding the guilt of his indiscretion that he began praising my virtues to all and sundry.

One might think men in authority have much more to converse about than their valet's qualities. But small talk over the card table covers many topics even for the grandest of mortals. Such gossip can be carried, as it were, like seeds on the wind, casual remarks germinating till what was trivial becomes altogether different.

The general spoke to an admiral who spoke to a diplomat who spoke to somebody else. The consequences of this chain of chit-chat were to be beyond imagining.

A FEW WEEKS LATER, as we loitered in St Petersburg, I carried the general's official mail into his study, as was usual each morning. One particular letter, delivered by courier, caught his eye. As I turned to leave the room, the general called after me:

'Kutaissa, wait a moment. There's a letter from the palace here.'

'Very good, sir,' I said, standing near the doorway in a respectful posture.

The general opened the letter and read it, his lips moving silently as he did so, a characteristic habit of his. 'This is strange,' he said, as if to himself. 'Very strange.'

The general was accustomed to dialogue with himself of this kind. It was not the cue for me to intervene but to stand still and wait. He read the letter again, held it up to the light to see the watermark, read it again, and ran a finger over the fine grain of the paper.

'I am to attend a reception at the palace, Kutaissa,' he said.

'Excellent, sir,' I replied.

'But you are to attend as well, Kutaissa.'

'Sir?' I enquired, the word strangled in my throat.

'I am commanded to bring you with me.'

'That's very strange, sir.'

'That's what I thought.'

'Perhaps there's some mistake, sir.'

He perused the script again.

'No mistake, Kutaissa. It says distinctly that I am to bring the man named Kutaissa to the reception.'

'But how do they know my name, sir?'

'That we shall probably find out for ourselves.'

(I was not sure what to think and thus said nothing.)

'The letter is from a secretary,' the general commented thoughtfully. 'Ah yes, the secretary to the Grand Duke.'

My grasp of the ruling hierarchy of Russia was vague. I had heard of the great Empress Catherine but the rest of the story was lost on me. My job was cleaning the general's boots and keeping out of trouble.

'The Grand Duke?' I uttered, in parrot fashion.

The general put the letter on the desk and leaned forward on his elbows.

—

'Kutaissa, you know so many things, I forget sometimes you are from another country. I shall have to educate you before we go to the reception and tell you what's what and who's who at this peculiar court of ours.'

'The Grand Duke sounds very grand,' I said, an attempt at humour.

'Yes, I think he *is* very grand. He is, so they say, slightly odd. They also say it is unlikely he will inherit the throne.'

To hear my general describing a member of the royal family to his servant as 'slightly odd' was intriguing.

'Who then, sir, would follow Her Majesty the Empress?'

'Ah, there you have an interesting question, Kutaissa. Rumour has it that Paul's son, Alexander, would be preferable.'

'Is there anything else I should know, sir?'

'Well, just in case you meet the Grand Duke Paul himself. I would point out that His Royal Highness is very fond of soldiers and armies.'

'Then such a man would surely make a marvellous emperor.'

'Possibly, Kutaissa, possibly.'

With that the general waved his hand indicating that our conversation was at an end and he had work to do.

I bowed and left him to it, my head buzzing with the mystery of it all.

OVER THE NEXT few days I made enquiries among certain acquaintances about the true state of the nation's affairs, not mentioning, of course, the invitation to the palace. The evidence which came up explained much of the general's reticence in talking about the Grand Duke Paul.

First and foremost, the man was renowned for his ugliness, in particular for his snub nose, a squashed plum sitting in the middle of his face. He was a short man, well below the usual height, resembling a dwarf. Legend had it that he was, furthermore, an idiot, one of those stunted imbeciles which the in-breeding of royalty regularly threw up.

Not only that, he was a *vicious* idiot, the soldiers of his private army being subjected to extreme discipline and insane punishments far exceeding anything in any other army.

In short, the man appeared to the general public like a creation from one's wildest nightmares. If ever he took the throne bloody chaos and anarchy would result. Such things had happened before. Russians were long accustomed to the follies and whims of rulers.

To meet such a creature would not be a blessing. But if the grand duke was as mad as some alleged it was not perhaps entirely out of character for him to summon a general and a valet to a reception in the same breath.

My main anxiety was that somehow Antonina was involved in this. A trivial complaint about a valet muttering veiled threats to her in the carriage after she had been violated by the valet's master would be punishable by death in my own country. The arbitrary power of monarchs is to do as they please, whether bound by law or no.

A sleeping serpent unravelled in my bowels causing me to feel slightly nauseous. For such a feeling I applied my usual remedy of honey and milk, laced with opiates and strong spirits. But the sense of fear remained.

—

OR THE NIGHT of the reception my general fitted me out in splendid livery so that, at my master's behest, I looked more like an officer than a servant. My green tunic fastened smartly at the neck was festooned with gold braid, my white breeches were set off by a new pair of gleaming boots.

The only things lacking were epaulettes of authority on each shoulder and the officer's hat with its gleaming imperial badge. Thus I did not look out of place when the general was attired in his extravagant best dress uniform, complete with ceremonial sword in a gilt scabbard, each detail appropriate to his immense authority.

On this occasion I rode with the general in his coach, sitting next to him, his usual aide-de-camp having been dismissed for the evening.

'Kutaissa,' he said fussily, as we trotted towards the royal abode where the reception was to take place, 'you will remember to stand discreetly behind me this evening.'

'Certainly, sir.'

'This is all quite irregular.'

'Yes, sir.'

'The whole thing is very strange.'

'Yes, sir.'

With that he lapsed into silence for the rest of the journey.

T THE PALACE (whatever palace it was I can hardly remember now) immaculate sentries saluted the general. Once inside the gilded hall a number of high ranking uniformed men approached my master.

None of them had their valet with them except the general. Several of them glanced curiously at me and looked for my badges of rank. Seeing none they studiously ignored me.

I stood doggedly behind my general like a bodyguard. Before long they accepted me as part of the furniture, though some jokes were made at my expense.

They were provided with drinks and the conversation became loud and hearty. I was conspicuously without refreshment but this kept my head clear and calm.

The general became more talkative with each cup he downed. Eventually he was so confused that he called me forward and introduced me to an admiral or two as well as various other distinguished personages, each of whom looked down their noses while I inclined forwards in a half bow:

'This is Kutaissa, my valet,' stuttered the general. 'I don't know what I'd do without him.'

'Quite so,' said his companions, shifting uneasily, unwilling to catch my eye.

Any attempt to move behind the general was now negated by my master himself, who kept insisting that I should meet this or that person.

My growing embarrassment was fortunately terminated by loud fanfares signifying the entrance of the Grand Duke Paul himself. All eyes turned to the royal party as they came into the hall.

At first it was difficult to make out the individual figures in the procession. But as they advanced closer I saw the central hero himself, wearing a military greatcoat with huge brass buttons and several large medals, a wide field marshal's hat pinned with an imperial star, a red sash round his body, riding boots which seemed too big for his small legs, and black breeches partly obscured by the greatcoat.

Halfway down the hall the grand duke swept off his hat with a flourish and bowed to the gathered crowd. We all, as one body, bowed even deeper in his direction. Now that his hat was off I could see his features in total clarity.

My first impression was of the width of his forehead, stretching back to the edge of a wig slightly too small for him and set half way along his pate, making him look older than his actual years. His eyebrows were set high above his rather pig-like, sombre eyes as if perpetually raised in astonishment at something he had noticed or heard.

His nose, ah yes, his nose – this appeared from the front flat against his face, as if someone had punched him and broken it in a fight. The length and breadth of his vast forehead dwarfed the rest of his features, making him look compressed, a tiny child's face surmounted by a vast dome, an image of a man seen in a madhouse.

But those peculiar drooping eyes were quick to focus at this moment on a pretty woman standing at the front of the crowd, her reverential bow causing her breasts to be extravagantly revealed. The grand duke stared with a strange vacant intensity, like some predatory animal.

After what seemed an eternity those lazy eyes swivelled round to the other side of the company with equal intensity, a lingering gaze as if he needed time to take in whatever sight he focused upon.

By now, in my unusual progress, I had seen a number of powerful men and in the case of my general had come to appreciate his special virtues and weaknesses.

But the presence of the grand duke was beyond any such

experiences. When that look fell on others one felt immediate fear that this individual was wearing the badges of office, the accoutrements of power. There was a terror within his person that waited, concentrated, intense, brooding, to break out into unpredictable action.

With a further flourish of the hat he entrusted the article to a servant, waved his arms, and the entire audience began their talking and drinking once more.

THE GRAND DUKE began to mingle with the guests, and the protocol seemed well understood by everyone in this gathering. My heart began to beat furiously. I gulped with nervousness and started to perspire.

The general noticed my discomfort. 'Bear up, Kutaissa. You have done well so far,' he whispered into my ear.

Hardly had he spoken when the small crowd parted, and the Grand Duke Paul approached the general. Fortunately at that moment I was indeed partially hidden behind my master. But as the general stooped to bow somewhat lower than perhaps was requisite, the prince's languid eyes fastened upon me, piercing to my very soul.

At close range his visage was overwhelming to one such as myself. It reminded me of when I had once come close in the fields to a venomous snake, though in that distant past the reptile allowed me to live.

In that instant as his eyes met mine I became aware of the enormity of the moment and thrust my head and upper body forward in ritual imitation of the general's posture in front of me. I hardly dared come back up again but kept my eyes towards the floor for as long as seemed necessary and polite.

The grand duke spoke:

'Glad you could come, General. I heard of your great success against the Turks.'

'I am too much honoured by your kindness, Your Royal Highness,' said the general, bowing again. I bent forward to mimic his movement.

'Is this Kutaissa?' asked the prince, my obeisance still in progress.

'Let me introduce, Sire,' said my general, 'Kutaissa.'

I bowed again.

'Ah, Kutaissa,' remarked Paul. 'I've heard about you.'

(His voice was small, high, and piping, slightly edgy, almost like a woman's voice.)

'Nothing too averse, I hope, Sire,' I said, astonished to hear my own voice emanating from some depths of surprise and horror.

To my amazement the grand duke laughed, a slightly disturbing chuckle as one might hear from a half-witted child. It went on further than any possible amusement and was echoed by the sycophantic response of those around us, as if the royal laughter must be admired and responded to by similar sounds.

'Nothing averse indeed. But what sort of name is Kutaissa? I've never heard of such a thing.'

'I'm from Turkey, Sire.'

'Ah yes, one of our enemies, no less.'

Here Paul laughed again at his own joke, once more inspiring guffaws from the company, his amusement going on and on.

'No, Sire,' I replied. 'I am in the service of our great General.'

Paul seemed slightly ruffled by this, a look of bewildered anger coming over his face, the transition being sudden, like a cloud passing across the sun.

'Great General indeed! But from tonight you will be in *my* service. How do you like that?'

I gulped, unsure of what to answer. This too was madness. The suddenness, the embarrassment in front of my master! But my general came to the rescue.

'Of course, Your Royal Highness, he would like that very much. I am highly honoured.'

'That's agreed then!' replied the grand duke.

Without a further word, he turned and stomped away, his large boots clumping like the steps of a crude farmer over the polished marble floor.

THE GENERAL TOOK me aside, visibly shaken by this development.

'My dear Kutaissa, forgive me. I had no idea this was going to happen.'

'Sir, can we not change this? Do I have to go?'

'I am sorry. The Grand Duke has spoken. The die is cast.'

'What will happen? What do I do now?'

'I don't know. Perhaps in the end you might return if the Grand Duke tires of you and throws you back into the pond from which you were taken.'

'I want to stay with you, my general.'

'I cannot go against the Duke. I have heard of this sort of thing before.'

'Thank you, sir,' I said, seeing the game was up. 'I'll write to you and let you know how things are.'

'I wouldn't if I were you. If you enter the service of the

court, be very careful. Don't commit yourself to writing. This is different from the army.'

'I understand,' I replied, though in truth I did not.

I could have thrown myself down at my general's feet in abject weeping. But I kept a straight face and bowed to my dear friend and patron for the last time.

At that moment a servant from the court approached us.

'Excuse me General, but may I escort Kutaissa to his quarters?'

'If you must,' said the general, somewhat crossly. With that he defied protocol and hugged me to himself like a father embracing a son.

I never saw him again. My general was that very week posted to some far eastern corner of the Russian empire. He died there of a fever three months later.

PART FOUR

GATCHINA

This unholy time is just right for my way of life.

Le Mondain (The Civilized Man),
VOLTAIRE

Y FIRST WEEKS in the royal service were steeped in fear, regret, and curiosity. Frankly, I was out of my depth. I was put to work preparing the grand duke's uniforms, polishing his buttons, boots and decorations.

It became necessary to learn the steps in the chain whereby his apparel such as shirts, undergarments, socks, towels, sheets, and so on, were taken to the laundries, and then returned to their master. Within a few weeks I was expected to supervise every aspect of this routine, a complex responsibility.

The process involved inspection of the vast rooms where the cleansing of garments and accessories took place. Dozens of washer women poked with long sticks into cauldrons of boiling water crammed with the filthy linen of the aristocracy. The smell, the heat, the noise, the clouds of steam, were akin to hell itself. The workers were scantily clad as they toiled.

I learned how the system operated. Even here were elements of corruption. The clerks who paid over the wages cheated the poor creatures, extorting fines for bad work, a sum which went straight to their own pockets. The payment distributed was well below the amount declared to treasury bureaucrats.

I made it my business to find these things out. It was not long before the chief clerk tried to incriminate me in their methods, assuming I would wish to trade a few of his profits for the price of silence. I procrastinated with the man, told him I had not yet found my feet, but would return to him later.

This seemed to please. He smiled, shook my hand, and

padded off in a state of elevated self-satisfaction.

The day came when somebody in authority considered me ready for duty as valet to the grand duke. In this role I was instructed by two sub-valets as to what was required.

Their explanations were politely reticent but they did let slip that a previous valet had been severely punished and stripped of employment for an infringement. His mistake may have been a word out of place or an unnoticed speck of dust on a shoe.

By the time of my first morning on duty in the grand duke's bedchamber I was prepared for anything.

My new master was snoring loudly when I entered, a foolish nightcap on his head the only part visible as he huddled beneath the copious blankets. The routine was to draw the curtains and to wait. Eventually with a final grunt and mutter the grand duke woke up.

'Good morning, Sire,' I said, bowing as I had been told to.

Without a word my new master extricated himself from sleep and climbed out of bed. Having procured a large chamber pot from beneath, he turned his back to me and passed water noisily into the receptacle.

With this task completed, the grand duke replaced the pot in its hiding place and turned to me, indicating I was to remove his nightgown. This I did, lifting it up gently as though dealing with a child.

After a few ablutions from a bowl of cold water, during which I sponged him down and dried him with a towel, we moved to the ceremony of shaving and dressing.

For the latter stage it was obligatory to assist him with each garment, including the wig, for he scarcely ever lifted a finger beyond what was necessary.

The final act of the drama was the fitting of the boots, the grand duke sitting on the edge of the bed for this to be enacted. Transformed, Paul moved to the full-length mirror to look at himself.

'Good!' he murmured. 'Very good indeed.'

'Thank you, Sire', I replied.

Then it was off to the state-room for breakfast, which on this particular day he took in isolation, apart from the servants, while I stood, hands behind my back over by the door.

The grand duke ate his morning meal with a loud squelching noise for his teeth were not good. He also slurped his drink, nobody ever having corrected his table manners.

But so far, so good.

A FTER A FEW weeks of service to the grand duke I had sorted the situation out. The man was undoubtedly odd, verging at times on a kind of insanity. His madness manifested itself in little things.

Sometimes he found it difficult to decide which boots he would wear that morning. At such moments his humble valet would have to humour him, assisting with the trying on of several pairs, most of which appeared identical in colour and design. (This was not surprising as every piece of footwear had been specially made for him by the same shoemaker.)

As various boots were fitted and removed, fitted and then removed, the grand duke was not averse to hitting me round the head with his fist. The first time he did this I was shocked.

But he never took particular notice of my discomfort nor any signs of regret at having perpetrated this assault on my person.

God help any serving wench or attendant who made a mistake at meals. Failure to comprehend an order or some minor error of conduct could result in the back of his hand across their face, no matter who was dining at the same table.

It was not that Paul enjoyed giving pain to his inferiors or even causing them embarrassment. Rather it seemed he was so unaware of the consequences of his own actions that he did things on the spur of the moment. Indeed, a few minutes later he might be patting the victim on the back, complimenting him for the excellence and competence of his service.

Reflecting on such incidents I had good cause to wonder how such a man might fare if he became emperor. The gossips among the lower echelons of the court were however strong in their belief that Empress Catherine would take steps to ensure her son would never rise to such eminence.

The present ruler had power within the constitution to select her own successor. It was well known that Catherine treated the grand duke with contempt and disdain terrible to witness.

But as far as my own relationship with him was concerned a number of interesting aspects became apparent. In particular Paul trusted nobody in the courtly circle, especially those meant to be his close, personal advisers.

He could not trust or love his mother in view of her seeming hatred of him. The memory of his father, whom he revered far more in death than he might have done in life had the man lived longer, was tainted by Catherine's own treacherous behaviour towards her husband.

Paul feared constantly he was in danger of poison, betrayal, accident, plots, or secret activities on the part of unknown assassins, His anxieties were rooted in the horrors of childhood when he heard on the wind so much about murders, removals, and tortures which befell men of esteem and power.

All this turned out to be my golden opportunity. The grand duke, against all the odds, trusted me.

Despite his lapses into bullying I sensed as the days passed that something about me lulled the grand duke into a sense of security. I realised this when he began to address me not as Kutaissa but simply as 'Figaro', the supreme barber.

He also spoke from time to time about various personal matters, at first as if he was alone by himself, musing out loud. But before long I ventured to answer him, and at such a point he responded accordingly.

'Figaro,' he began one morning. 'When we go to Gatchina you will meet my wife.'

'I look forward to that, Sire,' I said, with a bow of my head.

'Yes, and I can tell you that I love her deeply.'

He turned to look at me full in the face and I kept his gaze without averting my eyes downwards. His ugly little visage suddenly resembled a desperate boy, seeking a companion.

'Such love is rare, especially in the court. Here most marriages are arranged, but *not* mine, *not* mine. Do you understand that?'

'Indeed, Sire,' I replied.

'My mother hates her. My first wife died in childbirth. Terrible agony. But I must forget all that. I love my wife.'

Such nuggets of information I kept to myself, like prime cards in a game where much is wagered. With the grand duke my intention, my necessity, was to know everything worth knowing.

THE TIME CAME for Paul's entourage to move to the fortress of Gatchina. Packing up and travelling was a massive task. Fortunately my lord and master was in a good mood on the occasion of leaving his mother's palace. Consequently he needed me in the preparations close by his side to fuss over him, leaving the hard work of lifting and shifting to everybody else.

From St Petersburg to Gatchina we took it easy, our extended caravan of fine horses and carriages, accompanied by cavalry and infantry, proceeding at a snail's pace.

As we neared Gatchina, Paul summoned me to ride in his coach. 'I want to see your face, Figaro, when we reach my little kingdom,' he exclaimed, a foolish smile on his lips.

How could one describe an experience such as entering the palace of Gatchina? Rows and rows of troops in Prussian uniform were lined up in front of the gates. They presented arms with the utmost precision, somewhere in the distance a mighty band played.

'My children!' whispered Paul as the coach door was opened by a young officer.

Wearing his large cocked hat, resplendent with cane and sword, high jackboots and the glorious uniform of Leader of the Preobrazhensky Regiment encrusted with half a dozen medals and emblems of bravery, Paul put on a suitably martial face and stepped forth to much saluting and fawning.

I stayed where I was and watched the proceedings. A Teutonic-looking man with a pinched, mean face and ramrod back, also in elaborate uniform, came forward to salute the grand duke. This was Baron Steinwehr, at that time in command of the garrison.

The welcoming procedures took well over two hours. There was much marching, firing of salutes, goings to and fro, parades hither and thither – the entire military paraphernalia.

When eventually our cavalcade entered the fortifications one could but exclaim at the enormous size of the place. The grand duke had his own castle complete with toy soldiers.

Later that night, as I helped him disrobe, Paul's face was flushed with wine and excitement.

'What do you think? Isn't this a magnificent place?'

'Like heaven, Sire,' I said.

'Heaven indeed, Kutaissa. This is my home. This is my domain.'

I had never seen him in such good humour. But it was not to last.

T HE NEXT MORNING, following the completion of my morning duties, Paul, suggested it would be a good idea if I spent the day finding my way round the Gatchina grounds. He advised me not to wear palace livery and not to appear too ostentatious.

In accordance with his orders I donned old clothes and set off to explore. The entire area of the huge parade ground was full of soldiers drilling, hundreds of them. Apparently they trained and marched from dawn till dusk. But Paul was waiting a day or two before resuming his usual role in their activities.

After an hour or two of watching the immense labour of the troops and, hardly failing to observe, in one corner of the square, some punishment squads at work on offenders, I began to find the military oppressive. I passed the sentries at the gate and walked out towards the general direction of the lake.

On this fine summer morning the prospect of escaping for

a while from the intense atmosphere of the palace filled me with joy. I proceeded along a wooded path with massive trees.

I had not gone far before I became aware of the rustling of leaves and cracking of twigs, and coarse voices. As I turned to face the commotion I saw a band of soldiers with bayonets fixed, advancing towards me. Their expressions were not friendly.

I stood my ground as they surrounded me, their leader a mere corporal but full of himself. He spoke first in German, a language I knew nothing of. That I did not respond seemed to make him angry. But when he began speaking Russian, in a peasant dialect even more incomprehensible, things got worse.

They threw me to the ground where a few pokes with rifle butts on ribs and stomach softened me up. Getting me to my feet, with several slaps round the face from the corporal, the questions began.

'Who the hell *are* you?' shouted the corporal. He aimed another blow at my face as I tried to answer.

'I am Kutaissa,' I said, intending to continue that I was the servant of the grand duke. But at the very mention of my name a dreadful growling emanated from the throats of these hooligans.

'He's a foreigner. He speaks with a peculiar accent.'

'Where are you from?' barked the corporal. 'East or south?'

There was a special terror in being surrounded by such as these. I could smell their filthy breath and unwashed bodies. For all their fine uniforms they were a rabble.

The corporal did not wait for an answer. Drunk on his power he snapped out commands in German which resulted in my arms being trussed like a chicken. I was thrust up the path down which I had so happily walked a few minutes before, and trundled back into the fortress.

Once through the gate they dragged me into a cell and cast me onto the floor. The soldiers administered a kick or two for good measure.

An officer was summoned to examine the prisoner though it took time to find him as he was engaged in supervising drill on the far side of the square. By the time he arrived my face would be well bloodied and I had lost a tooth. The soldiers carried me to the interrogation room and sat me in a chair, my hands still tied so tightly behind my back that it seemed blood could hardly pass through the veins.

The officer entered, the guards jumped to attention with Prussian zeal. The officer's uniform was immaculate, not a grain of dust, not a blemish, his helmet gleaming. His military moustache was a caricature of his profession. But his eyes were hard as diamonds, and the lines of his mouth were cruel.

He stood and looked at me, holding silk white gloves in his right hand. The corporal came in and gabbled at him, now speaking in Russian, looking pleased at the brave capture of this enemy.

'He said, sir, his name was Kuta, or something. We caught him in the woods, sir, skulking around. We brought him in, sir.'

'Thank you, corporal,' said the officer.

A chair was brought into the room for the gentleman to sit down.

'What have you got to say for yourself?' he asked, his speech clearly that of an educated man.

'Could you untie my hands, sir?' I said. 'I am hardly likely to escape.'

The officer motioned to one of the guards who came forward and did as I requested. The pain in my hands was unbearable as the circulation surged through.

—

My wrists had indentations and white jagged lines where the rope had bitten into the skin.

'You are a foreigner,' said the officer. 'What were you doing in the woods? That part is off-limits to civilians.'

'I am Kutaissa,' I said, tasting the blood on my bruised lips. 'I am valet, barber, and personal manservant to the Grand Duke of Russia.'

'You are a servant to His Royal Highness?' The officer laughed aloud. 'Where is your livery? You are dressed like a peasant.'

'I arrived at Gatchina only yesterday. I was going for a walk.'

'Really? But surely Your Royal Master would have told you of our strict regulations here. That is if you really are who you claim to be.'

He paused for a moment or two.

'You will stay here. I have things to attend to.'

The officer left the room, the guards snapped to attention. We waited. I rubbed my chafed wrists and looked at the soldiers, intending to recognise them when this matter was sorted out.

After an uncomfortable quarter of an hour another officer came in, this time of a higher rank. 'Are you the man named Kutaissa?' he asked.

'I am Kutaissa, sir,' I said, 'personal manservant to His Royal Highness, the Grand Duke. I have been treated very badly.'

'I can see that,' he replied. 'But these things happen. We have our orders. We cannot be too careful. There are spies everywhere.'

'Then I am allowed to leave?'

'Soon. What I do not understand is how you come to be in this situation. Why did you not explain to the patrol the facts of the matter?'

'It is difficult, sir, to have a discussion when rifle butts are hitting you in the stomach. They gave me no chance to answer. My master will not be pleased.'

The man looked stern but was not put off.

'I think he might be. We have proved our efficiency. Sorry it had to be at your expense.'

With that I was permitted to rise to my feet, though feeling weak and feeble. A carriage was provided to take me across the square to the grand duke's quarters.

Y good fortune, on entering the private rooms after my ordeal, I ran into Paul. I was a sorrow sight, still bleeding and wretched.

'Figaro!' he shouted. 'What happened to you?'

'Sire,' I said. 'The soldiers arrested me, accused me of being a spy, set upon me in the guardhouse. I was interrogated. They abused me. I told them who I was. They didn't believe me.'

Paul emitted shrieks of high-pitched laughter.

'Ah, my poor man! I was testing our defences. You must agree you do have a rather suspicious appearance.'

'Sire, I expect these men to be punished.'

'They will be. Severely punished. While they were beating you, half a dozen real spies might have slipped through.'

Paul could not contain his amusement at my expense. But mindful that to lay rough hands on a servant is tantamount to insulting the master, he urged me to clean myself up, put on my livery, and accompany him to the guardhouse to pick out the soldiers concerned. This chore I carried out with the greatest pleasure.

—

In the company of the grand duke and a small squad of his personal bodyguard, we took a carriage back across the square, the men following on behind at the double. The two officers involved were fetched into the presence of His Highness. I inspected the soldiers who had apprehended me.

A particular delight was to select the idiot corporal whose incompetence had landed me in this mess. As far as possible I tried to identify the other members of his patrol. But for good measure I also pointed a finger at the guards of the interrogation room who had tied my hands. With a dozen men or so now chosen, Paul, the two officers, and the offending soldiers, moved to the punishment area of the square.

Here it delighted me to watch my assailants stripped to the waist, tied to a block, and duly provided with no less than twenty lashes for an offence against proper military conduct.

Their officers watched with indifferent expression as if used to all this. The work was carried out by a most capable sergeant. By the time he had finished we were all exhausted and ready for lunch. The miscreants, with salt rubbed in their raw wounds, were penitent but in no condition to walk or speak.

Thus, on the first morning in Gatchina I learned something about the place and about my master I would not easily forget.

GATCHINA WAS NOTHING but a madhouse, a military one at that. It was here that Paul's soldiers were dragooned and disciplined to his heart's content. The officers were disreputable, cashiered or dishonourably discharged from more prestigious armies. The men in the ranks were criminals and vagabonds, scum from every nation.

I wondered how the empress permitted this miniature army to flourish like a cancer in the heart of her empire, not far from the seat of power. The answer was that anything her son did was not taken seriously. Time after time Paul volunteered his army to fight alongside Catherine's own regiments in every kind of skirmish that ever arose. He was always turned down, commanded to keep the men where they were.

Such rebuffs made him train the poor brutes of Gatchina harder, prolonging drill, route marches, polishing of brasses, boots, buttons, swords, helmets, the endless cleaning of barracks and latrines.

Paul, once in Gatchina, changed from self-indulgent fop to Prussian maniac. His voice, ever high-pitched, now twanged in mimicry of how he thought soldiers should behave. His utterances became crisp and cryptic, speaking in short strangled sentences.

'Fetch my greatcoat!' he would bark while I was already holding the garment ready for him to slip into it.

The correct answer was to reply, with a slight click of the heels, 'Yes, Sire!'

My arrival at Gatchina brought me into proximity with Paul's wife, the former Sophie Dorothea of Würtemberg, now the Grand Duchess Maria Feodorovna. From the start she treated me as if I was mere dirt.

One morning she came down the corridor accompanied by three ladies-in-waiting as I was on my way to Paul's bedchamber. As is customary I stood by the wall and bowed my head to allow her to pass. Instead of continuing on her regal way, she stopped in her tracks and swung round towards me.

'And who are you?' she said, her voice as soft as the rustle of silk and as sharp as steel. (A pointless question for she knew exactly who I was.)

'My name is Kutaissa, ma'am!' I whispered, not daring to raise my eyes.

'Kutaissa! Oh!' She broke into trilling laughter, and turned to her attendants. 'His name is Kutaissa!'

Like tame parrots, they mimicked her merriment, as if an amazing joke had been spoken.

I didn't begrudge them their moment of humour at my expense – their reckoning would come later. It is the place of servants to snigger when their employers sniggers, to weep when they weep, in all things to act as a mirror to their mood.

'Why do you speak in that strange accent?' said Maria, turning back to continue her torment. This was richly ironic coming from her whose German accent was audible in every word she uttered.

'I apologise, ma'am. I am from a far country.'

'Turkey, I suppose. Like the bird. Though I never liked the sound it made nor the taste of its flesh.'

This was the occasion for further amusement, peals of jollity ringing through the corridor from all four of them.

I bowed my head and replied, 'Yes, ma'm!'

She flounced on with the entourage, her point having being made. Slightly smarting from such gibes I proceeded to Paul's bedchamber and, having knocked, entered.

'You're late, you're late,' snapped Paul, though he knew that I was not.

'I am sorry, Sire,' I said, bowing towards him, 'but the

Grand Duchess addressed me in the hallway.'

'Ah, so you have met the wonderful lady.'

He paused, staring at me as if to say 'I told you so'. 'Well, what did you think of her?'

'It would be impertinent of me, Sire, to advance any opinion.'

'Not at all! Come on, tell me what you think. Isn't she beautiful?'

'The Grand Duchess is radiant beyond what my poor words could ever express.'

'Tell me more. You are a man of the world. People don't always speak their minds to one such as myself. Tell me, in all honesty, man to man, what did you really think?'

As if to relish my answer Paul came close towards me, placing his two hands on my shoulders, and looking me straight in the eye.

'The Grand Duchess is the perfect image of womanhood. Her Royal Highness is the greatest beauty in the world.'

'Yes, she is. But tell me more.'

'The Grand Duchess has a beautiful voice. The voice of an angel.'

'Oh, yes, yes,' he exclaimed, his face bright with excitement. 'You are such a good judge of people. What would I do without you?'

'You are too kind, Sire,' I replied.

He dropped his hands from my shoulders and turned away.

'Ah,' he said, as if the previous conversation had never taken place. 'These boots I am wearing are too tight. Polish the pair I wore yesterday. I'll wear them instead.'

'Indeed, Sire,' I said, glad to be back on solid ground.

HORTLY AFTERWARDS PAUL gave me my new name. It was one afternoon, just as he came hot foot from the parade ground and was preparing to sign a sheaf of requisitions for arms and supplies. Looking up from his desk he gestured me to approach him.

'I have decided on an important matter,' he said, as if about to declare war or ascend the throne.

'Indeed, Sire,' I replied.

'I have decided to change your name to Kutaissov. It's more Russian. 'Kutaissa' has a feminine ending, it's embarrassing. That's why you keep getting into trouble with all sorts of people. Have you any objections?'

To me such matters were not worth a feather. If he wished to change my name to Caligula or Nero it would not have bothered me.

'Sire, thank you. This is a great honour.' I bowed from the waist. He liked that.

'Well, that's settled. But not quite.'

'Not quite?'

'No, not quite at all! Let me ask you this. What religion are you?'

I gulped, caught off guard. It was a subject never previously mentioned.

'Sire, I am…' I hesitated.

'Yes, spit it out man. You must know what religion you are. Are you a Christian man?'

'I was not raised as a Christian, Sire.'

'Well, what were you? What are you?

At this moment his elbow caught the pile of papers on his desk and sent them cascading to the floor.

'I'll pick those up for you, Sire,' I said, beginning to bend down to begin the task.

'Good God no! Let's settle this. First things first. This is more important.'

'Well, sire. I follow the religion of the Ottomans.'

'Yes. What religion is that?'

It occurred to me that Paul was unaware of any religion existing in the world beyond that which he followed himself.

'It is the religion of the east, Sire.'

Paul was now becoming irritated for he banged with his fist on the table, toppling a few more of the precious papers.

'But, damn it, man, what religion is that?'

'We follow the teachings of the Prophet, Peace be unto Him, and the Word of God, which is the Holy Koran.'

'Hmm...' Paul sat back in his chair, as if deep in thought. 'Well, does this book of yours differ from the Bible very much?'

'Sire, I have never read the Bible.'

'Well, I have been talking to the Grand Duchess. She thinks it's time you became a Christian, like the rest of us.'

'That might be difficult,' I said.

'Put it this way. When I married the Grand Duchess she joined the Russian Church. She had to give up the other. I demanded it. In the end, it was easy enough. She came over. Now she loves it.'

'Could I not remain as I am?'

Paul thumped the table again.

'Of course not! We all have to be the same here. Dammit, I need you by my side. I've got used to you.'

'So I have to change my religion?'

'Yes. The Grand Duchess thinks it's necessary. And I do too.'

I had no wish to discard my faith like worn out clothes to suit this madman. To stay in his service I already practised a hundred subterfuges and dissimulations.

I tried to buy time, to enable him to forget about the matter:

'Could we think about this for a few days, sire?'

'No, the matter is out of my hands. You must make up your mind. I need to tell the Grand Duchess. She cannot abide having other religions she knows nothing about within the palace walls. But if you change, as we require, the problem will no longer exist.'

In that moment I decided to pretend on this issue as with others. One could speak words, make promises, and lie at the same time, as men always do.

Paul was drumming his fingers with impatience on the finely polished desk.

'What do I have to do, Sire, to fulfil these obligations?' I asked meekly.

'That's more like it. I ask the world of you and you give me what I ask. I like that in a man. You are willing to become a Christian?'

'I await your command,' I said.

'It's easy. I'll arrange for you to have preparation with a priest. It shouldn't take long, and then, hey presto, you are one of us.'

What an ignorant madman the emperor was. All things were baubles to him, toys to divert the mind, tools to manipulate others.

Wealth, religion, power, authority – these were for him spume on the sea, gossamer in the fields, to be taken and blown on the breeze.

In that moment I hated him with every fibre of my being.

THE NEXT DAY I met Father Nikolai, whose task it would be to shepherd me into the embrace of the Russian Church. He lived just outside Gatchina but was summoned to the fort to attend and begin the induction whereby he might coach me into the mysteries of their strange beliefs.

Our sessions were held in the chapel. Father Nikolai possessed a distinguished face, his ecclesiastical beard giving a beatific serenity to his presence, a man seemingly without vanity. But who knows what went on under the surface?

Sufficient to say I was drawn to him from the start. If any man could tempt me from the faith of my ancestors, Father Nikolai was as good as any.

'What do you believe, Kutaissa?' he began.

This was difficult as I believed in very little. Belief in religious matters was less 'belief' as such than taking for granted certain ideas embedded into village life.

I had to be careful with my answers.

'We believe,' I said, cautiously, 'there is one God, and no other.'

'Good!' he said, smiling. 'We believe the same.'

'Does that mean then,' I asked, puzzled, 'that our God and your God are the same?'

'Indeed they are,' he said, his eyes twinkling. 'If there is one God for you and for us, it must be the same.'

This was reassuring though it proved to be a prelude to much hot air and peculiar superstitions. In particular I disliked kissing icons and giving them veneration which seemed to me some kind of blasphemy. But what the icons represented, it seemed, were actual people who had existed hundreds of years ago and represented the basis of belief. I had never heard of any of them and could not remember ever hearing about them.

As we spoke I discovered that in those elements where I could not possibly accept Father Nikolai's beliefs, he read me like a book. I had become accustomed to deceitful people. With Nikolai deception was not possible.

As he was a man who could not be fooled I found it expedient to find out where I stood with regard to one or two things. Thus I posed the most significant question.

'Father Nikolai, you have been asked by the Grand Duke to bring me into your church. Does this mean you have to tell him how I am getting on with my lessons?'

He smiled at me as if I were a small child.

'My son, to speak to a single soul about your progress, or lack of it, would be against my conscience. My lips are sealed. You must trust me.'

I was intrigued to know whether he was deceitful like the rest of society or whether truth was his real creed. After everything I had experienced I had no desire to put trust in any man.

So I replied with another question, teasing out whether I was suspended above an abyss, or a disciple with an honoured teacher:

'Am I an evil man, Father?'

He paused before answering.

'I think you are capable of evil. Perhaps because you have been forced to live among evil men.'

I launched out onto a further branch of a perilous tree:

'Is Gatchina evil?'

'There is evil wherever men gather together. Gatchina has as much or as little evil as any other human place.'

I was not used to thinking in such terms. My position was

that of a ship sailing close to the wind in order to reach its destination. Queries about the existence of the wind, its source, had never been part of my vocabulary.

Before we finished the first session, after three hours of debate, Father Nikolai leaned forward and took my hands in his:

'I know now what kind of man you are. But remember, to enter my church you don't have to understand or believe every single detail.'

'But the Grand Duke has told me I must come to you, or I shall be cast out.'

'Precisely!' he replied, with the hint of a chuckle. 'That is why, after all the talking back and forth, you *will* join us. Even a priest can see the wood for the trees.'

It was perhaps that remark which made up my mind.

SOMETIMES FATHER NIKOLAI saw me twice a week, on other occasions only once. After three or four such meetings it was clear that the further the sessions progressed the more confused I became.

Father Nikolai was a learned man. He was also persevering.

'My son,' he would begin, 'you are too anxious. Faith is a matter of acceptance rather than understanding. Surely that's not difficult to grasp.'

To prove his points he would quote from a number of saints, Saint Irenaeus of Lyons, Saint Maxim the Confessor, Michael of Tver, Dimitrius of Thessaloniki, Sergius the Abbot, Saint Hermogen, John of Kronstadt, Saint Justinian, Saint Basil the Great, Saint Cyprian of Moscow, and a score or more of others.

Whatever they said (or Father Nikolai said about them) went in one ear and out the other. Quite why I was expected to give these characters the benefit of the doubt was obscure. But when I nodded in agreement Father Nikolai became very affable.

Thus there was a solution. Agree to everything, toss in a polite enquiry from time to time, seem pensive, and this was taken as improvement.

'How do we know he said that?' I might ask.

'Because it was written down,' replied Nikolai.

'But what if the person who wrote it down changed it in some way?'

'Because he was a holy man who was saying these words.'

At this stage a subservient dip of the head was sufficient for Nikolai to move to the next subject.

Eventually we progressed to new aspects – the nature of sin, redemption, resurrection, heaven, hell, priests, communion, forgiveness, angels, saints, false gods and goddesses, icons, procedures, beliefs, confessions, etc.

Whatever I knew of my old faith now appeared to be simplicity itself. But in my head matters became jumbled and muddled. I wanted such discussions to be over and done with.

In the end things were rushed along. On the appointed day a large circular font, draped with white sheets, was set up in the Gatchina church. I knelt in front of Father Nikolai. A small congregation of soldiers, their wives and children, a few of the servants, and some villagers from round about, watched the ceremony.

Father Nikolai said a few prayers, and then, in a religious voice, chanted, 'Who are you?'

'I am one who desires to know the true God and seeks salvation.'

'Do you reject the faith, festivals and ceremonies of your previous faith?

'I do!' (Such a vow cut me to the heart, as I renounced my former life, my childhood, and all I ever believed or half believed. But no matter.)

'Do you truly believe in the Nicene Creed, the sacraments thereof, and do you swear to uphold all Christian beliefs?'

'I do solemnly swear.'

Father Nikolai then bound me to the new faith with chains of iron:

'Do you swear to renounce all previous faiths or thereby bring upon yourself the wrath of God?'

'I do.'

I was led to the font, where I was taken behind the screen and given my new baptismal name of Ivan Pavlovich Kutaissov. I immersed myself in the chilly water while the congregation sang the hymn '*Ye that Have Been Baptised in Christ Have Put on Christ*'.

After the ceremony Father Nikolai embraced me, called me 'my son', and advised me to go to regular confession to absolve my sins.

In return I inclined towards him, thanked him for his kindness, and in my heart resolved never to go to confession.

THUS CHANGED I continued in my service to the grand duke. Like a child eager to please a parent I looked for differences in his behaviour towards me now.

But for Paul life flowed on like a river. What had been said or done yesterday was tossed aside. My 'conversion' was complete. From his point of view no reason existed to dwell on such matters any longer.

But there *was* something else on his mind. One morning as I attended in his bedchamber he turned as if to engage me in chit-chat:

'I have a matter I wish to discuss with you.'

'Sire?' I replied.

'Have you ever thought of taking a wife?'

He chuckled as if the very idea was ridiculous.

'No, Sire. I had never thought of such a thing.'

He sat down in his favourite chair and leaned back:

'*No, sire, I had not thought of such a thing,*' he repeated, mocking my voice. 'Well, perhaps you should think of such a thing. Perhaps it *is* time to think.'

My mind flashed back to years ago when another superior suggested a similar matter. As then, so now, my answer was the same.

'I am not sure I can afford a wife, Sire,' I replied.

Paul laughed.

'Of course you can. Besides you deserve a rise in your stipend.'

'That is very generous.'

'Not at all. A mere flea-bite, I assure you.'

He looked up at me, his tired eyes fixing me in a stare. I glanced modestly downwards. 'Would you allow me to advise you?' he said.

'Of course.'

'I have a woman in mind that might be suitable.'

'Indeed, Sire?'

'Yes, very, very suitable.'

The grand duke was full of surprises but this surpassed all of them.

'May I know more?'

'Well, there is a small problem. You would be marrying above yourself.'

To this there was no acceptable response except a further question.

'Perhaps my increased stipend would help, Sire?'

Paul found this highly amusing and guffawed, ending his laughter with a slight coughing fit as some wisps of wig powder floating in the air caught the back of his throat. He took a sip of wine from a glass on the table and recovered his voice.

'Not in this case. The lady has money enough for both of you.'

'Who is this lady, Sire?'

'Ah, I can see you are interested.'

'Indeed, Sire.'

'She is one of the ladies in waiting of the Grand Duchess. Of mixed parentage, Russian father, German mother.'

'Is she a lady of beauty?' I said, trying to sound light-hearted.

'Beauty? Perhaps not. But sound in wind and limb, very sound.'

'How old, Sire?'

'I would estimate her age at around thirty-six, or perhaps a year or two either way.'

This would place her at several years older than myself. I had no objections to that.

'The lady in question is a widow and has two children, a daughter and a son.'

I realised that for some reason it was important to Paul that this matter was resolved soon. Having pitchforked me into his church, he was now matching me to a mare. But what had I got to lose? I have no false pride. Life is a wheel of destiny which revolves and who knows whether or when one's fortunes will rise or fall?

A MEETING WITH THE woman in question was arranged. It took place in one of the smaller salons of the palace. I put on my finest livery, brushed my hair and polished my shoes.

The lady was half an hour late. I waited in the salon agog with curiosity. Eventually she knocked on the door and entered.

Thirty-six years old she was certainly well past. Her age was more like midway between forty and fifty. On that point Paul had gilded the lily.

She had blue eyes, a magnificent head of blond curly hair, well cushioned bosoms, and the air of a woman of the world who could tell a fool from a wise man.

She curtsied to me:

'Monsieur Kutaissov,' she said, 'The Grand Duke has suggested we should meet.'

Her voice was pleasant, each word delicately articulated.

'At your service, Madame,' I responded, bowing to her.

Her name was Natasha. Her husband, a military officer, had been aide-de-camp to a number of eminent men. Alas, he had been killed in an accident on manoeuvres.

She was a lady of means – the rich texture of her dress and sumptuous necklace gave the game away. Yes, she had served in the grand duchess's entourage, perhaps more as *confidante* than lady-in-waiting.

I understood what Paul had meant when he implied that I would be 'marrying above my station in life'. My own experiences with women had been servant girls, washer women, peasants, the occasional prostitute, a farmer's spouse, and, of course, Mehmet's daughter, my own dear half-forgotten wife now in her grave.

Natasha listened to anything I said with polite attentiveness and spoke concisely with an exquisite turn of phrase. I gained the impression she could have been, at least at one time, a courtesan, trained to please men in the arts of discourse, dining, pleasantries, dancing, etc. That this paragon was being given to me on a silver platter was tempting.

When she left I could smell her perfume wafting in the air like a remembered dream. For days to come I could think of nothing but her.

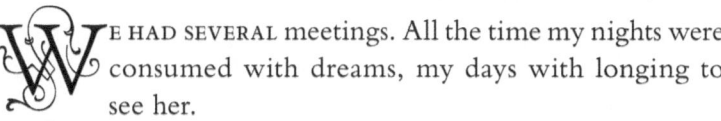

E HAD SEVERAL meetings. All the time my nights were consumed with dreams, my days with longing to see her.

'What did you think of the lady in question?' asked Paul one morning after breakfast.

'Very good, Sire. Very good indeed.'

'I heard that you have had one or two meetings.'

'Yes, sire.'

'And do you think she might make a suitable wife?

'I hardly dare to contemplate the matter. She is magnificent.'

'Well, commit your hand to her, show her your cards. Don't linger too long. There may be pirates in the vicinity, or wolves. Who knows?'

With this he chuckled and gave a grotesque wink.

AFTER SOME WEEKS I decided it might be time to test which way the wind was blowing. So I arranged a rendez-vous with Natasha in the gardens near the ornamental labyrinth.

She arrived late, in a red dress with a blue shawl, bright as a bird, her mood jolly. We entered the labyrinth, moving further into the high twisting hedges.

'We shall get lost in here,' she whispered.

'Hopefully,' I said.

We walked without speaking. Having turned a dozen corners, and now within the depths of the foliage, I stopped and fixed my gaze upon her.

'Madame,' I said, 'I must declare my affection for you.'

She shrugged her shoulders, not sure what to reply.

'Madam, I have fallen into an enchantment.'

Still she said nothing.

'Madame...' I slipped to one knee, looking up. I clasped her hand. 'Madame, I am your servant. I think only of you.'

Natasha raised me up.

I brought her close to me, my hands feeling the warmth of her dress:

'Madame, I want you. If you'll have me.'

A slight sobbing sound came from her. When we moved apart, her eyes were full of tears:

'Oh, Kutaissov, you are a strange man. I've never met anybody like you. They say you have the Grand Duke in the palm of your hand, that you are the only one he trusts.'

I knew she was referring to remarks by the grand duchess. I pressed on with my case:

'Madame. I am in love with you.'

'You don't know what love is. You are not that kind of man.'

'I hope I have not lost my heart in vain. I will ask you once more. Will you take me? If not, we must part forever.'

'I will give you an answer soon, I promise.'

We re-traced our steps through the labyrinth. If she had slapped me round the face I could not have felt more downcast.

WHEN I ATTENDED to Paul's needs the next morning I put on a melancholy air. He noticed at once:

'Is my little Figaro slightly out of sorts this morning?' he asked.

'Yes, Sire. I'm afraid I had difficulties with the lady.'

'Ah, the lady! Well, that *is* serious.'

'Yesterday I asked her to marry me.'

'Splendid,' said Paul, clapping me on the back. 'Then congratulations are in order?'

'No, Sire. I think she has doubts.'

'Doubts?'

His placid expression changed in an instant to a mask of fury. He stamped his foot and marched backwards and forwards, hands clasped behind his back.

'Doubts, eh?' he growled. 'We'll see about that!'

THE NEXT DAY I received a message from Natasha in her tiny handwriting:

My Dear Sir,

I must apologise for my hesitation in replying to your request. It was due to confusion in my soul, quite separate from what I feel for you, concerning my recent bereavement from which I am not yet fully recovered.

However, I have reflected on the matter and arrived at a conclusion.

I have decided to accept your gracious proposal of marriage, and pledge to you my allegiance and honour, as well as my gratitude for your declaration.

Natasha

Natasha's letter was followed by an invitation to have dinner with her.

I INFORMED THE GRAND duke of this development and obtained permission to leave Gatchina for an evening. When not on duty with the grand duchess, Natasha lived in a cottage, half an hour's ride from the fortress. Her dwelling stood in a forest clearing remote from other houses.

Her two children, Tatyana and Boris, were tongue-tied and fidgety in my presence.

'This is Tatyana,' said Natasha, presenting a girl of some eleven or twelve years of age, with blushing cheeks, long plaited hair, and eyes as blue as her mother's. The girl did not speak but performed a kind of curtsy, shuffled her feet, looked at the ground, and gave a bat-squeak of a giggle.

'And this is Boris!' exclaimed the mother, bringing forward a boy a few years younger than his sister.

He stared at me, not a trace of a smile on his features, and solemnly bowed his head.

'They are very shy,' whispered Natasha.

At dinner the children sat opposite each other while I faced Natasha at the far end of the table. A maid brought in cabbage soup and black bread. We ate in silence apart from the occasional clatter of spoon against dish. Next came portions of beef and dumplings, with glasses of southern wine.

The siblings began sidelong glances at me, especially after requesting a second small portion of wine, which their mother granted. The boy spoke first, clearing his throat as if to get rid of nervousness:

'Sir,' he began. 'You work in the palace?'

'Yes indeed.'

'Do you know the Grand Duke?'

'Yes. He's my master.'

'Do you see him every day?'

'I do.'

Boris paused to absorb this information. Natasha smiled encouraging him to continue.

'What sort of person is he?' asked the boy.

'Very grand!' I said.

At this the girl decided to join in.

'Sir,' she said, her voice as small as a mouse, 'is he frightening?'

I could not restrain from laughing for she had hit the mark:

'Sometimes,' I replied. 'If I don't do my job properly.'

'What sort of thing?' asked the boy.

'When I forget to polish his boots.'

'And do you ever forget?' he enquired.

'Never,' I replied. 'It's more than my life is worth!'

At this Natasha laughed too and the children joined in, as if I had made a joke of great humour.

The maid brought in apple pastries topped with raisins. Tatyana and Boris set to with a will. Natasha urged them to take their time and not gobble, instructions which they wisely ignored.

After the meal we moved to another room, leaving the maid to fuss away the plates and forks. I settled into an armchair, with Natasha on the sofa opposite.

The children were still sizing me up, looking anxious. I made no effort to ingratiate myself with them. There would be time for that later.

Quite soon they were dispatched to bed. The maid was summoned to supervise them. After a short interval they returned for their mother's goodnight kiss, the girl in a white dressing gown, her brother in his nightshirt.

Natasha hugged them and they embraced and clung to her, embarrassed to see me watching them.

'Goodnight,' they murmured.

Tatyana came to deposit the lightest of kisses on my cheek. The boy was in two minds whether to follow suit. Choosing discretion over valour, he decided merely to bow in my direction.

He went out of the room aware that my eyes were on him but returned to put his head round the door:

'Sir, would you tell me more about the Grand Duke next time?'

'Of course,' I said. 'Anything you wish to know.'

He nodded and departed.

As quietness crept over the house, the childish voices fading at the maid's behest in the distance, Natasha filled up my glass with wine. As if in a game of chess, we waited for the next move.

'Lovely children,' I said.

'They are shy,' she replied.

'Was their father kind to them?'

'Yes. But he was often away with the army.'

In the lamplight Natasha's face shone as if in a beautiful painting.

'Thank you for your letter,' I said.

'Thank God it was safely delivered,' she whispered as if nervous of being overheard.

'What made up your mind?' I asked. 'You were not sure at first.'

'I needed time to think.'

'Did the Grand Duchess mention the matter?'

'Only in passing.'

'Anybody else?'

Her expression became agitated.

'Somebody might have mentioned something.'

'*He* did!' I said cryptically.

'Yes.'

'Why does *he* want us to marry?'

She was now sobbing. A handkerchief was extracted from a pocket. She dabbed at her eyes.

'Because…' she said, unable to continue the sentence.

I laid my hand on hers.

'Just tell me,' I whispered. 'Let me know what this is.'

'I don't think you understand him,' she replied, softly as if fearful of being overheard. 'You think you do, but you don't.'

'Perhaps not…But if you know something, then tell me.'

As if in answer she stroked my face with the soft palm of her hand.

'Poor Kutaissov. I don't know what to make of you. You know so much and yet so little.'

'I am willing to learn,' I said.

'Our dear emperor is not like other men. If he gets the simplest thing in his head he acts on it. Some can distinguish between important matters and trivial things. His Majesty cannot.'

'I know that!' I said. 'He is my master after all.'

'But I *will* marry you. I have no choice.'

Natasha licked her lips as if her mouth had gone dry with fright.

In that moment all was changed. She was mine. Whether Natasha wanted to marry or not hardly mattered. The grand duke had laid his commandment on her. She would be mine and I would be hers.

I trotted back to Gatchina late that night through the forest paths under a bright moon, a victor more than a lover, intoxicated not by wine but by a surfeit of desire.

U P WITH THE lark, I walked to Paul's bedchamber the next morning with a new spring in my step. He was fast asleep, snoring like a baby pig, his nightcap slightly askew, a touch of dribble slipping down his chin.

The very act of drawing back the curtains was usually

sufficient to wake him. This morning he snored on for several minutes.

I had my instructions. Thus once the room had been tidied and prepared, I touched his shoulder with a quiet 'Sire'. His hand snaked out from beneath the blankets and seized my wrist. His eyes opened with a look of terror.

'Thank God it's you!' he muttered. 'I had an awful dream.'

'What was it this time, Sire?' I said gently, a nurse speaking to a waking child.

'Horrible! I was in battle, trapped, waiting for the death thrust from a bayonet.'

I noticed beads of sweat on his brow despite a slight chill in the room.

'That's a terrible nightmare, Sire,' I said

'Am I a coward?' he whimpered, like a boy wishing to be told he was not.

'You are the bravest man I know, Sire,' I replied, lifting my voice.

'My wife says I am a coward.'

'I am sure she did not mean such a thing,' I whispered, knowing that the grand duchess offered many adverse opinions in the heat of the moment.

He released the iron grip on my wrist. Swinging his legs out of bed, he allowed me to hold the chamber pot in front of him and directed a dribble of urine into it, watching his own progress with interest.

That little chore completed, I moved across the room to get his water ready for ablutions and strop the razor for the ritual shave.

He lapsed into silence for the remainder of the ceremony. I got him into his fine silk underwear and helped him put on the uniform. He loved this part of the game, preening himself in the mirror. Then the boots, tight and bright, the polished leather gleaming like a black mirror.

When all was to his satisfaction, and this morning it was, he stomped off to breakfast with his wife, leaving me to tidy his wardrobe, make his bed, empty the pot, and make sure that the whole paraphernalia of shirts, breeches, belts, boots, braces, and buckles, were ready for the next day and the day after that.

I DID NOT USUALLY accompany the grand duke to his daily military routines on the square. My own duties kept me too busy to be watching march-pasts, the changing of the guard, the procession of the band, and the punishment parade.

For Gatchina the rest of the day would be followed by more training. Ah, the training! Never in the world were there so many troops exhausted by that which was meant to make them fit in the first place.

The poor devils, all two thousand, were roused by bugles from sleep at an obscene hour, having been chased into their bunks not long previously. In Gatchina an eighteen hour day was normal, that is to say eighteen hours of barking and shouting by corporals, sergeants, sergeant-majors, regimental sergeant-majors, junior officers, and others.

Paul from the lofty elevation of his prize horse was perpetually seeking the displaced button, the patch of mud on trouser leg or boot, a rifle not at the authorised angle, and other imperfections visible only to a military eyeball.

When flag-raising, parading, saluting, shouting, wheeling, etc., were duly completed, the real hard work began. Much of this consisted of struggling across boggy, ploughed fields with frequent commands to dive face down into the filth, followed by further rising, ducking and diving.

Each man possessed ceremonial uniform (tall pointed hat, high boots, gauntlets, hair set in wax, dressed with flour, a pigtail down the back) for morning parade. For dirty, down-in-the-mud manoeuvres they wore fatigue tunics and leggings as they endured another day in hell.

The entire madhouse was governed under the joint tyranny of Arakcheev and Steinwehr.

Count Alexi Arakcheev's black eyebrows, thin soldierly visage, and vicious stare were sufficient to daunt Satan himself. His military slogan, repeated *ad nauseum*, was 'Twelve hundred men moving twelve hundred feet must suggest one man moving one foot'. (God help the man whose foot transgressed this code.)

In his favour, Arakcheev was a man of iron, unflagging as he toiled daily in the vineyard of soldiery.

On the other hand, the ladies of the court, headed by Maria, regarded him with contempt. The grand duchess described him as 'educated at the cost of a copper and a bushel of oats, with the appearance of an ape, the gait of a bear, a voice like a bull, and, in private conversation, incoherent'.

But if the grand duchess despised Arakcheev, she hated Baron Steinwehr more. Rumour had it that the man, a well-born Prussian, was once cashiered from King Frederick's army for drunkenness.

Despite all this, Steinwehr poured a daily potion of Prussian poison into Paul's compliant ear. The corrosion entered the grand duke's circulation in full measure. Paul's mind, as a consequence, was full of Germanic dreams and stupidity, fantasies he was able to play out to the full with the Gatchina garrison.

Is it not strange that a lunatic such as Paul was well supplied with companions who encouraged every evil tendency? In all the world there are many fine generals and officers who combine discipline with mercy, order with logic, organization with compassion. But in Gatchina a giant hand seized the place and twisted it into every ugly shape. With men like Arakcheev and Steinwehr at his elbow, Paul was prey to every whim they cared to push down his throat.

As for myself I did not have much to do with these gentlemen. But I made it my business to discover every detail about them that could be had by gossip or chit chat, some of which no doubt contained elements of truth.

However, in the business of power, lies and rumours are helpful. As the months passed those two army dictators would not have slept well at night if they had known how much information, hearsay, and legend I had amassed about them.

I met them from time to time. Steinwehr's cropped head, short neck, and cruel eyes, were ideal for his profession, his appearance a caricature of the traditional Prussian officer and one of nature's born bullies.

He came to Paul's bedchamber one morning when I was giving the grand duke some final touches to a new uniform. Steinwehr entered the room, clicked his heels and saluted, arm pushed out like a Roman greeting.

'Ah Colonel!' said the grand duke, surprised at the commandant's intrusion into the holy of holies. 'What can I do for you?'

Steinwehr gave me a ferocious glare as if I was a piece of dirt on a uniform.

'Sire, I have private business to impart.'

(His grasp of the Russian accent was inferior to mine I

was pleased to note.) Paul knew what he implied but would not be budged:

'Oh Colonel, you can say what you like in front of Kutaissov. I have no secrets from him.'

The pig grunted with displeasure, his massive shoulders miming a shrug.

'Sire, I came to ask for your advice about training. Half the men are down with some cursed infection.'

The cursed infection turned out to be a form of mild dysentery, an ailment which makes a large military parade appear even more comical than usual.

Paul frowned and looked at me:

'Figaro, what would you do?'

Steinwehr's face indicated a bubbling up of rage. How could a barber be asked about military matters?

'Don't worry, Colonel,' said Paul gaily, adding fuel to the fire, 'he was once a military man himself.' He gave a little chuckle, straightened his wig, and stared at me:

'Well, let's have it, we are waiting for an answer!'

There are many occasions in the grand duke's service when it is best to bite one's tongue and say nothing. In this instance a reply was necessary. I cleared my throat and dived in:

'Sire, in battle men still have to fight whether infected or not. So I can see no reason why training should be discontinued today.'

'Excellent! That is the answer I was going to give!' He turned back to Steinwehr. 'So, Colonel, what would you advise?'

'Whatever you say, Sire!' said Steinwehr in his clipped military voice.

A sensation of unpleasantness came off him as if from some

inferior perfume. His eyes lighted on mine for a single second, an indication that he would like to have had me flogged for insubordination but could not.

He saluted, wheeled round on his heel, and trotted away, his backside tightly contained within ample breeches.

When he had gone Paul looked at me with some admiration:

'Good advice! I must seek your counsel more often on such matters. You have the art of putting things in a nutshell.'

'What a splendid man Colonel Steinwehr is!' I said slyly. 'No wonder Gatchina is so efficient with men like him in charge.'

'An excellent man. I hope one day he will be by my side in battle.'

'Yes, indeed, Sire,' I replied.

If the grand duke could not see that he had created an enemy for me, I wasn't going to tell him.

BUT IF I made the occasional enemy the grand duke also helped me to find friends.

One morning he ordered me to seek out the residence in Gatchina of Fedor Vasilyevich Rostopchin, the son of a junior officer in the Russian army, now risen to a position of authority.

The previous day Rostopchin had suffered a bad fall from his horse and was nursing his bruises in bed. The grand duke thought that with my barber's skills I might be able to help him.

Rostopchin's house was quite modest in size but richly furnished and carpeted in elegant style. A manservant met me at the door. I was escorted to the relevant bedroom where my would-be patient was pale, gasping with pain.

'I am Kutaissov,' I said, 'valet to the Grand Duke.'

'Ah yes. I heard you have powers of healing.'

'My virtues must not be exaggerated,' I said with a slight bow.

'I hope you can do something. The Grand Duke gave you high praise.'

'His Highness is too kind,' I whispered. 'Whereabouts is the pain most intense?'

He indicated that his back and neck were affected. With his manservant's help I got Rostopchin upright, removed his shirt with a slight apology for the inconvenience, and gently examined the sensitive region. There was bruising along the line of his right shoulder and he could scarcely move his head. His right arm had taken the force of the fall and was also red and purple with bruising.

I had seen cases like this before in my village. No bones had been broken in this instance and the shoulder was not dislocated. I engaged in a modicum of massage round the back of the neck and along the line of the spine.

At first he groaned and grunted as my fingers probed and pushed. Gradually he relaxed and could even twist his head slightly from side to side and up and down.

For good measure I placed a tight bandage round his shoulder and neck and put his right arm in a sling.

'That feels better already,' he said. 'Kutaissov, you are as clever as the Grand Duke described you. What do I owe for this service?'

'Sir, you owe me nothing. I assure you in four or five days you will be back in the saddle as if nothing had happened.'

Rostopchin was so delighted that he asked his manservant to fetch some wine. I sat by his bedside and we enjoyed a long and earnest conversation. He told me how he had gained the grand duke's favour by an unusual gift. When Rostopchin was on detached service in Berlin, he had won a considerable sum of money in a game of cards.

The Prussian officer who lost was unable to fund the debt. In settlement instead of money he offered a thousand toy soldiers of the highest quality.

Rostopchin accepted the payment. By some devious means Paul heard of this little army and asked to see it. Rostopchin gave the toy soldiers to the grand duke and was immediately promoted to a higher rank.

The man had a witty way of telling a story. He caused me to laugh out loud several times, his occasional gestures of a wink or half-smile adding a layer of meaning to his brisk soldierly speech.

Neither did he hold back information. Before I left I learned that he hated a number of Catherine's courtiers, felt that he should have been promoted by her for his services, and recognised the grand duke's oddness and weaknesses.

Yet nothing treasonable was actually said. Rostopchin had the gift of being able to express what he meant without spelling it out. You felt you knew what he intended to say even if he never made things crystal clear in precise words.

Such a talent seemed most enviable.

TWO WEEKS LATER a most august personage visited Gatchina. This was none other than Alexander, Paul's son and (as whispered in certain circles) the next Tsar of Russia.

For his stay in Gatchina the whole military establishment had to be at the point of perfection. The grand duke wished to impress his heir and became fussy to the extent of mad intolerance. Thus the number of floggings within the barracks increased as the welcome day grew near.

The grand duke was not averse to slapping me round the face if he imagined the riding boots had any blemish (which they did not) or a single button on his tunic did not shine like a silver coin (having previously been polished to the point of perfection).

Any such physical abuse was however quickly forgotten. Within a quarter of an hour he could be putting his arm round my shoulders or offering me a glass of wine.

Paul moved in and out of contrary feelings and emotions without logic or reason. He had become accustomed since childhood to getting his own way. Now I took the brunt of his behaviour whatever it happened to be at that time of day.

On arrival Alexander took the salute of the troops as they staged an immaculate march-past, the band, slightly out of tune, blaring out a vigorous patriotic theme.

Dozens and dozens of polished boots paraded as one, bayonets glinting in the early weak sunlight, the multiple heads of wretched soldiers inclined to the right as they trotted past the podium.

The throng took some twenty minutes to get all uniformed bodies to traverse the parade ground though I could swear that some of the especially smart units appeared to come into view twice. But such ceremonial events are usually confusing.

I was mesmerised by the banging of drums, the tooting of trumpets and the menacing sounds of men raising and then dropping their legs brutally in a rapid goose-step.

After the parade I was invited to a brief reception in the fortress. Everyone was there including of course the grand duchess and her extensive entourage, as well as the military commanders of the garrison and Alexander's own retinue of courtiers and hangers-on.

In a ritual line-up I was introduced by the grand duke to Alexander, following on in sequence from Rostopchin, Arakcheev, and Steinwehr.

'This,' said Paul as I approached the critical moment, 'is Kutaissov. I told you about him.'

I stooped low in front of the guest of honour. He was taller than Paul with quiet, shifty eyes, many medals, and golden epaulettes. His head was going bald with little clumps of hair stretching back on either side, displaying a wide forehead. His expression was doleful and depressed as if already he suffered the weight of the world on his shoulders.

To my surprise he shook hands with me:

'A great honour, Your Royal Highness!' I murmured as I bowed again.

'So you are Kutaissov. My father holds you in the highest esteem.'

'Thank you, Sire,' I said.

His voice was deep and controlled as if all his life he had been taught to be aware of the impression he was creating.

That was all there was to it. The next morning he left Gatchina.

His hasty departure put the grand duke into a dreadful mood. For several days I was walking on egg shells, as it were, fortunate to get no further chastisement this time than the rough edge of his tongue.

FATHER NIKOLAI BEGAN preparations for my wedding. I thought marriages were a matter of simple vows. I was mistaken.

He described it as the 'Sacred Mystery of Marriage' and wove a beehive round this. Marriage was not only a kind of contract between man and woman but an image of God and the Church.

Through this hoop I had to jump, my mouth mumbling assent whether I liked it or not.

Natasha accepted whatever Father Nikolai had in mind. I begged to differ but kept my doubts to myself.

When the happy day dawned, I met my bride at the door of the Gatchina chapel. She wore a fulsome white dress trimmed with lace sleeves and a head-dress with a veil. I wore my splendid quasi-military best dress suit of livery designed by Paul specially for the occasion.

His wedding gift to me was a pair of riding boots, made to measure, of the finest leather, given to me a week before so I could get used to such finery.

After a blessing from Father Nikolai, rings were exchanged and placed on our fingers. We processed to the innermost sanctum, the priest intoning a psalm as we walked. Among the congregation were the grand duke and his wife, Arakcheev and Steinwehr, with sundry courtiers and servants.

The couple proclaimed in front of the assembly their intention to be joined as man and wife. When Natasha pulled back her veil she seemed sad, her cheeks stained with a tear or two. As we mouthed the vows I noticed Paul nodding earnestly, a sickly smile on his face.

We were given candles, emblems (so Father Nikolai had said) of the Light of Truth. To me they were just candles.

Crowns were held over our heads, a symbol of martyrdom in the old church, a reminder of death among the new.

After readings from the scriptures concerning wifely sub-missiveness and the turning of water into wine, a cup of wine was blessed and lifted aloft. The bride and groom shared its contents, taking turns to drain it to the dregs.

The taste of wine on our tongues, we then trotted after Nikolai in the so-called 'Dance of Isaiah' three times round the holy table. Those present showered us with rice and flower petals. Behind us the crowns were suspended by assistants.

More prayers were said, the crowns taken away, and we stood before the altar, while final benedictions were sung. She and I were now as one in the eyes of God and man.

All those in attendance came to offer congratulations, led of course by Paul and Maria, the grand duke bestowing a gentle kiss on the bride before hugging me to him.

The grand duchess appeared before me. I bowed to her as if in a daze.

Next came Steinwehr, his dark voice whispering 'Congratulations Kutaissov,' though his cruel eyes did not reflect the sentiments of his mouth. The rest, including Rostopchin, came up in strict social order, each mindful of Paul's presence and his languid gaze.

A celebratory feast had been set out in one of the salons. We sat at a long table full of rich food and wine. After we had eaten and drunk a little, Paul rose to his feet.

We followed his example and rose like startled birds, till he seated us with a peremptory wiggle of the index finger of his right hand.

'Dear friends and comrades of Gatchina,' he began, 'welcome

to the wedding of Kutaissov and Natasha, loyal and faithful servants of the court. We wish them long life and prosperity.'

The glasses clinked in a toast. The grand duke remained standing.

'You will all know what trust is necessary in the organisation of our great palace and fortress at Gatchina. It is some time since Kutaissov came into my service. Before that he was a valet to one of our greatest generals. It was through such recommendations that it was decided to employ him at Gatchina, constantly by my side.'

Once more the glasses clinked and were re-filled.

From my seated position next to Natasha, I was uncomfortably in the line of Steinwehr's vision. From time to time he cast an unsmiling glare in my direction.

Fortunately, drunkard that he was, the colonel was already in his cups. By his side sat Count Arakcheev, tilting his head back as he put the glass to his thin lips.

Grand Duchess Maria sat composed and inscrutable while her husband spoke his words. Paul cleared his throat and went on speaking:

'I have a wedding present for the bridegroom and his bride. From now on Kutaissov is appointed to be Steward of the Royal Household.'

A clatter of applause rang out and again a toast.

Natasha, ill at ease, looked flushed and anxious. But she forced a wan smile and nodded as this unexpected news of my promotion was announced.

I was breathless with excitement and shook my head from side to side in disbelief. The Steward of the Royal Household was a position of authority, extending to the task of choosing servants for employment or preferment as well as being responsible for a host of other considerations around the palace.

'Kutaissov will remain in his post as my personal valet. But I would advise all of you to tread carefully henceforth. For he will have my full attention for the decisions he will take.'

The company applauded, the clapping going on for some time. Steinwehr too was putting his hands together, but so gently as not to make any sound as his palms clashed.

Paul, standing straight and pompous, to the full stretch of his insubstantial height, lifted his glass high in a final blessing.

We all stood up and imitated his gesture. In the background a small military band began to play.

Natasha and I obliged with a marital dance together before the dignitaries took to the floor.

WE SPENT THE next few days in Natasha's forest cottage as a kind of a honeymoon before taking up my extra duties at Gatchina. Her children had gone to their grandmother for three days to permit a little privacy.

It is a strange moment when a bridegroom confronts his bride for the first time in the silence of the bedroom. Fortunately Natasha knew what was expected.

She quickly divested herself of her clothes. Covering her flesh shyly with a flimsy night-gown, she slipped between the silken matrimonial sheets. It was but a moment before I was in beside her, my blood hot and lusty.

Within minutes we were locked in union, my hands exploring her highways and byways, my lips testing the softness of her neck and breasts.

It was not the coming together of lovers but something more mechanical, an acknowledgement of our responsibilities to consummate what Paul had arranged and brought into being.

To tell the truth my head was full of my unexpected promotion. Since my 'conversion', and now the marriage, things had advanced unexpectedly. All was now grist to the mill.

'Are you happy, Natasha?' I asked.

'What is happiness? she replied. 'Do I have a choice?'

'You have as much choice as I do,' I said.

She did not answer.

I took her again into my arms.

'I don't know you,' she whispered, after the engagement had thrust itself to a conclusion.

'Perhaps you will learn to love me.'

'I'm not sure. Are you a person worthy to be loved?'

I thought about that. It was something I had never been asked before.

'Who is worthy of love? Perhaps nobody is worth loving.'

She laughed, a hollow laugh, with no humour in it.

'Is that what you think of yourself?'

'Of course,' I said.

'Then there is no hope for you.'

'Ah, but love comes despite that. It is a flower that grows by itself. Love comes naturally or it never happens.'

'In that case, I will never love you. Not as a woman ought to love her husband. But I shall be a good wife.'

'I shall try to be a good husband,' I replied, my voice trembling.

N MY RETURN to Gatchina, the grand duke, with other matters on his mind, seemed to have forgotten I was ever married. He made no mention of it.

Meanwhile the grand duchess, soon to give birth, was making heavy weather of everything. Her perpetual grumbling was more than Paul wished to endure and he became most off-hand. Off-hand with his wife meant he was not pleasant towards anyone else.

One morning as the grand duchess came slowly down the corridor, her pregnant condition most apparent. I stood head bowed by the grand paintings to allow her progress. I could not help but notice a lady-in-waiting tripping along behind her like a vision of springtime. There was a freshness in her demeanour which aroused something in me.

The following day I saw the very same lady in the library, sitting at a table with a book of poetry. Her absorption in reading gave me an opportunity to scrutinise her from behind the shelves.

Before long I approached this paragon of loveliness:

'Mademoiselle, may I sit opposite you?'

She glanced up, blushed, and gave me permission to take my seat in an educated tone of voice, softly spoken.

I was already won over. Her brown hair flowed invitingly over her shoulders, her hands were finely formed. Her lips parted like a prime rosebud, her eyebrows were exquisitely plucked, her eyes of the deepest blue.

'What are you reading with such devotion, Mademoiselle?' I enquired.

'It's poetry,' she said. 'My favourite poet, Aleksandr Sumarokov.'

'How wonderful,' I replied, with not a clue who Sumarokov might be. 'I love his poetry too. It is some time since I read any.'

'You are Master Kutaissov, adjutant to the Grand Duke!' she said, with a shy giggle.

'At your service, Mademoiselle,' I answered. 'Would you read me a line or two of these verses?'

'Oh, yes,' she whispered, the sigh of pleasure in her voice catching me unexpectedly in the region of the heart.

'Please do!' I entreated.

She turned the pages to look for a particular poem.

'Should I begin, sir?' she asked.

'Oh yes. Do please begin.'

I watched her prepare herself like an actress.

Slightly lisping, she began to read. I was enchanted by the beauty of her diction, the utter sensuality of the words in her mouth:

Hopelessly I hide my heart's pain,
Hopelessly I try to seem serene,
But I cannot be calm again
I cannot with this sorry scene,
My heart by sad laments,
My eyes by floods of tears
Give away all my secret torments,
You made me full of fears
You robbed me of my liberty.
You brought me this cruel destiny,
You disturbed my soul's serenity,
You gave me to captivity,
All delight has turned to misery…

My soul is held captive by you in this place,
I see before me nothing but your lovely face,
Inflamed with passion what can I do
But remember I cannot forget you.

As she finished, bright tears came into her eyes. When reading the words 'heart', 'soul' or 'passion', she placed her hand on her left breast. Such was her emotion I almost wished to weep in sympathy with her.

'That is so…beautiful,' I said.

'Oh it is, it is,' she whispered, another tear trickling down her face.

'Are you indeed in love?' I asked mischievously.

At this she stared at me with the full force of her sea-blue gaze:

'Are you not Master Kutaissov, valet to the Grand Duke?'

'Yes, I am!' I replied.

'Then you should know my name. I am Catherine Nelidowa.'

'Catherine! That is a lovely name. The same as our beloved empress.'

'Surely you have heard the rumours?'

I assured her that I had heard nothing.

'But my lady, the Grand Duchess, tells me that you know everything.'

'I am not sure of that,' I replied.

With that she scooped up her book and with the tiniest bow of her head began to weep again. Rising abruptly, she uttered some kind of apology and hastened from the room without a further word.

THE FOLLOWING MORNING I casually mentioned this encounter to Paul:

'Sire, I met a most enchanting young lady yesterday in the library. She read me a poem. She was very moved by it.'

Paul became annoyed:

'I never knew you liked poetry. You have very little poetry in your soul that I ever noticed.'

'Perhaps I could begin to learn, Sire.'

'I presume you are referring to the lady-in-waiting, Catherine.'

I nearly fell over with surprise:

'Indeed, Sire, the very same. What a beautiful young woman.'

'Beautiful indeed. Surpassing all others!'

'Indeed, Sire? Then you have noticed her?'

'Noticed her? She is my mistress. I am in love with her.'

I hesitated just long enough for Paul to cast his eye on me:

'Sire, I do beg your pardon for my indiscretion. I never realised...'.

'There are some things that even you will never know. But now you know all about this. So there's an end to it.'

'But, Sire, is the Grand Duchess aware of your feelings on this matter.'

Paul frowned.

'Don't be naive. You of all people! Of course she knows. In her present condition she believes it is good for me to consort with a beautiful woman. They are friends together. Catherine is not a servant. She is an intelligent woman of beauty. You'll see plenty of her in the future. If I were you, I would not get on the wrong side of her.'

'No indeed, Sire!'

Ah, what a mistake I could have made with Nelidowa. One

false move, one suggestive word. But I did not. My hands were clean. By luck I had steered clear of the rocks.

It was a lesson to take to heart (or at least bear in mind). With all this business of courting Natasha and getting married I had neglected to discover everything that should be known by one such as myself in the swirling undercurrents of the court.

Such a mistake should never happen again. (Of course, it *did* happen again. But that is something for another time, another place.)

I DECIDED TO TURN the Catherine Nelidowa affair to some kind of advantage. Paul's carelessness allowed me to achieve this in the best possible manner. By chance he let it slip that he was meeting the lady in an antechamber quite near the top of the building.

Why he should have given this information to me was strange but immaterial. It may have been a way of flaunting his manly prowess and rubbing my nose into the fact I had not known of his affair when I had such a reputation for knowing everything that was going on.

Apparently the grand duchess, in a manner of speaking, 'approved' of the affair, which is to say she could do little to prevent it. With this in mind she had given a kind of 'permission', a 'sanction', providing Paul was not indiscreet. Thus Paul was made to feel indulged by his wife and at the same time slightly guilty, a fine combination.

Adjacent to the back of the antechamber was a disused stockroom. Clearly at one time a thin partition wall had been added to make two rooms out of one. The stockroom was now neglected.

The antechamber, on the other hand, was well furnished for a royal liaison with a sumptuous bed, fine chairs, paintings, a dressing table, wardrobe, Persian carpets, exquisite bed linen, etc. Though I could not *see* what was going on when Paul and Catherine carried out their assignations, it was possible from inside the stockroom to listen to every word spoken between them, to even the subtlest whispers of lovers.

The usual chorus of amatory sounds echoed freely, cooing and cuddling language, quasi-baby noises, even the occasional rustle of silk against moments of silence before the grunting and squealing began again.

But it was the conversation that concerned my attention. Eavesdroppers may seldom hear anything good about themselves but there can be exceptions:

'That Kutaissov!' said Catherine, during the pillow talk. 'What sort of man is he?'

'Ah, Kutaissov, my Figaro!' replied Paul. 'What would you like to know?'

'He seems a strange man. I can't make him out.'

A pause as if the Master was formulating an answer.

'Strange? I never considered him that way.'

'Well…he is a mixture of charm and guile, flattery and a kind of rudeness not appropriate to his class.'

'He is from Turkey,' said Paul. 'They are different from us. That is why I trust him with my whole heart.'

It was Catherine Nelidowa's time to pause. After Paul's endorsement she surely could not pursue the path of denigration. But a woman is no more logical than a man.

'Yes,' she said, 'but I find him rude. It is as if he considers himself superior to everyone around him.'

Paul let out a peal of high-pitched laughter.

'Ah, you have mistaken his nature. He is the most attentive and obedient of servants. He caters for my every need without a word of complaint. He would do anything for me. He is the most pliant and willing of men.'

Catherine would not give up however:

'Sire, it was that encounter in the library. He seemed to be – how should I say? – above himself. He did not afford me sufficient respect. After all, he is but a servant!'

'There you are mistaken,' said Paul. 'He *is* a servant, yes. But I have never met a person quite like him. He is able to advise me on the most delicate matters of state. I trust him utterly. A prince of the royal blood must be able to trust the man who shaves him in the morning.'

At this point they relapsed into kissing and cuddling with much giggling from her and sighing from him. He swore immortal love to her and she to him.

I would have to persuade her I was not who she thought I was, even though I am exactly that. I possessed no great opinion of my own self. I am but a mirror to Paul's own moods. Such a mirror is a rare commodity.

But what if she, through a lover's whims and stratagems, turned him against me? It was, all in all, a tricky situation.

FOREWARNED, I WAS now in a position to do something about the matter. I pursued a simple plot. Firstly to Paul I praised the virtues and beauty of Catherine Nelidowa incessantly, saying what a wonderful, educated, gracious, dignified, and comely girl she was.

'Oh Figaro,' Paul remarked more than once, 'I think you are half in love with Catherine yourself!'

'Indeed no, Sire', I replied. 'I see her as a kind of perfection. I am happy and content with the wife that Your Royal Highness recommended to me.'

'Ah yes,' said Paul, a little dreamily, as he entered into what passed for profound thought with him. 'Marriage at first is such bliss. But the magic wears off. And that's where Catherine Nelidowa is so good. She gives me everything lacking when wives become pregnant and the grim realities of nature and birth take over.'

'Indeed, Sire,' I said, knowing that Nelidowa's charms might also soon displease this foolish creature.

The second initiative was with Nelidowa herself. Having heard from the horse's mouth her opinion of me, I counter-attacked. My obsequiousness to her was finely judged. It could not be excessive but had to be definite.

Before long I am sure she believed Paul must have spoken about my behaviour to her, for she expressed surprise at my courtship of her good intentions.

'Monsieur Kutaissov!' she exclaimed. 'When we first met I quite misunderstood your nature. But now I see you are a genuine person of great merit.'

'Thank you, madam,' I replied, aware that if she truly believed that she would believe anything on this earth.

When I again took up my listening post in the stockroom, the conversations indeed took on a quite different aspect from her former criticisms.

'I think Kutaissov is quite amazing,' said Catherine. 'I have watched him closely and now agree with you completely. He is a servant of integrity and a certain amount of charm.'

'Believe me,' replied Paul, 'I am a true judge of a man's character. In my position I have to be. My Kutaissov is one of the finest men you could ever meet.'

With that the couple took to billing and cooing.

I smiled, happy with the progress I had made in a few weeks. From now on I would rely on Catherine Nelidowa to promote my cause.

It is delightful how a little listening in unexpected places can work miracles.

PART FIVE

St Petersburg

*Tyranny is a habit capable of being developed,
and at last becomes a disease.*

The House of the Dead,
FYODOR DOSTOYEVSKY

THE MOMENTOUS MORNING of Wednesday, the fifth of November 1796, was bitterly cold. More to the point, Paul was in a terrible mood. The nub of the matter was another of his awful dreams:

'Sire, please tell me about it,' I pleaded.

'I cannot!' he said, his body shaking as if with a feverish trembling.

'Are you ill, Sire?' I asked, as he descended from the bed in his nightshirt.

'Not ill, just troubled.'

He crouched on the sofa like a hunted animal, his thin legs white and pathetic. (It is fortunate the populace do not see their aristocracy at such moments for it would spark instant revolution.)

We proceeded with the toiletry. With his constant moving and shivering the act of shaving him required all my skill.

'Is the razor sharp?' he asked suddenly.

'Very sharp, Sire,' I said.

'You should cut my throat!' he exclaimed, emitting high-pitched laughter as if a great joke had been made.

'I would lose my job, Sire!' I said, entering into his macabre spirit.

He cackled some more before telling me to hurry things up and not dawdle. The pale fear returned to his face:

'It was a dream,' he said, as if speaking to himself. 'But such a dream. Worse than I have ever known.'

I am no believer in the significance of dreams. They are mere clouds which float in our sleeping hours.

I doubt if we dream when we are dead. So why should the fantasy of night so concern us? But it was necessary to comfort this sick fool:

'I am sorry to hear that, Sire,' I said, wiping his face with a warm towel.

He brought his hand up to mine and held it for a moment, pushing the towel to his skin as if for further reassurance.

'What would I do without you?' he whispered. 'You are the only person I trust on earth.'

'Thank you, Sire,' I replied, aware that such words were as thin as paper. In a few moments he might take to slapping me round the face or chastising me for some imagined stain on a clean uniform.

I dressed him as speedily as I could. He still shook in anguish but fell to silence as we completed the task. I kept my eyes down so as not to meet his frightened gaze. There were moments when Paul was a caged tiger that at any moment might lash out. A curious tingling was in the air, brought about by his dream.

Such follies went back to his childhood. But we all have tragic upbringings in this day and age. Who can say what would be ideal? Whether bred in palace or pigsty, we grow up blighted, deformed by what the world does to us, united in the common anguish of childhood whatever blood runs in our veins.

Paul departed for breakfast with the grand duchess. I thought no more of it and proceeded with my duties in the bedchamber and the household.

The rest of the day proceeded as usual with the grand duke engaged in his military games while I feathered my nest in pursuit of whatever came along.

It was one of those evenings when my presence was required to supervise the royal dining. The meal, from my vantage point a little way back from the table, appeared excellent. The menu included rich vegetable soup followed by fresh roasted venison.

Curiously, however, nobody seemed to be interested in food for hardly a morsel was touched. Paul rejected the soup and merely nibbled at the venison leaving a quantity uneaten on his plate. The grand duchess, staring at Paul's irritable expression, was also off her victuals. Nothing, save a little wine, passed her lips.

During the meal the true hubbub began. A messenger came to me with a letter for Paul. (It was accepted that urgent messages at such a moment would only be conveyed to the grand duke by way of Kutaissov.) I read the import of the matter and was not pleased.

A courier had arrived hotfoot from St Petersburg to inform Gatchina that Count Platon Zubov was on his way and would be with us soon, accompanied by soldiers. My task was to communicate this bulletin to my master.

My first thoughts were not good. In effect I was anxious. If it was Empress Catherine's intention to arrest her son for whatever offence she had cooked up, this would be the way things were done.

I could imagine how all my efforts over the years might be in vain. In the forthcoming avalanche Kutaissov would be swept from his perch along with his employer.

As I fumbled for a way to tell Paul he turned in his chair towards me, having observed the ritual of the messenger's entrance.

'Well, let's have it. Tell me what you know!'

Before I could move a step his face remained as distraught as that morning during the toiletry. My feet seemed mired in treacle as I walked to him. He must have seen the blood had drained from my face for he looked me in the eye and burst out, 'In God's name, man, what is happening? You look like a damned ghost!'

I leaned over and whispered in his ear:

'Sire, I believe Count Platon Zubov is calling within a short time. He has been dispatched from St Petersburg.'

'*Believe*? You *believe* that Zubov is here within the hour? Give me that paper, you fool!'

He snatched the parchment from me. Holding it a hand's breadth from his face he read it, forming his own conclusions. His response was panic. He jumped to his feet, shifting a fine plate and a wine glass to the floor, the shattering sound echoing madly.

'Dearest one,' he shouted to the grand duchess, 'We are lost! Zubov has been sent. He will take me. The dream was real. I knew it. We should have gone elsewhere. To Berlin. It's finished. We are lost.'

He clamped his hands behind his back, put his head down like a chastised dog and began walking backwards and forwards like a child pretending to be a general.

At that moment I knew Paul was entirely mad through no fault of his own. Any sane man would have summoned Steinwehr and put the troops on alert. It would have taken a whole army to subdue Gatchina. But Paul, military man that he pretended to be, never even thought of defending his position.

In the midst of this chaos Rostopchin, breathless and

uniformed, hurried in.

'Sire, Count Platon Zubov has arrived with fifty soldiers. He has news concerning the Empress.'

Rostopchin's calm manner of speaking quietened the situation down. That voice just could not be taken seriously as the harbinger of doom.

Paul stopped in mid-stride to pay attention to the count; when the message was completed he took to walking up and down again. It was ludicrous.

But as nobody knew what was happening except that Zubov was indeed here and Paul was in disarray, we all remained miserably aware the worst was possibly about to befall every one of us. I wanted to whisper in Paul's ear that our Gatchina defences should be set in motion. But as I moved towards him he pushed me aside with a curt, 'Not now!' before scampering from the dining room.

The grand duke had hurried off to greet his unwelcome visitor in the library. Paul hated aristocrats who had bedded his mother. Platon Zubov (Catherine's favourite among her lovers) was foremost among those he loathed and feared.

Who, after all, could tell or even imagine what pillow talk might have ridiculed the son of Catherine, words that could never be retrieved?

When the pair emerged after ten minutes discussion I was in position just outside the room. Zubov looked intense as if about to attend his own funeral.

Paul beckoned:

'Ah, Kutaissov,' he said, 'we must leave at once for St Petersburg. Get the carriages ready.'

'Yes, Sire,' I said, catching a rather steely glare from Zubov, a man whose very being I detested. Such a man could sweep me from my perch like a condemned chicken with one flick of his little finger.

Paul took me to one side and, as if speaking to an old friend rather than to a servant, whispered:

'I need you more than ever. My mother is near to death. It may be a plot to trap me. But I have reached my forty-second year and God has helped me so far.'

In the candle-lit hall of the library entrance beads of sweat ran down his forehead despite the chill in the air.

I TRAVELLED THAT NIGHT in the grand duke's hooded sledge with my master and Count Rostopchin. Paul huddled himself in furs and blankets and said not a word all the way from Gatchina to St Petersburg.

It was a fearful journey across the snow and we went so fast that the accompanying sledges were soon left far behind. If Zubov had planned an ambush we would not have had a chance.

As it was, in the light of an ominous moon, Paul's face by the sledge window looked like a pallid corpse with its dead eyes open. The chill thrust itself into every bone and joint, an unforgettable ride into the grim darkness.

Rostopchin (believe it or not) fell asleep an hour into the night, shrilly snoring till I discreetly shoved an elbow into his side and feigned sleep as he awoke, startled.

As we approached the outskirts of St Petersburg I imagined the shapes of trees were horsemen or warriors, and the sky full of blood. From time to time wolves howled as if pursuing us.

It was all a sleepy delusion. I was becoming frightened of

my own shadow as we moved to whatever crisis awaited us in the city.

At the Winter Palace Paul stepped out to a full guard of honour from Catherine's elite grenadiers, their uniforms shiny with frost, faces pinched with almost unbearable cold. They had waited for hours to greet him in order not to be caught unawares.

The officer in command was confused by the presence of only a single sledge. Paul did not bother to explain but cast a peremptory glance over the bearing of the soldiers. With such formalities concluded we were escorted to Catherine's bedside.

Illuminated by ecclesiastical candles of remarkable proportions, the empress lay unconscious on her back as if waiting for a lover. A number of ladies of the court, handkerchiefs pressed to their faces, waited by the bed. Muffled sobs and sighs rent the air but subsided as Paul's austere face stared at them.

A fire blazed, fuelled by a heap of neatly cut logs. The air was stuffy, a mixture of incense and physical decay, as if dirty clothing had been left too long in a cupboard.

Paul moved on past his mother into Catherine's tiny private study next to the dying room. I followed closely behind while Rostopchin stayed near the empress, gazing with trepidation at the monarch's waxy face.

Candles in profusion had been lit. Servants bustled back and forth, carrying plates of food and cups of wine. Paul seated himself in the large chair behind the desk, took a slice of meat with some bread and stuffed it into his mouth. Even before he swallowed it, he reached for the wine, noisily swilling it round his mouth, gulping it down, liquid and food alike, in one noisy swallow down the gullet.

A procession of ministers entered having filed past the

empress with a nervous respectful nod in her direction as if she were still conscious.

The waiting women at the bedside were not pleased by this parade of business. But they could do nothing to stem the tide of those wishing to ingratiate themselves with Paul.

The final visitors were three doctors, their trade characterised by black gowns, long beards, and a clerical dignity. They bowed before Paul who was still munching at the food and therefore unable to speak comprehensibly. He gestured to command them to speak.

'Your Royal Highness,' one of the doctors began, his voice trembling like a girl, 'we entertain no great expectation of Her Majesty's continued state.'

'How long?' said Paul, his abruptness compelling another of the trio to take up the tale.

'That we cannot say, Sire. She is in the hands of the Almighty.'

Paul reached out for more of the food set out on silver salvers on the desk, selecting a morsel or two as if dining at Gatchina, choosing only the best.

'Are you hungry after the journey, Figaro? Take some food and wine, man!'

The doctors looked at me in amazement, turning their heads in my direction in unison, wondering how I would answer such a command.

'Thank you for your kindness, Sire,' I said. 'But for the moment, my appetite has left me.'

'Strange,' said Paul. 'I took you for one who looks after his stomach at all times.'

He nibbled on a piece of bread indicating to the doctors with a wave of the hand that they could leave now.

They had one more thing to say and hesitated before saying it:

'Yes?' said Paul, emitting little flecks of food as he spoke. 'Say it.'

The third doctor bowed low before speaking:

'Sire, may we humbly suggest the Last Rites should be administered as soon as possible.'

'Of course,' replied Paul. 'I thought that had already been done. For God's sake see to it!'

They hurried out, pleased to be dismissed from the unfamiliar presence.

I watched Paul as he continued with the drink. His wits adrift in the night, a flickering heartbeat away from the throne of Russia.

He showed no obvious emotion whether of remorse or pity, only a kind of bewilderment.

THAT NIGHT, ON the initiative of Arakcheev, detachments from the Gatchina fortress arrived in St Petersburg. In a few hours their Prussian uniforms, with tight tunics and stiff gauntlets, were prominent throughout the palace as our men occupied the lower quarters, ordering food, drink, and candles, manhandling the maidservants, and finding no reason to restrain their raucous voices.

Naturally the faithful grenadiers on parade outside became the butt of their humour. There was much talk of 'toy soldiers', 'fancy dress', and 'the army facing demobilisation', as the Gatchina vagabonds threw their weight about in the most unmilitary manner.

What was worse (or impressive, depending on your point of view) was that more and more of them were rolling into town, many much the worse for drink even before they came.

Paul decided to stay in the study, sleeping fitfully from time to time, wedged in the chair. At other times he stared blankly round the room as if unable to take in whatever seemed to be happening or where he was.

I decided to make a short reconnaissance of the situation. None of us knew quite what was going on. But it seemed probable that Paul could become emperor within hours. After years of telling everyone that her son would never be emperor of Russia, Catherine's sudden apoplexy had changed the rules of the game.

Between pouring wine and sipping it are many accidents. Perhaps the wily Catherine had made secret plans for a counterplot. In such a contingency my neck would not have been worth a single glass bead. Therefore into action.

Down near the entrance to the palace our Gatchina soldiers were keeping a tight hold, having mounted a guard inside the doors, and ensured the grenadiers were kept outside in the cold.

Arakcheev had taken the precaution of keeping the grenadiers lined up as if to welcome newcomers.

In so doing, he made sure that every man-jack of them was neutralised by the presence of mocking Gatchinites. It was not a pretty sight but the method was effective.

The grenadiers were cold, starving, and tired, in no mood to put up any opposition. For the first time I felt admiration for the Gatchina forces. Scum they were. But just when such a force was needed they came up trumps, loyal both to Paul and their commanders. If we were going to die the next day we would be in good company.

I was impressed by the deference the soldiers afforded to my own person, saluting and clicking their heels. They had been well briefed concerning the emerging court pecking order. This was a most promising omen.

Just inside the palace entrance loud squealing, laughter, and shouting came from a side office. Out of curiosity I passed through a jostling crowd of our men and peered round the door. A couple of dozen Prussian uniforms were there with a few girls, skirts askew, pinned to the floor with bare-buttocked Gatchinites on top of them, the women shrieking madly, the soldiers cursing and laughing, the victims finding no mercy from their tormentors.

I left in haste knowing I might require favours from these men within the coming day. To interfere with their sport might be possible, disciplined oafs that they were and accustomed to obedience to every whim of their officers and betters.

However, discretion warned me that their good will towards me was well worth the maidenheads of a handful of kitchen maids.

That the conduct of these men was disrespectful to the dying empress did not enter my mind. It could be argued that our men were already in a new world. For them it was as if Catherine had died and their hero was installed as ruler of Russia. They were indulging in a kind of celebration.

Such was the heady madness of that night. With the palace well-fortified and more Gatchina rogues entering by the hour, the situation appeared to be under control from the perspective of security.

Thus I let sleeping dogs lie, preferring to conjecture about the next step. I had already formulated a few plans.

DECIDED MY TRUE place was by Paul's side. I retraced my steps to the dying room, pushed past the crowd of courtiers and sycophants (whose grief was becoming more strident by the minute) and, without knocking, entered the study.

Paul was alone, awkwardly seated on the chair. He turned his face towards me as I went in, his expression so wan and forlorn I wondered if his wits had already burst their dam of reason once and for all.

'Who are you? I command you to identify yourself!' he grunted, though his voice was trembling and not at all commanding.

'Sire, do not trouble yourself. It is your faithful Figaro come to comfort you.'

'Oh thank God you are here. I can't sleep. I think the food I ate was bad. Perhaps they are poisoning me.'

I moved closer to him and examined his complexion, his lips, his eyes, and his mouth. There were no discolourations as might have been with toxic substances. His pulse was fast but regular. He took deep frantic breaths now and again but otherwise no cause for alarm.

'Sire,' I whispered, 'there are no adverse signs. I believe you are in good health. But these circumstances are difficult. The loss of a mother is, I believe, one of the worst things a man can ever go through.'

'Is she dead then?' he said, looking around as if in a new panic.

'Not yet, Sire. But her death is surely coming.'

'What can I do? What can I do?' He reached out and clutched my hand. 'Don't leave me here. I need you.'

'I am here, Sire, but with good news.'

'Good news? What good news?'

I paused a moment. His fingers tightened on my arm. By the candlelight reflection his eyes bulging with fear, his tight, rotund face like a white mask at a carnival.

'The palace is secure. The Gatchina forces are here and consolidating their hold on the city.'

'Thank God for that,' he said. 'All that training paid off.'

'Yes, indeed, Sire,' I said. 'Down below they look magnificent.'

His eyes seemed to get bigger, like a boy contemplating an enormous apple pie.

'Should I go and inspect them? They may need a glimpse of me, a touch of me, a small gesture to inspire them.'

'I think not, Sire, at the moment. They are engaged in their duties, vigilantly guarding the palace in all directions.'

'Then I will not distract them with my presence,' said Paul pompously.

'Thank you. Let us stay here for now. I think the position is good.'

'Ah...'

He let out a weary sigh and, without a further word, dropped back his head and began snoring, his mouth wide open.

A small dribble of saliva trickled from his lips to land in a white pigeon-like dropping on the top golden button of his otherwise immaculate uniform. I wiped it with my handkerchief.

PAUL'S SLUMBERS PROVED to be unusually lengthy considering the lack of comfort when falling asleep in a wooden chair. Occasionally he groaned as if about to wake, but the snoring returned, first in irregular rhythms and (soon after) with a steady swine-like grunting of happy oblivion.

From time to time I dozed off myself, stretched out on a chaise longue against the wall of the study. From such a light nap Paul eventually woke me:

'Quickly, you must help!'

'Yes, Sire, certainly,' I said, aroused from a recurrent sliver of dream agitating my mind like a buzzing bee.

'Why are you asleep? Are you not guarding our person?'

'Of course, Sire. I just rested a moment.'

I noticed a pile of official papers heaped on top of the desk in an untidy cluster.

'I found it, I found it,' stammered Paul.

'Very good, Sire,' I said, without the slightest idea of what he was on about.

'The letter, Kutaissov, the letter!'

Unsteady as a drunkard I got to my feet. Paul thrust into my hand a parchment written in Catherine's unmistakable script. My reading of Russian handwriting was not good though I could by now read a book or printed document with reasonable fluency.

'Master, what does it say?'

Paul's eyes were full of tears threatening to overflow his cheeks. But there was anger and contempt there also.

'This letter disinherits me. It says Alexander is to rule instead of me. That I am not a fit man to govern.'

'What will you do, Sire?' I asked. 'Something must be done.'

He snatched the letter from me, looking down as though it were some malignant spirit threatening to destroy him.

'What would you do?' he said. 'What, in heaven's name, would you do?'

My blood pounded in my veins as if I were fighting a duel.

I took a sharp deep breath.

'Let me have the letter, Sire,' I said. 'I will destroy it.'

'Good, excellent!' he replied.

He threw his arms round me. When this was completed I took the letter and tore it into dozens of pieces. Frenzy took us over. Like warriors bent on pillage we began to tear apart every single particle of paper.

When each document had been reduced to fragments I brought over a porcelain chamber pot concealed under a curtain.

With the application of candles he and I burned in the pot all the evidence which might deprive Paul of the throne. It took a while. By the end we were laughing like children, so loudly I worried its noise would penetrate the solid oak door to the death chamber beyond.

I had a further anxiety.

'Sire, are these papers duplicated elsewhere?'

Paul continued chuckling:

'Not at all! This is Catherine's private office. I used to play here when I was boy pushing a model elephant round the floor. She trusted no-one, especially not the scribes. Once again you have done me great service. Thank you.'

'Your Majesty,' I said, bowing low to the floor, 'You are my Emperor. I shall serve you with all my heart forever and ever.'

'Amen,' said Paul.

With that he turned his back on me and passed water noisily onto the ashy fragments in the pot.

'Your first duty in my reign,' he said with a smile when finished, 'is to dispose of this royal water and the strange black substances floating within it.'

'Gladly and willingly, Your Majesty,' I said, moving to the window to empty the contents out into the snowy courtyard.

SHORTLY AFTER DAWN the grand duchess arrived at the palace and was escorted to her suite by servants who treated her as if she were empress already.

Paul went to talk to her. He may have been mad but I knew he was not foolish enough to tell her about the destruction of Catherine's letters.

I passed through the death room several times. The company seemed to change every hour as if those in attendance were so overcome by grief they could not bear to linger. Catherine lay on the bed, as she had the night before, her eyes open, her head on a golden cushion, the mouth twisted to a distorted smile, her breathing hardly discernible.

You might think she was dead already. Candlelight gave her the appearance of a gremlin or hobgoblin, as if make-up had been embalmed but had gone wrong, too much white paste having been added.

But for the moment she survived. If a miracle occurred and she emerged from the coma, many of us were doomed. I yearned for her demise, prayed it would be soon.

Ladies in waiting crowded round the bedside. They were not sure who I was or what I was doing there. Some of the weeping girls were comely. I cast a keen eye on one, a little slip of a thing with blonde hair and blue eyes like a crystal lake. She saw me looking and blushed. I smiled, as far as it is decent to smile at a deathbed, and inclined my head towards her.

She raised her handkerchief to her eyes in a pretence of excessive weeping.

IN BETWEEN TIMES I attended to matters of business. For example, I went to see Count Arakcheev and made sure his troops were ready for anything. It was a cat and mouse game and one could hardy be too explicit or outspoken. But Arakcheev was shifty and anxious and knew what I meant.

'I have to tell the Emperor his security is good,' I said.

'He's not emperor yet!' he whispered, looking to left and right as if for conspirators.

'Not quite,' I replied. 'But I have seen the Empress. The end is near.'

'Ah well!' said Arakcheev. 'It will be expedient to serve our Master.'

Our eyes met. He nodded, gave me a sly salute. We had at last achieved a perfect understanding.

CATHERINE KEPT US waiting far longer than anticipated. Our vigil, on and off, lasted from the cold bitter dawn right through the day until ten that evening. So much the better for me. I had arranged appointments with bureaucrats, household managers, estate administrators, one or two military gentlemen, suave courtiers, bankers, even the mayor of the city. It was best to take precautions.

The situation could get out of hand. But I was doing my best to make sure the transition would be smooth.

Their response was confused. They didn't know me from Adam and knew next to nothing about Paul either. My task as a go-between was to assure them we had their interests in mind, with no conflict or lack of discretion.

My foreign accent bewildered them no end. One or two

had no knowledge Catherine was ill. Their manner quickly altered when I remarked that I had just emerged from the inner sanctum where our beloved empress was taking her agonised last breaths in the presence of her devoted son, soon to be emperor.

It was not exactly entire truth. But facts were only slightly garnished to bring such lackeys to an appreciation of the appropriate mood for these days.

They had a problem even remembering my name. I made sure not one of them would forget it in the future, writing it down if they so wished. They appeared flattered that I was eager to recruit them as allies and impart secrets to them which no others knew.

I described myself as one of the grand duke's premier advisers, being careful not to jump the gun and refer to him as emperor. But I proceeded without any hedging or fudging of the fact that Paul's reign was about to begin and that they should cut their cloth accordingly.

'It will be a new and happy reign,' said one old fool, elegant in fine clothes and large old-fashioned wig.

'We must expect respectful and wise change,' whimpered another.

By the end of that day, through the labyrinth of whispers, gossip, and rumours, my chosen informers had begun to set the scene for Paul's imminent advent.

CATHERINE'S DEATH IN itself proved to be no great drama. The crisis had come earlier at around six when her eyes closed, her breathing became laboured, and her face was twisted by a last spasm from the exhausted heart.

At ten the doctors listened to her chest and felt her pulse. Nothing, nothing, nothing, or so they said. The mighty ship had finally pitched to the bottom of the eternal sea.

Paul and his wife made a fine show of entering the death room, the former not sure whether to weep like a child or look like a dignified monarch. In the end he combined both, alternating massive sighing and crying with an expression of aloof indifference. The ladies of the bedchamber were not sure what to make of it. Each bout of Paul's visible grief impelled them to produce more handkerchiefs and renew their sobbing.

This little ceremony over Paul moved to different rooms in the palace to allow undertakers to deal with the corpse and to prepare himself for the ritual of the oath of allegiance.

The little man was acclaimed emperor of all Russia just after midnight in the main hall, the entire contingent of minister, officers of state, courtiers, and servants, having been assembled to witness the historic moment. The Lord Chief Justice administered the oath which Paul repeated back in such an insubstantial voice that only those within a short distance actually heard what he said. This restraint was later attributed to the excessive grief that our new dear emperor experienced at the demise of his great mother, bereavement restricting his throat and causing him to whisper.

A SANE MAN MIGHT have retreated to bed for a few hours after the tempestuous progressions of the previous hours. Paul decided to work through the night, preparing emergency laws to be implemented immediately.

He summoned me before the travail began:

'I wish to appoint you as Master of the Wardrobe, your duties to begin forthwith.'

I thanked him and knelt to kiss the newly anointed hand.

The vagueness of the responsibilities of the Master of the Wardrobe ensured there would be ample room for manoeuvre in every direction. For example, the post enabled its recipient to have a supply of ready finance through which stipends could be paid and other payments facilitated.

'Your Majesty,' I said, 'this is a historic night!'

One of Paul's ambitions was to be as 'historical' as possible. Such a comment caused him to beam like a child receiving a birthday present.

'You are our closest adviser, Kutaissov,' he said. 'I would like to make you a minister of the crown. But such a thing would be unpopular with the Russian nobility. They don't like foreigners much except in the army. So you're better off without a portfolio. We will need your advice about everything.'

'I shall do my best, Your Majesty,' I replied.

Together we moved to his new office, a magnificently immense room on the second floor.

'Here the world will be turned upside down,' said Paul, with a wave of his hand to indicate this extraordinary splendour. Without a further word he sat down behind the desk and arranged a few sheaves of fine paper to complement an elegant quill pen and a massive inkwell.

I expected he might have called his ministers to him. Instead he began writing page after page in his small hand, spacing out the commands so that only one or two orders filled a page. I stood for at least an hour watching him scribble away, his features made even more pallid by the flickering candlelight.

Finally, with an elaborate signature, he completed this

preliminary list of imperial wishes, stood up, and presented me with the dozen pages.

'Read that!' he said proudly. 'Have we not made a propitious start to our reign?'

'We have indeed, Your Majesty,' I replied.

'These are a few little forethoughts. That is before we get down to the main business. I've been mulling these things over ever since I heard my mother was dying.'

I glanced at the first page, expecting sweeping reforms, gigantic changes, requests for new taxes to be levied. Instead a different programme was being put forward. The gist of the matter was as follows:

I   Commissioned officers serving in the Russian army are instructed henceforth to wear civilian clothes when on leave.

II   The official uniform approved by the Gatchina fortress handbook becomes the standard dress of the entire army including the guards and grenadiers. There are no exceptions.

III   War with Persia is suspended immediately.

IV   All ministries must begin work each morning at six o'clock.

V   Sessions in the Senate must begin each morning at eight o'clock.

VI   The wearing of round hats, low collars, tails, waistcoats, trousers and boots in the street is forbidden. All subjects must wear three-cornered hats, starched high collars, tight tunics, breeches, gaiters, and square-toed shoes which are the only lawfully permissible wear.

VII   The hair of all subjects in the street must be thoroughly powdered and brushed well away from the forehead.

VIII   A special unit of three hundred men is to be set up to regulate orders in Articles VI and VII.

IX   Tailors, hatters and shoemakers are to apply to the appropriate offices for lawful patterns of clothing and footwear.

X   On seeing any member of the Imperial Family, subjects in the street must stop while passengers in horse-drawn carriages must immediately step down and bow.

XI   Any subject wishing to organise a dance, concert, wedding or funeral must first obtain permission from the local police station. An officer will be dispatched to each event to observe that the conduct of any such event is in accordance with loyalty, propriety and sobriety.

XII   Any infringement of the above statutes is punishable by imprisonment of not less than a year and not more than thirty years, depending on the offence.

Having completed the deciphering of these edicts, I glanced up to see Paul smiling from beyond the huge desk:

'There it is. The smack of firm government, is it not?'

'Certainly, Your Majesty,' I gulped. 'Congratulations on such a list of initial commands.'

'There will be more to come, of course!' said Paul. 'I want you to get these matters drafted into legal language. Make sure they are officially announced first thing in the morning.'

'Certainly, Your Majesty. But would you not like the advice of your ministers on these matters. Some of them might have interesting insights and even suggest further orders.'

Paul frowned.

'Ministers don't make laws. At the moment, with these elementary matters, there is no desire to consult anybody.'

It was obvious which way the wind was blowing. I saluted the emperor with a sweeping bow. He lifted his hand and motioned me to go in a way I had not seen before − a quick dismissive flick of the fingers. No mistaking its intention.

I hurried from the office and made my way to the heart of the administration in the bowels of the palace. Because of the empress's death, even at this hour of the morning a few clerical servants of the realm were lounging about down there.

Having gained their attention, I issued the emperor's instructions and went over the papers with them, word by word. There were two young men and an older man.

As we worked through the list the older man could not refrain from a wry smile, a response which encouraged the striplings beside him also to smirk.

Putting on a severe expression, I placed my forefinger on Article xii and looked at the older man:

'Did you smile, sir?' I asked, in a low voice.

'No, Sire,' the poor man said, 'I did not. I am only doing my duty.'

'Good!' I replied. 'Because if you smile at the Emperor's orders again, sir, I will not be held responsible for what happens. Do you have children?'

'Yes, Sire. Six children, two boys and four girls.'

'Well, sir, if you cherish their company, refrain from smiling.'

'Certainly, sir.'

With that I left them to put the document into legal words. In one and half hours I went back to them. Their new text was now transformed and ready for the penal code. The text was officially announced from the high point of the public gallows an hour or two later.

It showed what could be achieved if we all co-operated.

KUTAISSOV,' SAID PAUL, one morning two or three days later, 'we have an important matter which must be expedited immediately.'

'Certainly, Your Majesty,' I replied.

A slight twitch had developed overnight around the emperor's left eye. That night he had hardly slept at all but traipsed round the room in his nightgown, writing down whatever came into his head.

'We intend to make it a double funeral,' he said.

'A double funeral, Your Majesty?' I asked.

'Yes, and a period of national mourning for both of them.'

'*Both*, Your Majesty?'

'Yes, for *both* at the same time. That would be fitting.'

I bowed my head.

'Indeed, Your Majesty, that would be *doubly* fitting.'

'I'm glad you agree. You do not find the concept disagreeable at all?'

'Not at all. Whatever you decide will be acceptable, to all of us.'

'Good. In that case, it is decided. Thank you for your advice.'

I paused.

'Your Majesty…'

'Yes?'

Paul looked at me as if we had not been talking previously, as if I had just come into the room.

'It would be an excellent idea, perhaps for the purposes of future historians, if each edict is put down in your own writing.'

'What a wonderful proposal. Of course. What a fool we were not to think of such a thing.'

With that he hopped in a sprightly manner behind the desk and began scribbling away. When he finished he handed me the parchment with the proud look of a scholar who had done his research. The manuscript gave instructions for the exhumation of his father, Peter III, and the order for 'the joint funeral of their Imperial Majesties'.

'Your Majesty?' I enquired carefully.

'Yes, what is it? There is so much to do, so much to think about.'

'Your Majesty commands a state funeral for your father and your mother.'

'Of course,' said Paul. 'What is amiss about that?'

'Nothing, Your Majesty, nothing at all. Except that your esteemed father has already been laid to rest.'

'Yes. But that was thirty years ago. That paltry ceremony was unequal to the respect my father deserved. We'll do it again. That will remind everyone of the emperor's achievements.'

Paul burst into an flood of tears. Bending his bewigged head, he thumped the desk with puny fists so hard I thought he might damage himself.

'You know the rumours,' he sobbed. 'That he died of haemorrhoidal colic – piles – awful things.'

'I have heard such tales, Your Majesty,' I replied. 'It must have been a painful death.'

'Fiddlesticks,' shouted Paul. 'It was nothing of the kind. Our father was murdered. *She* killed him.'

Such rumours were common knowledge. What was true or false was hard to come by. What mattered was what Paul believed.

'Now comes the reckoning. We shall dig him up and plant him in glory. His funeral will overshadow hers. She will become as nothing in the light of his glory. She *is* nothing – nothing but a murderer.'

Paul came from behind his desk and hugged me, burying his face into my shoulder. At such moments he became a boy again, anxious for his own life, uncertain of everything. I embraced him till the tantrum abated. Then he eased himself away, staring with his tired, watery eyes.

'What would I do without you?' he bleated.

'Your Majesty,' I replied, 'I will do this for you. I will obey your will in everything. Leave it to me.'

I hurried off to find the appropriate churchmen and ministers of state to arrange that the remains of Peter III were exhumed from the Annunciation Church of the Alexander Nevsky Monastery to be re-interred with the greatest honour in the Cathedral of the St Peter and St Paul fortress in St Petersburg.

Under the emperor's signature and seal I issued instructions for the abbot and monks of St Alexander's Abbey to be present at the grand funeral, not a single one of them to be absent.

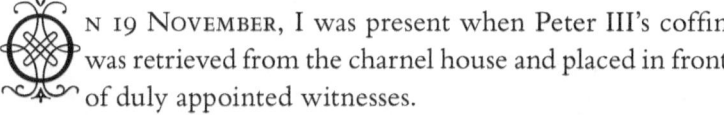

N 19 November, I was present when Peter III's coffin was retrieved from the charnel house and placed in front of duly appointed witnesses.

As the lead casing of the plain box was cut open by the workmen a foul odour spread through the room, infiltrating our nostrils and causing gasps of horror from all present. The body had not even been put in a winding sheet but lay there in its grey nakedness.

With difficulty the corpse was scooped from its rest and transferred, bit by bit, to a magnificent new receptacle set with gold and lined with choice velvet.

The former emperor's skull lay there, its mouth open as if laughing at its own spectacle, the rotting bones spread in some disorder below it. We held perfumed handkerchiefs to our noses. By Paul's order the coffin remained open. It was placed on a dais draped with royal purple surrounded by a guard of praying monks whose noses were clearly less sensitive than most.

That afternoon the whole royal family, with the exception of little Princess Olga, were brought to the abbey to pay homage. Paul led the mourners in. The archbishop gave him the crown of Russia, which Paul placed ceremoniously on the grinning skull.

Some days later the news was given out that the casket with 'the translation of the august remains' was to be transported from the Abbey to the Winter Palace.

Y now the whole of the Gatchina garrison had moved to St Petersburg. It was these ruffians on the day of the funeral who lined the route to pay their respects.

***

On one of the coldest days I had ever known every person of the court (young or old) was required to follow behind the former emperor's gun carriage.

At the Winter Palace, where every patch of walls, floors and ceilings had been covered in black cloth, the coffin was placed next to that of Catherine's.

At an especially tedious service for the dead Paul delivered a prolonged epitaph. He hardly mentioned his mother but praised the achievements of the dead Peter, intoning his farewell to his father in a monotonous whine that sounded at least to my ears as particularly mad.

Glancing round at royals and commoners, most of them with their eyes prudently cast down, I had the feeling that each of them had seen in their emperor exactly what his servant Kutaissov saw. As if further proof were needed of the craziness of the day, the sight of two coffins being carried side by side towards the crypt would have been sufficient to convince.

Across the way I observed Platon Zubov, Catherine's last lover, consumed with grief, his body shaking in the anguish of memory.

It would be best to deal with such as him as soon as possible.

IN THE PURGES which follow a change of power a measure of discretion is advisable. By this I mean two distinct schemes must be planned. When removing the sediment of the previous regime, care must be taken.

Thus Zubov would be told one thing but something else would actually happen. My initial problem was to convince my master of the need for such a strategy. But Paul was already so drunk on the wine of power that he accepted almost anything from my lips as pure gospel.

The morning dressing session was the best opportunity for such machinations. Often a bad dream or two had again tipped the emperor into a state of panic.

Paul's remedy for such a condition was to issue edicts and devise further edicts. But he had to be reminded from time to time that ruling was not just a question of giving out official orders. Within forty-eight hours he had done enough of that, sufficient for most rulers for months.

While powdering his wig that morning I turned to him as if to mention something significant. He noticed the eagerness of my glance.

'I see from your face you have some advice for me.'

'Not really. I am too humble to offer advice. Your ministers can do that for you.'

'My ministers are a collection of addled heads,' said Paul. 'I wouldn't trust them to carry a bucket of piss across a room without spilling it.'

'Well, Your Majesty, a certain matter did flit across my mind.'

Paul executed a little dance, like a boy promised a treat.

'Oh, tell me, tell me! Stop teasing me. What is it? I demand to know.'

'Just a small nothing that entered my foolish head,' I said. 'Perhaps I should not even mention such a thing to you. Your Majesty is far too wise not to have thought of it already.'

'Ah,' said Paul, still in a childish manner, 'a guessing game, eh?'

'Not entirely,' I replied.

I adjusted his wig and placed my hands on his shoulders as he sat facing the mirror in his full dress uniform ready for breakfast.

'Oh those barber's hands of yours,' he sighed. 'They are so relaxing. Press my shoulders. Comfort me. Only you can do that.'

I applied a gentle pressure on the royal shoulder and neck muscles.

'My God! If only you had been born a woman. What a companion, what a wife, you would have been!'

In the mirror I noticed that Paul was dribbling. I removed the saliva with a silk handkerchief before once more tightening my grip on his epaulettes and neck. It was like stroking a pet cat, making it purr with pleasure.

'Your Majesty, before I forget. May I mention that small and insubstantial matter?'

'Of course, of course,' sighed Paul, slightly off-guard with the tenderness of my massage.

'Well, it's a question of Count Zubov.'

'Zubov!'

Paul stood up. In the mirror I saw his face change to fear and loathing:

'Zubov! Never mention that man's name to me. I hate him. I hate him.' He sat down again, red with anger.

'I saw him in the chapel. During the funeral,' I said.

Paul lost his composure. He was now dribbling down his chin quite freely. I dared not touch his face again with the silk handkerchief.

'Was he there? How dare he? The usurper. Creeping into my mother's bed.'

'Precisely!' I said. 'He *was* there. I thought it presumptuous at the time. But I suppose we must all pay respect to the departed.'

'She killed my father, and then favoured *him*. That I will

never forgive.'

Paul wrung his delicate hands, squeezing them together, upset, the muscles of his face twitching.

'Well, Your Majesty, I think such a man needs careful handling.'

'Handling? What you do mean? Why don't you speak more plainly? *Handling*?'

'Yes, I will speak plainly.'

'Good. Proceed without delay.'

He turned in his chair to face me. I sat down in the gold chair opposite. It was a sign we were to talk.

'Your Majesty, I must tell you this. Zubov and his cronies are still powerful. They must be dealt with.'

Paul's face showed amazement.

'I never thought of that. You mean…That such a man could be a threat?…To my very throne?'

'Of course! The memory of your mother is strong. These men represent strong interests. They do not represent yours.'

Paul rose to his feet and paced the room, up and down, up and down. Perhaps on this occasion I had expressed my views too strongly for his nervous disposition. A man such as Paul could rapidly become anxious, bereft of confidence, in short, unhinged. But the brain storm did not last long this time.

In due course he returned to his chair like an obedient pet, and in a low voice asked simply, 'What should I do?'

This was sufficient for me to put forward my plan to settle with Zubov, once and for all.

'Your Majesty, I think we can solve this easily.'

'*Easily*?'

'Zubov and his companions are reeling from the death of your mother. Now is the time to strike.'

'But how? Without leaving one's flank exposed?'

'*Easily*. This is what we must do. Zubov is in a state of fear. Therefore Your Majesty and the Empress should call at his house by appointment.'

'Enter the snake's den?' said Paul.

'Yes. Go to him in the fullness of authority. Tell him he is forgiven for any past doing and that you are not a man to harbour resentment.'

'But I do harbour resentment!' said Paul. 'The man bedded my mother, for God's sake. They will have spoken of me after their rutting and cavorting. He will know my secrets. She will have told him everything.'

He looked close to tears.

'Of course!' I replied. 'What Count Zubov did can never be forgiven. But that is the beauty of my plan.'

'Beauty?' squeaked Paul, as if this was an inappropriate word in such a context.

'Yes, Your Majesty, *beauty*! Firstly you enter the snake's den. You charm the snake with your words and forgiveness. The snake curls up and sleeps, his venom extracted with sheer gratitude on his part. Then comes the most beautiful part of all.'

'What is that?' said Paul.

'We examine the documents Zubov left at the palace in his role as High Steward. We look at them, ledger by ledger. Even the Archangel Gabriel would make some errors. But with Zubov such mistakes will be on a large scale and catastrophic.'

'Who will do this?' said Paul.

'The independent auditors preparing the ground for your successful reign. They will find in those ledgers more than enough to get rid not only of Zubov, but his two brothers also, and perhaps most of his friends.'

'Marvellous,' said Paul, clapping his hands together as if at the theatre. 'Of course, the man is a bachelor. So we don't have to worry about his wife and children. He has none. For all practical purposes my mother was his wife, may she be cursed in hell for it!'

'Well done, Your Majesty! Let us go forward with this. No time must be wasted. Within a week, a month, six weeks, Zubov would be back to his old tricks. At the moment he is off-balance, disorientated, lost. Let us do this as soon as possible.'

FOR THE REASON of avoiding embarrassment I did not attend the tea party at Zubov's house. But I heard from private sources that Zubov was so worried before the visit at the prospect of arrest and humiliation that he had a little accident in his breeches. (Such gossip may be mere rumour! But I hope not!)

At court it was common knowledge that Zubov informed his associates he was so relieved at the apparent pardon that he had felt like falling at His Majesty's feet. A fine spectacle that would have been. Paul might have kicked him in the face.

For the second part of the drama, there was neither rumour nor room for error. Zubov was caught with his dirty trousers truly down round his ankles. The ledgers were crammed with evidence of corruption and greed. Not only had Zubov paid unnecessary stipends to his relatives. The books, which never lie, showed he continually greased the palms of various courtiers, individuals whose identities were now known to us.

Within a week Zubov and his tribe were embarking on a journey of exile, deep into the countryside a thousand miles or more from St Petersburg. Zubov had enjoyed his fun in Catherine's bed. Now he paid the price.

His Majesty was so elated he presented me with a magnificent mansion, one of the finest.

My wife was delighted to move in there. Personally I hardly ever bothered to sleep in our new dwelling. The Zubov affair so inspired me it seemed best to keep close to my master and take up a suite of two or three rooms in the palace.

Strangely enough this suite may have been Zubov's former quarters, situated conveniently with good access to the royal bedchamber.

I COMPILED A LIST of those who were to fall, and of some (rather less) who should rise. Paul was engaged in the self-same sport, though his victims were selected more for vengeance against his mother than any thoughts of protecting or bettering himself.

First on his mind was a sick, grey-haired woman, the Princess Dashkova, now living in seclusion in Moscow. Her friendship with Catherine had stimulated much gossip years back. Paul believed Dashkova colluded in his father's murder though the truth was as ever hard to come by.

'She must be punished,' said Paul one morning, in that tone of voice which really enquired my opinion of the matter.

'Certainly,' I replied. 'Your Majesty always knows best.'

'What would be a suitable retribution?'

'For what particular sin?'

Paul frowned as if dealing with a foolish child.

'For the sin of knowledge. Knowledge we are not supposed

to have is a sin.'

I paused to think about the meaning of this enigma.

'Ah yes, knowledge, Your Majesty. Knowledge would be dangerous.'

Paul smiled, laughed.

'There you are. You see everything is simple. Only certain people should know particular things. If others find out such things, it is dangerous.'

'In that case,' I murmured, 'the punishment should be severe.'

'Indeed. There – you understand everything. So suggest an appropriate penalty.'

I thought for a moment. But I had already made up my mind.

'Exile, Your Majesty. That would suffice. But not too far.'

Paul was not pleased with this answer, the concept of 'not too far' not being in accordance with his beliefs of how a ruler should act.

'Not too far? She possesses knowledge that could ruin me, and you talk about not too far'.

I tried again.

'A ruler should be merciful. Mercy shows the true strength of a ruler.'

'Now where did you get those ideas from? It's not like you to spout such nonsense. To rule is to be strong, to be clear, to be straightforward. Mercy is something else.'

With that he dismissed me from his presence as if my advice had been too lily-livered. I learned a good lesson from that moment.

Yet I felt the case of the Princess Dashkova was indeed difficult. She was frail with illness, a living skeleton, or so I heard. Any kind of exile would kill her off.

Nevertheless when later I returned to the emperor's presence, he showed me a letter he had sent to the governor of Moscow. I read it with some trepidation.

Paul had no inkling how such a message revealed the worthlessness of his judgement. Worst of all was one passage which instructed the poor governor to 'tell her that she has to go and live on her estates in the north because of what she did in 1762. Tell her to go at once.'

After the slight displeasure Paul had shown towards me previously, I decided to praise him rather than risk deeper offence. Dealing with Paul was like flying a kite – each little change in the wind could bring you down to earth. A sensitive nose for the direction of the wind was one of my virtues.

'Splendid!' I intoned. 'It combines firmness with judgement, expediency with discretion.'

'I will write that down. I like the expression – 'expediency with discretion.'

He duly copied the phase, reading the words back to himself with a smile.

THE GOVERNOR OF Moscow at the time was a man named Orlov, (though no relation as far as I knew to either General Orlov of the Don Cossacks, or Count Alexis Orlov). Perhaps he had assumed that name somewhere along the line to improve his chances, one never knew the true background of such people. He had once been in charge of a large prison south of St Petersburg. On the back of that appointment he had clawed his way into administrative posts of various kinds until landing the supreme prize.

I heard later that Governor Orlov carried out his orders precisely to the letter. The winter was as cruel as it ever could be. Despite the winter chill Orlov insisted that the princess should pack her bags immediately and leave the following dawn.

It was not Orlov's fault that her carriage broke down and could go no further than it did. Princess Dashkova was forced to sleep in a peasant's hut for several nights while the surrounding village came to her rescue and repaired the vehicle. By then strong representations had been made to the court.

Paul was compelled to modify his position by heart-felt entreaties and weeping from the empress. Browbeaten by his wife, Paul cut a sorry spectacle in the morning.

'You know,' he murmured, almost weeping, 'you were absolutely right to suggest I should have been more lenient with the Princess. As it is I have permitted her to reside not too far away. Is that wise?'

'Very wise. I believe you intended such an outcome all along, at the same time giving a clear warning to all your enemies.'

'Good God!' he exclaimed. 'It's unimaginable how you read my thoughts. Whatever would I do without you?'

I decided to leave that question unanswered.

THE WIFE PETER had so kindly chosen for me, my dear Natasha, proved to be a most appropriate wife. She made no undue demands and did not complain when for days or weeks at a time my duties with the emperor kept me from attending upon her.

Natasha understood that any neglect of her needs was a

necessary aspect of my ambition. Being the emperor's servant involved my whole purpose in life. To let things slip would be to cut one's own throat. She knew that.

Of course her previous husband had been a successful soldier till he got his head blown off in battle. Occasionally between this former paragon and her present husband Natasha would make subtly veiled comparisons, as between perfection and imperfection.

I took little notice of these petty jibes. If they stung like a wasp from time to time that was only to be expected. When a man marries a being from a superior social caste he must expect a few caustic comments.

Besides in Russian society I was rapidly gaining ground. My daily proximity to the mighty sovereign was enough to impress most of the courtiers even at the price of stimulating a surfeit of envy.

At times I discerned that Natasha was herself finding a new respect for the stranger she had married. Whether she showed this openly or not remained a matter of some indifference to me. I had entered into matrimony in order to fulfil the will of the emperor. That part of the bargain was sealed and delivered. Whether she despised me or loved me was not within my gift. I could but persevere and hope for the best.

Natasha's daughter, Tatyana, was in another category. In a short time she progressed from a shy duckling to become a most pleasing swan. Her blonde hair had grown into attractive tresses falling to her shoulders. For me she could do no wrong. I spoiled her every time with gifts and kindness.

'Father, will you buy me a pony?'

'Yes, of course! What colour?'

Or perhaps it was a new dress she wanted, or some jewellery, or a piece of furniture for her room. Whatever she asked for she was given.

Natasha showed no disapproval at this. She never asked me for anything, having money of her own. If she had asked me for anything she could have had it. But Natasha provided for herself.

To be with Tatyana was a joy. When out for a walk together we held hands. She loved this attention and would gaze at me with that look which surely one day would win all hearts.

As for her brother Boris, he was more distant. Sometimes he sought my advice on matters such as becoming a soldier or taking up a profession. He often asked about my early life. But Boris was really more interested in the emperor and details of men and women at court.

I tried to be discreet with him as well as moderately truthful.

As PAUL's EARLY weeks in power passed among clouds of activity, his perception of what was real and what was false began to change. I noticed most mornings how thoughtful and dreamy he remained, a man scarcely awake.

Never accustomed to everyday humanity, his overheated brain conjured up images of his own grandeur. Paul could never see the wood for the trees. He confused important issues with trivia and vice-versa. The trivia were matters of revenge for his father's demise, the important issues, statecraft and policy, being beyond his grasp.

Fortunately the 'overheated' aspects of his brain could be cooled with an application of flattery. One could praise his bearing, his diction, his understanding of human nature, his choice of clothes, his breadth of knowledge about history, literature, and philosophy, his love of the empress and his mistress, Nelidowa.

Eventually it became necessary to find new tunes and not go day after day harping on the same subjects and praising the same things.

Even Paul in his insanity appreciated variety. Quite by chance I found a topic which combined praise with clear action.

One of the serving maids, Galina, a sweet girl with a piping voice and rosebud lips, was overheard telling her companions that a sentry at the Summer Palace had seen some kind of vision.

Such stories circulated like wildfire, growing till they flared out of all proportion. I summoned the wench to my office for a chat. She came in nervously, wiping her hands on her apron.

'Close the door!' I said. 'I wish to speak with you in private.'

She approached the desk. I gazed on her slim figure, her fresh clean face, and her anxious expression.

'Do you enjoy your work here?' I asked, not wishing to frighten the wretched little flower.

'Oh yes, sir,' she trilled, 'It is everything I would wish.'

'I have heard good reports of your work.'

'Thank you, sir. That's very kind.'

'I was thinking of offering you a promotion.'

'Thank you, sir,' she said.

'But first you have to answer a few questions.'

'I'm not very good at that,' she said.

'It's a very easy question first.'

She clasped her hands together as if offering a prayer.

'It is said you knew a soldier who received a vision.'

Galina looked alarmed.

'It wasn't me, sir, it was a lot of people. They all heard the same story.'

'Tell me what story it was. Only tell the truth.'

She became flustered, tongue-tied.

'Spit it out, girl! Tell me what you heard.'

'It wasn't much, sir.'

'Whatever it was, tell me. That is if you would like your promotion.'

She hesitated as if trying to remember a favourite nursery rhyme or something someone said a long time ago.

'I heard it from several others. It wasn't me who spoke to the soldier. It was somebody else.'

'I understand that.'

'They said this soldier, on guard at the Summer Palace, saw a vision.'

'A soldier saw a vision?'

'Yes. He saw Saint Michael the Archangel.'

'Do you believe this?'

'Some girls do. The soldier did. So they said.'

'You don't think the soldier was trying to deceive anybody.'

'Oh no, sir, he wouldn't do that.'

I relaxed back in my chair and smiled.

'So, Galina, you know this soldier then.'

'No, sir. Not me.'

I rose from my chair and went towards her.

I placed my hands on her shoulders and kissed her on the cheek. She stared at me, a touch of loathing in her face. I kissed her on the lips and touched the smooth skin of her throat. She stood as still as a sacrificial lamb.

'Now, tell me the truth,' I said slowly. 'You know this soldier?'

She gulped before letting out a cry of, 'Sorry, sir, yes I do.'

'Is he your lover then, this soldier? No lies now!'

'Yes, sir. We are getting married soon.'

'That's better. Now tell the truth. What was the vision about?'

'He saw him, sir. He really saw him. It was the Archangel Michael, in shining armour, smiling on St Petersburg.'

'Good,' I said, and went back to my chair.

I scribbled a note, signed it and stamped it with my own seal of office, and gave it to her.

'I want you to go to the barracks and bring your soldier back with you. This piece of paper is all you need. Present it to the guardroom. Make sure you are back within the hour.'

She took the message with trembling hand and almost ran from the room.

Within forty minutes she returned with a handsome young soldier from the palace guard in full dress uniform obviously put on in haste for one button on the front of his jacket was undone.

'Private Smirnov, at your service, sir', he said in a quiet voice, standing smartly to attention.

'Do up that loose button, private,' I said. 'You can't come into this office looking like that. Galina, you may go. I trust you not to mention this to anybody outside this room. Gossip can be dangerous.'

'Oh yes, sir. Thank you, sir,' she whimpered.

The soldier worried at the front of his uniform with anxious fingers. Galina escaped like a mouse from my presence. The button duly fastened, I allowed a few moments of silence and stared at him. His eyes were fixed on the wall behind me at the height of the man. His bearing was excellent. A man to depend on.

'Private Smirnov, have you ever been in a battle?'

'Yes, sir. Seven times, sir.'

'Then why are you still only a private soldier?'

'Got into some trouble, sir. Nothing too serious, sir.'

'If you answer my questions, we might be able to see about that.'

'Thank you, sir.'

I glanced down at my desk and took up my pen.

'What's this about a vision, Private Smirnov?'

'Yes, sir. A vision, sir. The other night, sir. At the Summer Palace.'

I scribbled on the paper, his exact words.

'And what did you see?'

'Archangel Michael, sir.'

He said the words in a matter of fact, clipped military voice, as if this was the most usual thing in the world.

'Why should you have a vision? And not somebody else?'

'Can't say, sir, beyond my understanding.'

'Had you been drinking that night?'

'Not a drop, sir. Dry as a bone.'

'What time was this vision?'

'At the stroke of midnight, sir. I saw the Archangel above the gate.'

'Have you ever seen anything like this before?'

'No, sir. First time, sir.'

'You realise this vision makes you a special person?'

He paused and blinked.

'Sorry, sir. Don't understand the question, sir!'

'Well, visions are not the sort of thing just anybody sees.'

'Oh, I see what you mean, sir.'

'Have you seen visions before?'

'Not to my knowledge, sir.'

The man was obviously too stupid to be lying. He believed

he saw what he saw.

I summoned a scribe who took down the man's version of what he had seen, word for word.

The written witness was as follows:

The Testimony of Private Smirnov, of the Royal Summer Palace Guard Squad, concerning a vision of St Michael the Archangel.

I hereby swear by Almighty God that on the night of 30 November 1799, while standing guard at midnight at the south gate I became aware of a tall figure on the palace wall above me.

I believed it to be none other than a vision of St Michael the Archangel and immediately presented arms in salute.

The figure remained before my eyes for several seconds and I laid eyes upon it as a sign of blessing on the emperor for all his good works. On the disappearance of this visitation I reported the event to my commanding officer, Lieutenant Gordanov, who smelt my breath for alcohol but could find none.

My officer neither believed nor disbelieved my story and came to the same spot where I had seen the vision. I was advised by the officer to watch in the same place for a further period of sentry duty and to contact him in case of further sightings. I was relieved at dawn after a total of ten hours on duty. No further incidents or visions occurred.

I have made a full account of this happening to Master of the Wardrobe Kutaissov and I certify that this account is the true substance and circumstance of what I have witnessed with my own eyes on that night.

(Signed) Private Smirnov

Of course we helped the poor fellow out with a word or two here and there as his military training rendered him almost inarticulate and he could only express himself in short sharp phrases.

I decided to take the information to the emperor without sounding out Lieutenant Gordanov, as the officer could be interrogated at a later time if needs be. It was clear that Gordanov had given the underling extra guard duty as a punishment for reporting the vision.

I intended that Paul, the most superstitious of men, should receive the testimony in its undiluted form.

With this in mind, I had the scribe write out the words on fine paper in his most elegant handwriting.

P AUL OFTEN EXPRESSED his dislike of the Winter Palace and believed he should, as an emperor, build his own palace. I chose my moment carefully. One morning, just before lunch when Paul was hungry and susceptible to suggestion, I knocked on the door of his state study. He was seated behind his desk with a remarkable mountain of paper in front of him, spilling over onto the floor.

'Ah, Kutaissov,' he said, 'would you clear this rubbish off the desk?'

I ignored this, moving with haste towards him. I had ruffled my hair before entering the room to give the semblance of disarray.

'Your Majesty,' I blurted out, 'a great happening has occurred which I thought must meet with your instant attention.'

Following a boring morning full of legal rigmarole and

committee meetings, hence the high hill of paper on the desk, Paul sat bolt upright in his chair:

'For God's sake, what is it?'

Paul at first believed I had sniffed out some dreadful plot, having endured a vicious nightmare around this theme during the night. His relief on finding it was good news rather than bad made him even more gullible.

I handed him the parchment with its bright black message inscribed in flowing large letters. He read it several times, his lips moving as he scanned the page up and down.

'By all the holy saints, what does this mean?' he said.

'It is a propitious omen, Your Majesty,' I exclaimed. 'Saint Michael the Archangel has come to offer the Emperor his protection.'

'Ooh...' he exclaimed, scratching his head. I pressed forward.

'Your Majesty...This indicates that it is time for you to embark on your largest project yet. The building of a palace, something glorious, to carry your reputation into history.'

The emperor bounded to his feet.

'You are correct. I will do more than that. I will build a castle, St Michael's Castle. I will rename my youngest son, Michael, in honour of this vision. This is a miracle. I shall begin work after lunch.'

Whatever expectations I might have imagined, Paul's response exceeded every one. The man was a bigger fool than anyone could ever know.

ANY CHESS PLAYER will eventually move a piece in error, thereby placing his position in peril. In the manipulation of Paul, I proved no exception. Once or twice I made mistakes.

I must first mention the strange situation in the palace after the death of Empress Catherine. Nelidowa, formerly an underling, assumed, after only a short time, a quite disproportionate significance at court, her elevation endorsed by Paul's wife to everyone's amazement. Catherine Nelidowa now accompanied Empress Maria to all important public events from church to dinner, from state banquets to tea parties. The two women became inseparable, chattering like eager schoolgirls.

The court could hardly be scandalised by all this. Everything was open and above board. Gossip inside or outside the palace became unnecessary. If courtiers wished to chew on the matter they could discuss truth instead of rumour.

I made two errors in that period. The first concerned the matter of the Order of St George, a medal introduced by the Empress Catherine, awarded only to the bravest soldiers.

One morning Paul sounded me out:

'Help me with this.'

'Yes, Your Majesty,'

'Have you heard of the Order of St George?'

'I believe I have.'

'It's a medal the Empress Catherine brought in for our best soldiers. It is worrying.'

'Why?'

'Because every soldier who receives this honour will think of her and not of Emperor Paul I.'

Paul paused and hummed a little patriotic tune:

'Politics, politics,' he said. 'They make things so difficult.'

'You could abolish the Order of St George and bring in your own medal instead.'

He pondered for a moment and then smiled:

'An excellent idea. I will proceed along those lines immediately.'

A strange anxiety entered my head. In truth I did not know the Order of St George from a children's toy at a party. But it seemed reasonable to expect medals could be divisive.

If you abolish long-cherished awards you anger those who already hold them while dispiriting soldiers hoping to win one. Instituting a new medal under a different name for the same deeds might breed resentment, envy, or nostalgia for the old order.

On the other hand my approach was to sail in whatever direction my master indicated. Lacking prior knowledge of a subject could lead to embarrassment, as happened here.

The situation became more difficult than anyone could have imagined. Empress Maria and Catherine Nelidowa were strongly opposed to any tinkering with this medal. From that point things began to go rapidly downhill.

The significant date was St George's Day at the end of November when the most courageous soldiers and sailors gathered at Kazan Cathedral. The occasion had been introduced by Empress Catherine as a holy feast. At a time of national mourning it was not expected that this celebration would take place. But the abolition of the ceremony of the Order of St George would have been too bitter a pill for hardened veterans to swallow.

Paul's view was that he would never wage war on another country. So military medals were now redundant. Empress Maria ventured forth with a quite different opinion. On this issue Paul affirmed he was not to be moved. The empress eventually gave up the unequal struggle. Unfortunately things did not end there.

Catherine Nelidowa now entered the fray. Her first step in the campaign was to write a letter, a document which caught my eye in Paul's office a few days later, a sweet little document, fragrant with scent and neat handwriting of extraordinary clarity.

I observed that Paul tore up the paper in a childish moment. So that was that, it seemed! But Nelidowa was not to be thwarted. When I next proceeded to the area behind their loving room to eavesdrop on Paul and Catherine, I discovered she had not given up. After much dalliance they eventually reached the subject about which I wished to hear.

'Darling, that was exquisite,' whispered Paul. 'What present can I give you this week to enchant your soul?'

'Your love is all I need,' replied Nelidowa, giggling a little.

'But I delight in giving you gifts,' said Paul insistently. 'You must want something!'

'You give me everything,' she answered, 'more than I ever thought possible.'

'Then ask me for something, for anything,' suggested Paul.

'Anything? Something?' she cooed.

'Something, anything,'

'A little something?'

'Anything!'

A long pause followed. Perhaps she was stroking his face. At last she spoke:

'A little thing,' she said, in a voice so soft I could hardly hear her.

'Anything you ask for — you shall have.'

Another lengthy silence.

'I wish to ask for something, dear one,' she said, her voice so seductive I would have given her the world and all the stars just for the asking.

'Ask. I promise it will be given.'

'It is not an easy thing,' she continued.

'No matter. I will grant you whatever you wish.'

Paul had launched his boats and now must sink or swim. Nelidowa delivered the message:

'You will grant me whatever I wish?'

'Of course, of course.'

I thought I heard a sigh, long and drawn out.

'Then grant me this,' she whispered.

'Of course, of course.'

'Please keep the Order of St George,' she said.

I waited for a distant explosion. There was none. Instead my name was awkwardly invoked.

'Kutaissov thinks it should be abolished.'

'But I think you should keep it. For the sake of all those brave soldiers.'

No reply came from Paul. Nelidowa continued her plea:

'If you abolish this order you will be accused of meanness. You will destroy the pride of the soldiers when they look at their black and yellow ribbons. You will make enemies in abundance.'

I could hardly believe my ears. Such impudence, such impertinence, such meddling in the affairs of state.

Even more extraordinary was that Paul did not reply. What could he be doing?

Instead of a tantrum, silence ensued. I deduced that they had returned to their love making. Confused, I pressed my ear close to the wall. I heard nothing. Paul spoke not a single word for or against her proposition.

When the details were announced a week later the truth emerged. The proclamation announcing the end of the Order of St George never appeared.

The ceremony in Kazan Cathedral took place and the Treasury funded an especially magnificent banquet.

Nelidowa had won.

IN MARCH 1797, Paul, his family and his retinue, accompanied by the ex-King Stanislas of Poland, set out for his Coronation to be held in Moscow. Paul, eager to consolidate his grip, had issued a proclamation as early as December 1796, that the glorious ceremony of his crowning would be held in the spring.

In a long string of imperial coaches over many days we made the interminable journey through thick snow and bone-aching winds from the comparative warmth of our northern palace to the gloomy quarters of the Kremlin.

On arriving in Moscow, our procession wended its way through almost empty streets, though surely it had been announced that His Majesty's presence was forthcoming.

We heard little cheering from the populace. This plunged Paul into one of his blackest moods.

On Easter Sunday, the acclaimed day, I attended in Paul's bedchamber to dress him and prepare him for the ceremonies ahead.

'Kutaissov,' he growled, 'Moscow has let me down. They think only of my dead mother. They have no respect for me. Such contempt will not help them.'

'Your Majesty,' I said, in the hope of soothing him, 'once the wonderful Coronation is completed, the entire country will fall at your feet. An anointed emperor is irresistible. They will worship you and cheer you to the rafters.'

He gave me one of those ominous glances.

'You are seldom wrong. In this instance I feel aggrieved and upset. My feathers are ruffled. My feelings are out of sorts.'

'That is natural. You have the empire on your shoulders and the responsibilities of state. But after today everything will be different.'

Paul sat down and put his hands over his face:

'If you only knew what was in my heart, how fearful I am, how confused.'

Such vulnerability was not to be encouraged. It could soon change to resentment or anger.

'Your Majesty,' I hastened to reply. 'You are the sovereign lord. You must not weaken. This is the turning of the tide, the start of springtime, the opening of the new book, the fulfilment of all your desires.'

To drive the point home, I descended to one knee in front of him. 'You are the father of the nation, Your Majesty. We all depend on you.'

He took his hands from his face. Paul was not weeping. He looked petulant like a spoiled child. The kaleidoscope of his madness threw up so many patterns.

'Get me dressed! I will be strong as an emperor is strong. I have great strength within me.'

He rose from the chair, and touched me lightly on the head in benediction as I maintained my suppliant posture.

'Rise up. We will be strong together, you and I. Sometimes I believe you are the only friend I have in the world.'

I fetched his ornamental robes. After he had taken off

his nightgown, I helped him put on the apparatus of dignified majesty.

When the task was finished Paul's dwarfish appearance
seemed even more diminished by the weight of the costume.
Like a midget clown hired in a circus to parody the image of
an emperor.

But I bowed deeply, and murmured with all the reverence I
could muster, 'Magnificent, Your Majesty, truly magnificent!'

PAUL'S CORONATION WAS the official act of blessing by the
Russian Orthodox Church. Only after this ceremony
had taken place could a new ruler be acknowledged as
politically legitimate. The superstitious belief held sway among
the church and people alike that no reign would ever have a
propitious voyage without such a ritual.

Obviously in the instance of Paul I no religious mumbo-
jumbo or black magic had the slightest effect on his progress
from madness to madness. If anything, the rites of Coronation
merely augmented the disastrous aspects of Paul's character.

The notion that the emperor was anointed and transformed
by God Himself was ludicrous. The changes in Paul inspired
by his Coronation proved to be for the worse. Anyway, the
charade proceeded that day and I witnessed every detail of it.

The Coronation party was met by officials of church and
state at ten o'clock in the morning at the Kremlin's Red Porch.
Paul took his place under a moving canopy accompanied by
thirty Russian generals. The empress under a similar but smaller
canopy followed behind.

From there the emperor progressed to the Cathedral of the

Dormition, passing rows of soldiers backed up by crowds who by proclamation had been ordered onto the streets.

Items of regalia in the parade included the Chain of the Order of St Andrew, the Sword of State, the Banner of State, the State Seal, the Purple Robe for the emperor, the Orb, consisting of a polished hollow ball made from red gold, encircled by two rows of diamonds and surmounted by a large sapphire topped by a cross, the Sceptre, a burnished shaft of three sections containing eight rings of brilliant-cut diamonds topped by the Orlov Diamond surmounted by a double-headed eagle with the coat of arms at its centre, the Small Imperial Crown, a special crown created for Maria, encrusted with diamonds but lighter than that intended for the ruler's head, and the weighty Great Imperial Crown, in the style of a mitre divided into two semi-spheres with a central arch between them topped by diamonds and a great jewel all the way from China.

The entourage following on included aides-de-camp to the emperor, generals, marshals of the army, ministers, the commander of the Horse Guards, and somewhere, among the distinguished throng, I was there in my finest attire.

Paul and Maria were greeted at the door of the Cathedral by the Patriarch of Russia and assorted prelates. The Bishop of Moscow, a fat man with a well-fed face, offered the Cross to Paul for a kiss. Another priest sprinkled the couple with holy water.

On entering the cathedral they venerated the nearest icons three times before taking their seats on the dais where two immense thrones had been constructed. Paul snuggled himself down into the throne like a little monkey unaccustomed to such a seat. I wondered whether any of those present permitted themselves a moment of inner humour at such a spectacle.

The service of Coronation began with the reading of the

Psalm 101, *I will sing of mercy and judgement...I will behave myself wisely in a perfect way.* After that Paul, in his quavery voice, stutteringly recited the Nicene Creed. Then came the incantation of several prayers, the singing of hymns, and the reading of appropriate scriptural excerpts.

Paul was robed in purple by the Bishops of St Petersburg and Kiev. The Patriarch laid his hand upon Paul's inclined head, and read two prayers. These intercessions pleaded for the anointed ruler to be full of the Holy Spirit, to help him judge the people in righteousness, to subject to his will all the barbarous nations, and to keep the new monarch within the shadow of God that he might continually do those things pleasing to God.

Such sentiments seemed absurd given the nature of the anointed. I could have laughed out loud. They might just as well have anointed a horse or a stray dog from the street. Did a single one of those officiating understand Paul was not worthy or capable of sanity? If they did, would it have made any difference?

After these antics, Paul took the Imperial Crown from the Patriarch's hands and placed it with some difficulty, because of its weight, on his own tiny head. The mass of adornment squashed over his narrow forehead like a child's imitation of the Magi of the Orient. More prayers followed and thus came the reception of the sceptre and orb.

Paul, overburdened with crown, sceptre and orb, positioned himself on the throne, orb in left hand, sceptre in the right. As Maria knelt on a purple cushion before him, Paul gave the sceptre and the orb to his attendants.

His own crown was briefly placed on Maria's head, before being put once more back onto the monarch's head. Paul then placed Maria's small crown on her head, with the chain of the

Order of St Andrew round her neck, accompanied by a purple mantle.

Next in the ritual Paul retrieved his sceptre and orb while the Cathedral choir burst into song, praying for many years of health and prosperity in the reign of the emperor and empress.

Outside the bells rang throughout the city, the populace cheered when they were urged so to do, a hundred and one guns roared in salute.

Paul knelt, gave his sceptre and orb to the attendants, then recited another prayer, followed by a general prayer read by the Patriarch.

The Orthodox Divine Liturgy was conducted. During this the process of anointment of the rulers took place, Paul being touched with holy oil on forehead, eyes, nostrils, mouth, ears, breast, and both sides of each hand. Maria was anointed on forehead only.

Outside a second salvo of guns erupted, while Paul took a sacred oath to rule with justice and fairness and to preserve the role of emperor.

The anointed emperor took communion having passed through the Royal Doors into the private sanctuary of the priests, where he partook of bread and wine in clerical fashion. Maria celebrated her communion, receiving bread and wine together on a spoon, outside the holy area, not being permitted to progress through the Royal Doors.

The couple returned to their thrones for further prayers after which homage was pledged by relatives and nobles.

Paul now turned to the people and read out the Succession Act, proclaiming that the crown of Russia would descend to the emperor's eldest son or to the next male member of the Romanov lineage. The document was placed in a silver casket and laid upon the altar as a holy object.

Paul proceeded to a further manifesto, giving the peasants exemption from Sunday work before announcing (in deference to the divine Nelidowa), that the Order of Saint George, Martyr and Conqueror, was to remain, in honour of those who had been courageous on the field of battle.

THAT EVENING A banquet took place at the Granovitaya Palata, the council chamber of the rulers of Moscow. It was my privilege to prepare Paul for these nocturnal rituals.

At first he was reluctant to divest himself of his coronation garments, preening in front of the mirror and muttering, 'I am now a true Emperor, a true Emperor.'

After an hour of this I began to fear the ceremony had unhinged his mind even further from its asymmetrical axis. He fixed me from time to time with an unholy stare and ever so gently waved his right hand in my direction. I took the hint and dropped to one knee, my head bowed.

Eventually he tired of these games. Without a single word he stripped off every single vestment, this time standing statuesque in front of the mirror without a single stitch as if he still wore the illustrious garments.

'The emperor's clothes!' he said suddenly, laughing like a girl with his high-pitched voice. 'Would you dare point out to me that we are naked?' he said.

'Your Majesty has no need of such instructions,' I whispered.

This pleased him for he bowed his head imperiously in my direction:

'Now you must dress me for my banquet. I am so looking forward to it.'

From the royal wardrobe I selected the finest dress uniform of the rank of commander of the Russian Army, a garb in which Paul always took pleasure. Once dressed he moved in a slightly less sinister way.

Though only true born Russians were eligible to attend the Coronation Banquet, Paul permitted me to be present at some remove from his personage. This suited me as from a reasonable distance I could observe the courtly throng, as well as the ritual presentation of foreign ambassadors and princes.

Later on, after the dining and speeches, we were summoned to follow Paul and Maria and Nelidowa into an adjoining chamber where dancing was to take place.

Intrigued by the spectacle I hugged the perimeter wall as the orchestra struck up. Paul and Maria pirouetted together alone on the floor, after which a mass of couples joined them, whirling and swirling in extravagant costumes, the men having acquired new wigs, jackets and breeches, the females sumptuous in rich finery.

Thereafter Paul took to the floor with Nelidowa, while Maria was escorted by various ministers of state and Muscovites of high ranks.

Shortly after I noticed a beautiful young woman in the company of an older man, presumably her father. What particularly drew my eye was the abundance of her long black hair descending in great tresses over bare shoulders. A bystander informed me that this was none other than Anna Lopukhina, daughter of Prince Lopukhin, who chaperoned her for the evening.

However, before half an hour had passed Prince Lopukhin

was replaced by the emperor himself, the splendid creature in his arms towering above him. As they moved together I noticed a trance-like joy transformed his features, his eyes fixed on her like a basilisk.

As was his prerogative, he detained her for several more dances, a phenomenon which did not pass unobserved by a number of people present.

Most exemplary of all was the fury on the empress's face, matched only by the distinct mask of jealousy displayed by Nelidowa who could not resist staring at the couple as they entwined closer.

After what seemed ages, Paul bowed to the lovely angel, and her father resumed his stewardship. It was not often in public that he dropped his guard thus. But now he was the anointed emperor and could behave however he liked.

JUST AFTER THE Coronation I landed in a deal of hot water due to a second mistake. Following the debacle of the medal this particular error nearly proved disastrous. It came about this way.

The ceremony, and all that went with it, put the emperor into a generous mood. The sun shone brightly the morning after through the curtains of his palace.

Following long established custom a measure of largesse was handed out by the emperor to commemorate his crowning. I heard the day before the Coronation that I was being promoted to Chief Master of the Wardrobe, an honour accompanied by a quantity of roubles and some trinkets such as signet rings and a silk purse embroidered with jewels.

I was not overjoyed. What I hoped for was a greater mark of Paul's respect. I yearned for an honour which would draw me out of mediocrity into the position some might consider I deserved. The coveted award in question was the Order of Saint Anne, given for honourable service in either civil or military functions.

The Order of Saint Anne, Fourth Class (I did not hanker for third, second, or first class), would have elevated me to the nobility. I knew men who had got it for far less distinction, individuals hardly known to the emperor. I thought hard about this matter and was confident Paul would hear my petition with sympathy.

I prided myself on being able to choose the appropriate moment of petition. It would have to be the right moment, when Paul, slightly off-guard, was lost in contemplation of his grandeur, and flattered enough to give gifts previously beyond the recipient's reach.

The omens were propitious the day after the Coronation. In the early light of morning Paul reprieved three men sentenced to the gallows, gave presents of fine chocolates to the empress, and remained calm when a stupid footman tripped over a chair and landed in the imperial presence on his back like a tortoise.

I went to dress the emperor. He was most affable, singing a line or two from a hymn used in the ceremony, smiling at me as I brushed down his uniform on completion.

'Ah, how good the world is!' said the emperor. 'Things will never be better than this.'

'Indeed!' I replied. 'From now on your star will rise and rise.'

'Perhaps, perhaps. You really think so?'

'Yes. The whole world will come to your court to pay homage.'

Paul did a jig in front of the mirror, wrinkling his nose and wagging his head from side to side:

'That would be admirable,' he said. 'The whole world. The whole of the empire.'

'Your Majesty is the envy of the world,' I said softly. 'Your place in history is assured.'

'I wonder if that is true?' replied Paul. 'I will never be able to match my mother's reign. That is something which saddens me.'

His face in the mirror darkened and sulked for an instant, as it always did when he thought of the Empress Catherine. (Of course, he was right. The emperor was a mere insect compared to her. But nobody would ever tell him.)

'But Kutaissov,' he said, turning to face me, 'you haven't thanked me for your promotion, or for the presents I gave you.'

I bowed deeply.

'Your humble servant is grateful for every small mercy. Your Majesty is immensely generous to his most obedient, devoted servant.'

Paul looked straight at me, putting both hands on my shoulders, his face so close I could smell the contagion of his breath.

'Is there something you wanted to ask? Are you are not satisfied with the gifts you received?'

His madness sometimes inspired him with perspicacity, an instinct for something in the air. This morning it was uncanny. The ideal moment had come to put forward my request.

'Your Majesty, I would be most grateful for just one small addition to the honours you have heaped upon me.'

He looked into my eyes.

'Speak up, man. Let me know your heart. You cannot keep any secrets from me. I know you too well.'

'Indeed, you know me better than my own mother ever did.'

'What is it? If possible you shall have it at this glorious time.'

'Your Majesty, I am too shy to ask for such a favour.'

Paul released me from his hold, putting his hands on his hips in a playful posture.

'All right. If it is some extra bauble or ornament or medal you desire, tell me. You have done me extraordinary service. I am grateful to you. I love you more than my ministers and I depend on you. Therefore, speak!'

I dropped to one knee and took the plunge:

'Your Majesty, thank you. My request may be too much. But I long for further honours from your hand. May I hope one day to be awarded the Order of Saint Anne?'

The emperor took two steps back. His face contorted into the most hideous anger I had ever witnessed. Whatever semblance of a smile had graced his lips vanished. A mask of horror possessed him.

'You impudent, greedy, vain bastard,' he said, and with his fist struck me across the mouth a powerful blow.

I staggered but did not fall. I felt the taste of blood in my mouth. A tooth was broken.

'Guards!' he yelled.

In five seconds I was seized in my kneeling posture by four soldiers who grabbed me and hurled me out of the room. I landed hard on the floor, hearing laughter and cackles of derision.

'I never want to see you again,' shouted the emperor, slamming the door shut behind me.

As I picked myself up the attendant military turned their backs on me as if I no longer existed.

I was dizzy with the blow. But the speed and force of my fall from grace made me even dizzier.

I LIMPED DOWN THE long corridors towards the empress's room. She was my only hope and it had to be done now. My mouth was pouring blood and tears filled my eyes.

As if by magic the doors of the empress's chamber opened before me, the lackeys in the hallway aware that this was a crisis of an unusual nature.

The empress was sitting in the centre of the gilded room, reading a book. She displayed no surprise as seeing me bloodied and tear-stained. I threw myself onto the lavish carpet at her feet.

'Forgive me. Please help me. His Majesty has struck me and dismissed me. I am lost forever. Please help me.'

I raised my head and noticed I had put a drop of blood or two on the white fleece of the carpet. Spreadeagled on the floor like a suppliant monk before the altar, I saw two other feet to my right, the presence of Nelidowa.

'Oh, your Grace, please help me. I have betrayed myself. The Emperor is angry with me.'

Two servants lifted me to my feet and placed me, fairly roughly, in a chair brought from across the room. I looked a dreadful sight, not at all the Kutaissov they knew and probably hated. The empress looked at me.

'What have you done now? What is the nature of your misdemeanour?'

She spoke gently. Perhaps all was not lost. Another servant gave me a handkerchief with which I doused the blood. I wiped my eyes with the stained silk.

'I asked for an honour beyond my station,' I whimpered. 'The Emperor has punished me.'

'Poor man!' said the empress. 'The Emperor is capable of great anger. You were wrong to ask more than His Majesty was prepared to give. But you do not deserve dismissal.'

I bowed my head and said nothing.

'Go to your room. Wait for my summons. I will try to see what can be done. But do not expect miracles. Even if this is the day after the Coronation.'

I slipped off the chair and knelt before them. Once more the tears flowed from my eyes in humiliation and fear of my banishment.

'Do what you are told!' said Nelidowa. 'We will try together to see what might be rescued from this.'

DURING THE NEXT hour or so the sound of loud voices came from the emperor's sitting room. Apparently the empress put the argument on my behalf, though she was appalled that I had requested the high honour of the Order of Saint Anne.

The emperor was not moved by his wife's entreaties. If anything he waxed more adamant that I was to be chased from the palace and punished further.

It was Nelidowa who tipped the balance. She blamed the emperor that he had been too indulgent with me for years, lulling me into a false sense of my rank. The emperor chided her for upbraiding him.

But his passion for Nelidowa addled his judgement. If she had asked for the moon he would have tried to acquire it for her.

Some hours later a servant was dispatched from Paul with a message. I was to go to the empress's chamber and thank her and Nelidowa for interceding on my behalf.

Once more I flung myself onto the sumptuous carpet.

I kissed the hems of their skirts, I pledged eternal gratitude, I thanked them over and over till they tired of my antics, sending me away with words of warning never to trespass in this manner again.

I LICKED MY WOUNDS for a while. The emperor's blow still ached. When I returned to his service he made no mention of my misdemeanours. Instead he flattered me with extravagant phrases about my eternal loyalty, my dependability, my steadfastness, my refusal to harbour a grudge, my patience, my resourcefulness, even my wisdom.

'Your Majesty is too kind!' I would murmur after each comment, and give an obligatory bow. The atmosphere had changed, surprisingly for the better. Paul now knew my ambition extended to the moon and planets. Given time, the stars themselves might fall into my lap.

But beyond the palace where Paul and I revolved in this strange dance that was neither friendship nor intimacy, mysterious currents were already on the move.

It took some weeks before the patterns of the tides could be calculated to my advantage. I am not even sure of when I became aware how certain politicians were eager to make their designs on Paul's favours pivotal on my own actions.

The trouble was that the Coronation had shaken things up. The court became as thick as treacle with intrigue and deceit. Certain political elements wished to manipulate Paul. They were thwarted this way and that by the influence of the empress and Nelidowa.

As for me, I was so intent on my own little games that I

almost stumbled on this one. I first heard things were moving in a peculiar manner when I chanced upon a palace whisper that certain men of power considered it odd I had not been honoured sufficiently in the Coronation lists.

The trouble with rumours is the difficulty of finding their origin. Snatches of conversation reported at third hand become clouds of vapour rising from a cess pit.

Even so such vapour indicates certain aspects of the weather Only a fool would fail to act concerning these omens.

I WAS FORTUNATE ENOUGH to trace some of these comments to none other than Prince Bezborodko. Raised to the aristocracy by Paul's Coronation honours, his diplomatic service stretched back to the Empress Catherine.

How can one best describe a man like Bezborodko? His Ukrainian face was blubbery with double chins and a large nose which portrait painters toned down. His blue eyes had the coldness of a fish and his lips were thick-set. Like every man with power and influence he wanted more.

How touching it was when I realised I had been chosen as the bait for a little plot he put together with some of his cronies. But at first I was as innocent of these machinations as a new-born lamb.

Bezborodko summoned me to his office. This was arranged secretly. (It was not intended for Paul to find out about our meeting.) I was asked to attend for 'discretionary purposes'. Bezborodko was not a man to be disobeyed.

'Come in, Kutaissov,' said the Prince as I was ushered into the splendour of his apartments. 'I've been intending to talk to you.'

He motioned for me to sit and positioned himself behind his desk, his icy eyes gazing steadfastly upon me.

'It is an honour, Your Grace,' I replied.

'Well, let's not waste time on that,' he said. 'I have things on my mind.'

I waited as he rustled through papers on his desk.

'You have been in the Emperor's service for some time, have you not?'

'Indeed, Sire, I have enjoyed that privilege.'

'Yet in the Coronation honours His Majesty appears to have overlooked some of the virtues of your employment.'

'I don't quite understand, Your Grace,' I said, aware that caution was essential.

'Well, it is customary at Coronations to reward one's servants adequately.'

'I have no complaints, Sire. I am now the Chief Master of the Wardrobe, a worthy position for a man of low birth.'

I admire your humility. But surely you expected more than just that.'

'Not at all. I am not an ambitious man. To serve the Emperor any way I can is the limit of all I desire.'

He cleared his throat and smiled slightly, as if detecting a lie:

'Your reputation has preceded you. I understand you have considerable influence over the Emperor, quite beyond the position to which he assigned you.'

'I cannot account for what my enemies in the court might say of me. I am but the Emperor's valet.'

He turned his head to look out of the window, the light bringing out the fat cheeks of his face and the excessive size of nose.

———

'But you do advise him, do you not?'

I paused a moment, aware of a trap opening up in front of me.

'Your Grace, I mainly advise on the placement of His Majesty's wig and the condition of his uniforms.'

'You are telling me you do not influence the Emperor in certain ways?'

'Not deliberately. That would be tantamount to usurping my role.'

'That is not what I have heard. What has come to my ears is different.' He paused then looked directly at me:

'Then who is the greatest influence on the Emperor?'

'I would imagine the Emperor's ministers are the most significant.'

'And after that?'

'After that, Sire?'

'Yes, who else wields 'significant' influence?'

'I presume, from my humble position, that this would be the Empress.'

'Ah yes, the Empress. And who, after the Empress?'

In the game of chess I was cornered. I was beginning to perspire with anxiety. But I made the move.

'After the Empress, Mademoiselle Nelidowa.'

Bezborodko stood up and clapped his hands together as if some important milestone had been reached.

'Exactly! Mistress Nelidowa and the Empress!'

'I hope I have not spoken out of turn,' I said, for the situation was rapidly escaping my grasp.

'Not at all. In fact you have been exceedingly helpful. But you can help me further.'

'By all means, if possible.'

'I know (and you know) that your influence on the Emperor is immense. It is common knowledge in the court. But some among us think the influence of Mistress Nelidowa is not entirely for the good. What do you think?'

I thought of Nelidowa's kindness when she appealed, with the empress for my forgiveness and reinstatement. Yet to this titan of power before me an answer was necessary.

'Your Grace, if this was ever discovered I would lose my position.'

'Be assured you are in no danger. I am a man of honour who knows how to hold my tongue. I need your answer.'

'In that case, I believe on occasion Mademoiselle Nelidowa's advice is not always as sound as it should be.'

'But should her advice, or even that of the Empress, be given preference over ministers?'

'Surely not. But the ways of the Emperor and the ways of the court are varied and unfathomable.'

He sat down again, seemingly more relaxed.

'Good. Now this is how you can help me.'

'I am willing to do so.'

'Do you remember the Coronation Ball in Moscow?'

'Some things I remember. But I did drink an excess of wine that night.'

'Do you remember the girl who danced with the Emperor?'

'Anna Lopukhina?'

'Exactly. Now if the Emperor were, should we say, to 'take' to her, would not Nelidowa's influence be lessened?'

'Inevitably.'

'Good. I appreciate something of what the Emperor sees in you. You are a man of wisdom and understanding.'

'Thank you.'

———

'What I would like you to do, as would several of my friends, is to open the eyes of the Emperor in this matter. Nobody in the realm is so well suited for this task. Your service here would not be forgotten. You understand me.'

'Yes.'

'Can you achieve such a thing?'

'Yes.'

'You will be rewarded for this. Not only will we be grateful but I think in time even the emperor will thank you.'

'I will do my best.'

'Good. None of this has been written down. As far as we are concerned this conversation never took place.'

'Of course not.'

'Then go to it. Report back to me when you have success. Which I am sure will not be long in coming.'

I left the room, my head buzzing with the implications of all that had been said.

I now had an ally in Prince Bezborodko, a man who could kill with a word but had placed his confidence in me!

THE DISPLACEMENT OF Nelidowa proved to be a comparatively straightforward task. Of course such things take time and a certain amount of luck. With Prince Bezborodko's support the game became easier.

When the empress's fourth son was born during the winter of early 1798 and Her Majesty's parents died within a short time of each other, Maria was (at least for a few months) a shadow of her former self. It was decided the empress should spend the summer at Pavlosk accompanied by Nelidowa. Meanwhile the emperor would progress to Moscow, a city whose inhabitants at last were becoming slightly more devoted to him than previously (perhaps because they knew so little about him).

One morning during our visit to the great metropolis, as I was attending to Paul's needs, he began a conversation about his subjects in Moscow:

'I am intrigued by a simple riddle.'

'Indeed? I am not adept at riddles, even simple ones.'

'Nevertheless, I will tell you.'

'I am deeply honoured!'

Paul paused to look at himself in the mirror. His face was pallid through lack of sleep and much travelling in the royal carriages in recent days.

'The riddle is this...I come to Moscow but rarely. Yet here they cherish me. In St Petersburg, where I spend most of my life, they are worse than ungrateful dogs.'

Silence hung in the air between us. Last time he talked about this subject he had expressed a contrary opinion.

He turned from the mirror towards me, his expression changing to irritability at my lack of response.

'Well? Any explanation of this sorry state of affairs?'

'Your Majesty,' I stuttered, 'I am sure your worthy subjects throughout the land bear an equal measure of respect and affection towards your royal person.'

It was not the right answer and not the solution he wanted. The emperor stood up. For a moment I thought he might strike me round the face. But this time he restrained himself, his anger projected through his voice rather than a clenched fist.

'I am telling you the truth. I want a truthful answer. If you find it impossible to speak the truth, you may as well become a barber at Gatchina all over again.'

I sank to one knee and bowed my head, a moment of wild decision filling my thoughts. A throw of the dice now might achieve my death or my salvation. I staked everything on a single comment:

'Sire, I hardly dare speak of this. But if you demand that I do, then the words must be spoken, even if they bring about my downfall.'

Paul dragged me to my feet, putting his face close to mine:

'For God's sake, man, you must speak or you're damned if you don't.'

'Then I will speak, as God is my witness.'

Paul sat himself down again as if awaiting a long narrative. What I had to say could be said briefly. So I blurted it out, the shadow of Bezborodko heavy on my mind.

'In Moscow they love you for what you truly are – wise, forbearing, the patriarch of the people. But in St Petersburg they are tired of being ruled by women. Why even the British ambassador saw the Empress and Nelidowa before entering your presence. That is the holy truth, Sire.'

(Of course, the last part of this confession was a partial lie. The couple had seen the envoy before the meeting, but only in passing, as it were.)

Paul stood up again, his face livid, his mouth tight, his eyes slightly bulging, almost a figure of comedy.

I fell to my knees and continued.

'Please forgive me for speaking the truth. If the Empress and Nelidowa were to hear anything of this, they would know it was your servant who gave you possession of this truth. But that would not save me.'

'You are a coward and a liar. But I tell you nobody in this

kingdom will ever accuse me of being governed by the counsel of women.'

With that he waved his hand towards me like a man warding off an intrusive wasp.

'Get out. I have things to do. I shall not hold this against you. But you are close to the wind. Be careful. I shall not warn you again.'

With that I beat a retreat from the royal presence. But the arrow had struck home. At risk, yes. At the very edge of the precipice I had survived.

I WROTE TO PRINCE Bezborodko informing him of the gist of this conversation, omitting a few of the less pleasant details. It had to be worded with special care, but I tried my best:

Your Grace,

I have spoken to His Majesty of the matters we discussed previously. His Majesty has expressed a strong opinion to move forward from his present situation.

Therefore the hunting season should begin as soon as possible in order to provide alternative game.

The quarry of which we spoke would be ideal for His Majesty and I believe the emperor would deeply approve in the long term of any such realignment.

I have pleasure placing the details of the arrangement into your Grace's keeping.

Your servant ever,

Kutaissov

I hoped this document was neither too short nor too obscure to communicate the force of our intention. Bezborodko was after all an intelligent man accustomed to diplomatic innuendo.

Within a few hours I received a message from the Prince which allayed my anxieties and set the course of action admirably:

> *My esteemed Kutaissov,*
>
> *Thank you for your message. The season will begin with a significant gathering at the ball the day after tomorrow. I hope you will be able to attend.*
>
> *Prince Bezborodko*

ACCORDINGLY I PREPARED Paul's garments for his appearance at the grand Moscow ball. He chose a combination of red and green, with a brilliant gold sash to distinguish him from the throng.

His honourable companion for the evening was Bezborodko himself who arrived in magnificent military uniform.

They departed in the royal coach. I followed in a second carriage bearing my little bag of necessities containing the wherewithal to re-powder the emperor's wig, administer smelling salts, brush down his clothes, re-polish his boots, and so forth.

Naturally the royal party arrived appropriately late, by which time the assembled guests were well primed for Paul's appearance. He entered the banqueting hall and adjacent ballroom in a blare of trumpets, his tiny figure upright but diminutive relative to the bulk of Bezborodko.

Armed with a tiny telescope I retreated to an upper balcony where I could watch proceedings from a recess without fear of intrusion. It was not long before I spotted the object of the evening's manoeuvres, Anna Lopukhina, accompanied by her father, standing to one side of the hall.

Paul's wandering eye found the object of his desire. She was brought over to meet him. They flounced away together in a dance, applauded by the crowd who seemed too nervous to approach the floor as yet.

Through the telescope I could see her beautiful face, her fulsome white neck and front, her elegant demeanour, and her pouting lips red as a flower, enough to tempt the devil himself.

After that first dance, Paul turned towards the audience. With regal gestures he indicated it was time for all the company to join in the festivities.

As if mesmerised he took Anna into his arms and swirled off again, this time two among the mob, his gold sash glimmering in the flickering light.

Perfect! I recognised his ingratiating movements. Always he drew the lovely creature nearer to him till his head was almost in her bosom.

She was taller than him and in such a couple there is an element of the ridiculous − the ageing monarch flirting and toying with a youngster. Some would have found it repellent. I felt more like laughing.

By the end of the evening Paul had fallen in love, irrevocably, utterly, stupidly.

T HE FOLLOWING MORNING Paul was humming to himself when I entered the royal bedchamber.

'Figaro,' he said, 'I had a wonderful time last night.'

'Indeed, Sire! That is good to hear.'

'Yes. It was one of the best evenings of my life.'

I bowed gently, waiting for more.

'I hesitate to tell you the details. But you may have guessed how happy I am this morning.'

'Naturally, Your Majesty,' I replied, 'I have scarcely ever seen you in such magnificent humour.'

'Ah then, you rascal, happiness shows!'

He pinched me on the cheek playfully. I inclined my head respectfully.

'But even happiness brings problems, great problems,' he mused.

His demeanour changed into slight melancholy, a transition I was hoping would not happen.

'Of course, Sire, but every problem has a solution.'

'By God, you are right. I must remember that when I am feeling overwhelmed.'

I waited a moment or two before speaking:

'Perhaps, I might offer some assistance with any problem. I can but do my best.'

'Oh, my Figaro, what would I do without you?'

With that he sat on the dressing table chair and began to weep.

'Sire', I said, going down on one knee, 'happiness and tears do not mix.'

'Ah, if you knew the greatness of my mind, you would understand.'

The tears increased, he was becoming nervous and irritable.

'Your Majesty, allow me to enter your confidence. What on earth is amiss?'

In an instant the crying ceased and he was back in another mood, this time confidential:

'I have fallen in love. But I cannot invite the lady in question back to St Petersburg openly. It would be too much. But I need her, I want her.'

In that instant I understood the deed of love had not yet been completed. The environment of Moscow and the presence of the girl's father were not congenial to a secret coupling. Here all was public and open. St Petersburg would be the place for conquest.

Again I paused before speaking. But Paul was looking at me as if seeking a way out.

'May I offer a suggestion?' I said.

'Oh, if only you could. Tell me what is best.'

'Unfortunately, I know little of the arts of love.'

'What's your answer? I want to hear it.'

'The solution is simple, Your Majesty. We will invite the lady to Moscow officially, by way of a humble secretary. Her father will come too, as well as her mother. In St Petersburg you will be master of the game.'

Paul smiled and rose to his feet:

'That's good. Why did I not think of such a ruse?'

He extended his arms and embraced me. Then he stepped back abruptly, a new question burning his brain:

'But what if the father will not countenance such a thing. I can't arrest him. She would hate me.'

I bowed tactfully.

'Sire, we promote him, we give him and his wife a bauble or two. The lady will be yours entirely.'

'I place this invitation in your hands,' said Paul, brimming over with excitement at the thought of the pleasure ahead. 'I rely on you.'

'Thank you, Sire,' I said, and bowed slightly lower than before.

THE COURT RETURNED a few weeks later to St Petersburg. Our little scheme was going well. But as it needs only one cloud in the sky to blight a summer's day. An unexpected development nearly spoiled everything.

I first heard about the matter from Iryna, a lady in waiting to the empress to whom I had paid some attention for several months. Iryna loved to chatter on about the empress. During one of our conversations she let the cat out of the bag.

It transpired that the empress and Nelidowa had been informed of Paul's behaviour at the ball in a letter from a courtier. The empress's anger exploded in an angry scene while Nelidowa remained placid.

The consequence was that the empress wrote a furious epistle to none other than Anna Lopukhina, warning her never to set foot in St Petersburg.

At some expense, having been tipped off, I was able to procure the letter from the post bag before it had been dispatched, making sure the letter found its way onto Paul's desk.

I went into the emperor's office just after he had read the letter. His face was tinged red and slightly purple with a rage such as I had never seen before even in this man.

He turned the heavy desk over, banged on the walls with

his fists, stalked up and down hither and thither, and called on the name of Christ to avenge all he had to suffer in the name of love.

'Do you know anything about this?' he barked, striding up to me.

'About what, Sire?' I bleated.

'This disgusting letter!'

'Letter, Your Majesty?'

He thrust the offending paper into my hand.

'Oh read it for yourself.'

I duly read what was there, the clear writing in black ink unmistakably that of the empress's own hand. It was a harsh letter, a hysterical letter, threatening all manner of reprisals to Anna Lopukhina if she were ever to be found in the vicinity of her husband.

'Come with me!' shouted the emperor, snatching the letter from my grasp. 'We have business to do.'

Quivering with wrath, he stalked along the corridors to the empress's room. Without knocking he flung open the door, and there, in regal splendour, sat Maria herself, in the company of Mistress Nelidowa.

'You're not fit to be an empress,' he bawled, waving the letter on high like a flag. 'You're a treacherous witch, a devil, a bawd, a scab on the face of the kingdom.'

With that he made towards her and would surely have struck her in the face had she not fallen back onto the couch in a dead faint, all colour leaving her features.

'You have killed her,' shouted Nelidowa.

It seemed for a moment the empress was indeed deceased from shock.

'Keep out of this, whore,' said Paul. 'Your days in the sunlight are over. Get out of my sight.'

In such tantrums were elements of pure comedy. But the look on poor Nelidowa's face was tragic. She ran past, crying bitterly.

It fell to me to minister to the empress as best I could. I fetched a glass of wine and held it to her lips. Momentarily her eyes opened, but on seeing my face, looking down from a close range, she let out a prolonged exhalation of breath most like a sigh, and fainted again.

'She is not dead, Sire,' I heard myself saying. 'Only in a faint.'

'Of course, she isn't dead,' ranted Paul. 'She has done this before. It's all a trick.'

With that he turned on his heel and marched out. Two ladies-in-waiting came through the door at the same time and he nearly barged into them. One of them, as luck would have it, was Iryna, who looked at me in an accusing manner. But what could she ever prove without incriminating herself?

I left the empress to the tender care of her servants, and followed my master almost running, such was his disturbance.

Once back in his office he told me to sit down and keep quiet while he dictated an edict of the day.

The empress's favourites such as Prince Kourakin and a few others were to be exiled. Baron Buekshoevden, governor of St Petersburg, who fawned on the empress like a lap dog, was sacked and the job given to Count Pahlen.

Nelidowa left St Petersburg the following day bound for some God-forsaken northern city.

Prince Bezborodko was delighted with everything, and

forwarded a sum of money to me by way of gratitude.

As for me, the unthinkable came to pass. In an act of sheer insanity the emperor raised me to the level of Count Kutaissov, an accolade well beyond my dreams.

Anna Lopukhina was eventually installed in St Petersburg. This involved diplomacy and deceit before the task was achieved.

Paul sent me in the first instance to Lopukhina's home to talk to her father, the chief of police in Moscow. Peter Lopukhin had a brisk, military manner about him. But now that I was *Count* Kutaissov and a messenger from the emperor, he curbed his lip and afforded me a measure of respect.

His house, not far from the centre of Moscow, was modest for a man of such influence. That was a good sign for anything we might offer him in St Petersburg would be impressive by comparison.

'I have heard of you, sir,' said Lopukhin when we were seated in his drawing room armed with glasses of good wine. 'You are highly favoured I understand by the Emperor himself.'

'I am but a humble servant,' I replied. 'His Majesty has been kind to me.'

We sat in silence for a while. I was in no hurry.

'We are in a difficult situation,' he said after the long pause. 'I think you know why.'

I nodded as if in agreement. He was nervous but continued:

'His Majesty is making demands we may find difficult to meet.'

'It may be possible to come to some agreement.'

'Let me explain the situation. My daughter is young. I have no wish for her to be exposed to the court.'

'That is a fair position, sir,' I replied. 'I have a daughter, I understand all your concerns.'

'I would prefer my daughter to remain with us in Moscow until she is older.'

I sipped my wine. The moments passed. We returned to a kind of quietness. I seized my opportunity:

'The Emperor wishes you, sir, to be promoted to a post comparable to his estimation of you. His Royal Highness would like your family to come to St Petersburg. There is no suggestion your dear daughter should come alone.'

As if in reply he rose to his feet and walked around the room. He seemed surprised, even dumbfounded. Such blatant bribery was not what he had anticipated. The temptation was too much.

He returned to his chair:

'I expected to continue in my position here.'

'The Emperor has expressed a desire you should work more closely on His Majesty's behalf in St Petersburg.'

'As his chief of police?'

I waited once more. The fish was now on the hook.

'The Emperor wishes you to become Procurator-General. You will work with Chancellor Rostopchin. A suitable mansion and a fruitful stipend are available.'

His face revealed everything. Lopukhin could not stop himself from smiling with greed. Before he could recover his wits or his equilibrium I thrust home the dagger:

'Sir, I have been authorised by His Majesty to offer you

this position. I have papers prepared for you to sign, if you are willing to please the emperor's will in this matter.'

'I have no other choice,' he murmured.

That was true. If I had failed in my mission or Lopukhin had been troublesome who knows what Paul might have done.

So IT CAME about. I returned to St Petersburg in triumph, Lopukhin's signature safely in my pocket.

Within a week or two the family moved north and Anna's father began his work. Lopukhina herself, in line with the bargain struck, moved into the palace and was given a suite of rooms.

One of the ladies of the court observed how Anna had 'such a lovely head, such lovely eyes, beautiful eyebrows, jet black hair, wonderful teeth, a very attractive mouth, a funny little nose, but not much of a buxom figure being somewhat slim in that respect'.

Paul was head over heels in love. So much so he became as silly as a youth. If Anna had a fit of the vapours he sat for hours by her bedside. Ministers and messengers could come and go but in such an emergency the emperor had no concern for mere matters of state. The rest of the world could go hang itself.

He awarded her the Grand Cross of the Knights of Malta, and asked the lady about her favourite colour. As a result he gave the palace guards new crimson uniforms.

If she cried on his shoulder, as Anna frequently did, he showered her with gifts and pampering, telling her time after time how much he loved her.

Paul, in his madness, had banned the waltz on the grounds that it was 'immodest'. When he learned this was none other than Anna's favourite dance the waltz was hastily reinstated as 'appropriate' for the court.

As ever there was a fly in the ointment. Anna Lopukhina had no desire to surrender her virginity to the emperor despite all efforts to bring her to heel. The whole thing became a kind of farce. Paul entreated and importuned, Anna refused to give in.

Worse still, Anna strayed. When she was observed flirting with young Alexandre de Ribeaupierre, aged seventeen, I got the young fool sent to Vienna to a minor post in the Embassy there.

Somehow soon after that Anna came into the company of Prince Pavel Gavrilovich Gagarin. The situation was so serious she came to see me. Fluttering her eyelashes and shedding tears she poured out a tale of woe:

'Sir, I am in love with Prince Gagarin, Can you help me?'

It was too ridiculous. How could I help her without jeopardising my own position? I advised her to seek His Majesty's advice on the matter, whatever the cost.

So Anna Lopukhina, with the assistance of even more tears, achieved the impossible. By some miracle of persuasion she gained Paul's permission to marry Gagarin. What promises and compromises were traded between them to achieve this strange state of affairs may only be guessed at.

What is certain is that having proudly become Princess Gagarina, and settled in a new residence on the Neva Quay with wonderful views over the river, Anna became less reluctant to yield her charms to the emperor.

Within a few weeks of her marriage it became customary for Paul to visit his paramour at least twice a week.

THINGS SEEMED TO be going well, my star was rising. Till the unexpected happened.

Prince Bezborodko, on whom I had lavished so much grooming, was summoned by Paul at eleven o'clock at night to run an errand. The emperor wanted the poor, sleepy man to proceed in haste to the residence of the Prussian ambassador. Bezborodko was ordered to command the diplomat to attend the palace immediately for a discussion of a significant matter.

Bezborodko, a proud man with some self-respect despite being at the beck and call of a degenerate ruler, refused to carry out the order that night, expressing a preference to postpone such a visit till the next morning. Paul went into a fit of temper and may even (according to some reports) have struck the prince.

Sufficient to say that Bezborodko hurried off into the darkness, spoke to some of his aides on what had transpired, became breathless and blue in the face, and dropped dead just outside the palace.

After Bezborodko's death everything became insecure, edgy, down-hill. Before that the outlines had appeared simpler. Now the plot thickened, I lost sight of essential matters, more was going on behind the scenes than I knew.

How could this happen? Partly it was my fault, and then again, events conspired against me. The death of Bezborodko set many things in train, decisions I had no part in.

Paul promoted Feodor Rostopchin to president of the Foreign Collegium and postmaster. Nikita Panin, whose uncle had been tutor to Empress Catherine, became vice-chancellor for a short time. Peter von der Pahlen was appointed as governor-general of St Petersburg.

Paul, as bemused by all these comings and goings as anyone

else, went into decline. In fits of confusion he got rid of the British ambassador, and appointed Pahlen to army duties before re-appointing him (twice) as governor of St Petersburg.

Paul became obsessed with a certain Napoleon Bonaparte (a military man 'after his own heart') at that time in the middle of conquering Italy and Austria:

'I am full of admiration for his military genius,' he kept saying, 'He is a man one can do business with.'

With that Paul looked at himself in the mirror and preened like a peacock. At such moments I doubt whether he even knew I was in the room.

P AUL BEGAN TO work more and sleep less. When I attended for his morning toiletries he was often already dressed in a general's uniform, his hair uncombed, his mouth flecked with dribble.

'Where have you been?' he asked at 5 AM when I arrived earlier than usual. He was at the writing desk, holding his quill, bent over a sheaf of paper.

'Your Majesty', I stuttered, 'it is only five o'clock. You do not expect my services before then.'

'But it is nearer half noon,' he replied, picking up a small clock on the shelf.

From where I stood near the door I could see the hour was indeed five past five.

'How foolish,' he said, 'I will destroy this clock. The hands are deceptive. I must have things that are reliable, like the men who serve me.'

With that he continued writing. I waited for several minutes before he addressed me again.

'Kutaissov!'

'Yes, Your Majesty?'

'I have drafted fresh orders. It's been hard work.'

'Indeed, it is hard to deal with such responsibilities.'

'Good. Now read this and tell me what you think.'

With a little flourish, he gave me the prepared papers. The spidery squiggle read as follows:

I.   *Importation of foreign literature is prohibited because of injurious consequences to national morality. Printing works are to be closed down with the exception of the Synod Press and the Academy of Sciences, to prevent material superfluous to national requirements.*

II. *All bookshops will be inspected for unwholesome products. New guidelines for bookshop censorship will be issued.*

III. *Private correspondence entering or leaving the country will be subject to scrutiny to discover culpable discontent.*

IV. *Permission to leave the country will be subject to supervision and journeys abroad by any citizens will be granted by licensed authorities. Police are commanded to be vigilant at docks and wharves to apprehend dangerous malcontents.*

I was speechless, uncertain whether to laugh or cry. Paul's eagle eye was concentrated in my direction. I dared not show the least expression.

'Oh come now! By your silence you indicate dissent from my edicts. Or is such quietness something else?'

I gathered together my thoughts, scattered like sheep:

'Your Majesty...I pause in admiration of your wisdom. These edicts are remarkable. But beyond my understanding.'

'Quite so! You are wise to know your place, even if you are *Count* Kutaissov. But I treasure your advice, now and always.'

I bowed, bemused by his folly. Not a great reader at all I regard most books as baubles to divert simple minds. The rest were so badly written they were hardly worth reading.

But what sane ruler would ever expect his subjects to require permission to leave the country? Who but a fool would close printing presses? Who was to judge which works or letters were dangerous and which were not?

Only a mad man!

PART SIX

TOWARDS THE ABYSS

And if you gaze for long into an abyss,
the abyss gazes also into you.

NIETZCHE,
JENSEITS VON GUT UND BÖSE

I HAD FURTHER TROUBLES of my own at this time. Among other things I fell in love myself.

One night at the theatre, accompanied by Natasha, I was introduced to a French actress performing the leading role in the drama. It was a worthless play (I forget the title and the author) but I did remark on the excellence of her acting.

Her husband was there, hovering like a ghost in the background. I was not impressed by his hangdog demeanour and dismissed him from my mind. But afterwards I could not stop thinking about Madame Chevalier, her performance and her charming manner.

'You are Count Kutaissov!' she had cooed in her soft French accent. 'I have heard of you, sir, and longed to meet you.'

Natasha took against her:

'That woman is dangerous,' she grumbled later. 'You should be on your guard.'

'Nonsense,' I replied. 'You are too jealous. You see something where there is nothing.'

As usual Natasha was right. There was something. But what was it?

A FEW WEEKS PASSED till, by chance, I met Madame Chevalier for a second time. Her company staged a short masque for the court, the customary tale of a young prince who falls in love with a peasant girl in the woods and lives happily ever after with her in his castle. Madame Chevalier played the girl's mother.

The emperor loved the presentation and applauded loudly, shouting bravo. With an extravagantly imperious gesture to those present he encouraged everyone to offer an excess of clapping and cheering. This went on for five minutes until Paul rose to congratulate the actors and the musicians for their performance. More applause followed, of course.

After this nonsense was over I took the opportunity to talk with Madame Chevalier. She was engaged in chit-chat with her fellow artistes, all excited by the emperor's response. Immediately she saw me she waved:

'Count Kutaissov, how good of you to come. Do you remember me?'

As Madame Chevalier was the most famous actress in St Petersburg her question was disingenuous. But people of the stage are prone to exaggerated discourse.

'What a wonderful play,' I whispered, kissing her hand and stooping low.

'Did you like it?' she said, her French voice making my knees tremble.

'Like it? We *adored* it. Especially the Emperor.'

At this Madame Chevalier took a tiny silk handkerchief and dabbed at a tear or two, overcome, it seemed, with emotion.

'Would you care to look round the art gallery while you are here?' I asked.

'That would be wonderful!' she exclaimed, waving her hands about in the French manner.

So I showed her the private paintings of the Romanovs, not too far from my own suite of rooms. An invitation to visit my chambers met with similar acceptance.

Once safely inside, with the door closed, she expressed delight at the majesty of the room, its curtains, decorations, more paintings, furniture, and its palatial elegance. From there it was but a step or two to reach the bedchamber. She followed me as if I were a guide to the secrets of the house.

'What a large bed!' she said, and sat down on it.

Without further ado I kissed her on the mouth.

'Oh, Count Kutaissov, what are you doing?' she murmured.

She put her arms round my neck. Somehow we fell together onto the bed.

Our clothes magically removed themselves from our bodies. Within moments we were naked beneath the silk sheets. She was exquisite, a professional lover, skilled in the arts of sensation.

'I am in love with you!' I whispered into her ear, imbibing her perfumed hair.

'And I with you!' she replied.

THAT EVENING MADAME Chevalier returned to her husband. I woke in the morning with a sense of joy, and wild jealousy at her departure.

Though I was now a count, my duties as valet continued perpetually. Soon after dawn I called at the emperor's quarters.

'Figaro, you old goat. We've been hearing tales about you.'

Dammit. The man was positively clairvoyant.

'Indeed?' I said, putting on an air of innocence.

Paul chuckled and winked:

'In this palace there are few secrets. You were seen! Or rather she was. Leaving your room. About nine last night.'

'Ah yes. Madame Chevalier. She came to tell me about life in the theatre, about which I know very little.'

'I am sure you know a great deal more now! More than you should perhaps.'

I bowed to him in a gesture of submission.

'Never mind, Figaro. You are as much a man as any of us. But that's enough frivolity. I wanted to ask you about something else.'

I inclined my head once more.

'Yes, indeed,' he said. 'I want to know about Count Pahlen. What do you think of him? Is he to be trusted?'

It was a good question. I had a good answer ready.

PETER VON DER Pahlen had been raised to the status of Count at the same time as myself. The association was not, I think, something he relished. But he kept his feelings to himself. Perhaps too much so, as it turned out.

Pahlen treated me with courtesy and what I interpreted as respect. He was a close friend of Count Panin, now vice-chancellor. But I never saw anything sinister in their amity as it is natural for lower dogs to lick the hindquarters of superior dogs.

I knew that Panin was in close touch with Alexander. In the palace I sometimes came across the two of them whispering in corners and corridors. On seeing me Panin usually bowed to the heir to the throne and hurried away. Alexander, on such occasions, ignored me, not even glancing at my humble stoop to his regality.

However Panin soon received his comeuppance. The

emperor followed the advice of his poodle, Rostopchin, by favouring a diplomatic accommodation with Napoleon whom Paul admired to the point of idolatry.

Panin wrote a memorandum setting out an opposing viewpoint. The emperor, in childish tantrum, lost his patience. He immediately commanded Panin to get out of his sight and join the Senate in Moscow.

In a few hours this order was rescinded. Instead the wretched man was expelled from court and sent into exile on his estates. Rostopchin, the glorious victor, was shamelessly cock-a-hoop while Panin spread his resentment the length and breadth of St Petersburg before he left.

As it turned out, he had more sympathetic friends than anyone might have guessed at the time.

AFTER PANIN'S HUMILIATION, Count von der Pahlen became an even brighter star in the Russian firmament. Altogether a man worthy of being cultivated. So when Paul enquired about Pahlen, I praised him and commended his services.

'Count Pahlen is one of your greatest admirers. He deserves encouragement,' I exclaimed.

On the strength of these few words the emperor came to rely on Pahlen as his grand counsellor along with Rostopchin. Nothing is ever ideal in this crooked world. But at least for me the pot seemed to be boiling happily.

How could I know that from this self-same pot we would all get our hands well and truly scalded?

WHILE PAUL HAD been informed about my affair with Madame Chevalier, my wife, Natasha, seemed to know just as much. On one of my rare visits to the family abode I sensed a bad atmosphere as I entered the house. A single look at Natasha's face revealed the entire story.

'Is there something wrong? Has somebody died?' I asked.

Her reply was to break down into tears, to cover her face with a handkerchief and sit on a chair howling like a chastised child.

'What is it?' I said, putting my hand on her shoulder.

'Don't touch me!' she sobbed. 'I never want you to touch me again.'

I retreated to the far side of the room and sat down on the sofa. I am not an insensitive man. I was neither proud of myself nor ashamed. (I thought at that moment of Madame Chevalier, her subtle attractions, her body, her voice.)

'Have you taken leave of your senses?' said Natasha, gaining strength through indignation. 'You may think yourself clever but you are a fool.'

I said nothing.

'I knew there was something between the two of you at the theatre. I knew.'

'At that time I had never met her before!'

'You are a liar. And a cheat. Your whole life is a lie. Your life is a cheat. The chickens are coming home to roost. I will never forgive you.'

I absorbed the truth in this declaration. In my situation what else could I have been but a dissembler, a flatterer, a man of deceit?

'Are you pretending you are in love with her?' Natasha was keeping up the attack.

'Not pretending,' I replied. 'I *am* in love with her. I did not mean to become so.'

'You are a double fool then. She has a husband and other lovers. She does not love you.'

'She said she did.'

'Then you are gullible. She is using you. I have heard about her goings-on. She is an actress.'

'What have you heard?'

'Too much. You can find out all the other things next time you see her.'

I waited for some moments. I never doubted Natasha was speaking the truth. Then I spoke:

'Dear Natasha, what do you want me to do? I have loved you. But this is different.'

'I don't want to see you or hear you or hear about you. You have spoiled it all. Perhaps later I shall feel better. I am upset beyond words.'

'Will you tell me when you are ready for me to come back?' I murmured. 'When you tell me, I will come.'

Natasha erupted once more into weeping.

'Go!' she said. 'Before I say words I may regret.'

I left the house. Her outburst shocked me. I hate to see women crying.

That was all there was to it. I closed the door quietly behind me.

P AUL'S PASSION FOR Anna Lopukhina continued to flourish in the most extraordinary way. In return for whatever she offered him, he showered her family with gifts.

One month it would be a small Russian estate at Korsoun (purchased at excessive cost from Prince Stanislav Poniatowski) followed the next month by the award of further honours to her father.

No wonder Sir Charles Whitworth, the British ambassador soon to be banished from Russia under a dark Napoleonic cloud, is alleged to have mused aloud whether the emperor was 'literally not in his senses'.

But generosity is a hard burden to shoulder. Lopukhin soon buckled under the strain. For example, he incurred displeasure from the emperor when as Procurator he issued a generous *ukase* forbidding corporal punishment of persons over the age of seventy. As Paul believed everybody should be flogged, the innocent as well as the guilty, the young and the old, such an amendment to his usual practices was not well received.

'What do you think of that, Figaro?' exclaimed the emperor one morning as I was shaving him. 'Allowing criminals to escape justice? I give the man rewards and he does that?

'Despicable!' I replied, careful as ever not to nick the imperial neck as it writhed in righteous horror at such lenience.

'But we shall let it pass!' he added. 'Every dog must have his day.'

Within a few weeks Lopukhin resigned from all his offices, having earned the gratitude (no doubt) of a host of ageing miscreants.

His daughter meanwhile continued to minister to her lover's desires, and presumably to her husband's as well from time to time.

Dear old Rostopchin, in one of his more poetic moments, sighed deeply and whispered in my ear, 'Such a romance – it takes us back to the age of chivalry.'

VER THE COMING weeks I tried to revive the joys of my own age of chivalry in the loving arms of Madame Chevalier. To avoid court gossip and visits to the palace on her part, I secured a tasteful mansion for her close to that which housed Anna Lopukhina.

But I was disappointed that she did not lodge there all the time. My informants reported that on certain nights when at the theatre the Madame did not return to the mistress abode. Those nights she stayed with her husband.

At first such excursions did not bother me. But as my passion grew in force I began to want her as my own entirely and completely. It became necessary, though unpleasant, to broach the subject.

I wound myself up like winding a clock. At last, one afternoon, following a wonderful session of passion, the words came tumbling from my mouth:

'Beloved,' I said, 'do you still see your husband?'

(By 'see' I intended of course to suggest more intimate behaviour than the mere act of visiting.)

She was surprisingly truthful in her reply.

'Yes, from time to time.'

'Do you intend to continue 'seeing' him?'

'Yes, I intend to. He is my husband.'

'But I love you. You are the world to me.'

'And you to me. But when I see him it's not like seeing you. Things are different.'

I pondered her reply. She was honest. It was the honesty that was hurtful.

'And with him…you share your bed?'

'Yes. Only for a while. He soon goes off to sleep.'

I let these cruel words sink in. Jealousy flared like a wound in my stomach.

'But what about me? Have you no thought for my feelings?'

'Of course. I give you everything. I give you love. My husband receives only the crumbs from the table.'

How I hated those crumbs, those moments of closeness another man enjoyed with my sacred beloved. Ah yes, but worse followed. It transpired another man had visited the Chevalier mansion that I had given her.

'Another man?' I gasped, breathless with disgust.

'Oh yes. Someone who could not be refused?'

'Who could *not* be refused? Why not?'

'It was not possible. Such was his personage.'

'Did you want to refuse him?'

At this a few tears came to her eyes. But she is an actress. Tears can come to her at her own bidding, as can any mood. Her trade is to dissemble, to make believe, to be another person, as the occasion demands. I also have to pretend day after day that I am something which I am not. But with my lover I wanted to be my true self, whatever that is.

'Yes,' she said, 'I would like to refuse him. With all my heart. But I could not. He came only once. He said he would come back again. That might be difficult.'

My heart ached with sorrow. I was lost in a world of mischief and deceit.

'Who is he?' I asked through gritted teeth.

'I dare not tell you,' she said, her tears flowing freely.

'Can I guess?'

'I cannot tell you his name.'

I buried my face in my hands. I felt as if I had died with jealousy. Then, as if mouthing a poem, she whispered his name, before giving way to an eruption of misery which could only be sincere.

'It was...Alexander himself.'

In that moment I understood everything. He was indeed the untouchable, the unnameable, that man whose whim would one day be the imperial command.

How and why the heir had crossed the river of decision to visit such a woman would remain a mystery. I presume he had seen her at the theatre. From that point his path may have been similar to my own.

'It could be useful,' she said. 'He said things. Secret things.'

'I'm sure he did!' I replied, full of scorn.

'I think he said things he shouldn't have said.'

'Did he say he was in love with you?'

'Not a word.'

'He must have said something. You gave yourself to him!'

'I had to. There was no choice.'

How often have we heard in Russia and in life, 'no choice'? The words tolled like a bell. But whatever we do we always *choose*, one way or another.

'What did he say then? What secret things did he say?'

'I'm not sure I should tell you. It could get us into trouble.'

'We're in enough trouble already. A little more will not matter.'

She paused as if to summon up courage:

'He spoke of the Emperor's abdication. It was mere pillow talk!'

I went white with fear. Any kind of abdication would mean a plot was in hand. Bloodshed and horror would plague the land. My head would be severed from my body.

'Abdication!' I said, my voice louder than I intended.

'Yes. Apparently Panin has something to do with it.'

I could not at first grasp even the simplest elements of what was going on. Whatever it was, this was even more important than my acerbic jealousy.

I gave Madame Chevalier a light kiss on the cheek, signifying my displeasure as well as my love and without another word hurried back to the palace.

N THAT SHORT journey certain thoughts came to me. If I took rumours of abdication straight to the emperor he might be in one of his worse moods. I would be blamed, horribly so. Better to find another intermediary.

Who more appropriate with whom to discuss this crisis than Pahlen, responsible for Paul's security and almost as close to the emperor as I was?

Without a moment's hesitation I directed the coach driver to drive straight to Pahlen's house. Fortunately Pahlen was at home and willing to see me. I was shown into the drawing room by a servant and waited only a few minutes before Pahlen entered.

The room was that of a rich aristocrat. A large portrait of Pahlen dominated the far wall. There were many books, a chess board set up with its ivory army, and a harpsichord in the corner.

The furnishings were luxurious, the walls lined with exquisite silk, and the chairs and chaise longue of the finest workmanship.

Pahlen's face was the model of serenity. His lips scarcely moved when he spoke yet his words were enunciated with crisp brevity. His eyes gazed at you with a gentle concentration. You felt at ease with him.

For the first time I realised how persuasive this man could

be and how valuable was my contribution in recommending him for promotion to the emperor.

'Do sit down,' he said in his calm voice. 'Let us drink some champagne.'

He poured the drink into a crystal glass. I sipped it anxiously.

'You look worried, Count Kutaissov,' he murmured. 'Are things becoming difficult?'

'I need your help. It's a matter of protecting the Emperor.'

He took a mouthful of champagne himself:

'Good stuff this, Kutaissov. French of course.'

I nodded assent. It is good manners to admire your host's offerings.

'Protecting the Emperor?' he said. 'That sounds serious.'

'Very serious.'

'Heads could roll.'

'Indeed.'

'Well, let's have it. What have you heard?'

I waited a moment or two to prepare my thoughts. This man was so easy to talk to. I felt at ease confiding in him.

'Sir, it's not easy to explain. My informants tell me there is some kind of plot going on.'

Pahlen leaned forward. His expression did not change in the slightest, He was like a doctor listening to a patient's ailments. No disturbance, no anxiety.

I continued:

'I heard a rumour. Something about Paul being asked to abdicate. I know little more.'

'Hmm,' he mused.

'It's just a rumour. But there's no smoke without fire.'

'Certainly not,' said Pahlen. 'You are always in a good position to hear such things, I trust your instincts in these matters.'

'Thank you.'

'But I think there is little cause for concern.'

'Really?'

'Yes. I have heard a similar rumour. I think there is little substance in it.'

'What should I do? Take it to the Emperor?'

'You would be a brave man to do that. You know what I mean?'

That I could be implicated with such a rumour had not escaped my attention.

'What can I do?' I said.

'Do nothing. Leave it to me. I'll sniff out the rumours and pluck out the roots.'

A burden was lifted from my shoulders. Pahlen was so logical, so reasonable, so assured. Imagining Paul's face if I ever presented him with even the merest hint of such a thing was indeed frightening. Pahlen would sort it out. I trusted him.

'Thanks for coming to me,' he said. 'You did exactly the right thing.'

'I thank you from the bottom of my heart,' I replied.

I left his presence with a sense of the greatest relief. It was not usual I placed any faith in individuals of the court. But this man seemed different from the others. If anyone could save me, Pahlen was the one.

PAHLEN WASTED NO time. When the following morning I went to carry out my duties with the emperor, he had already been visited by the gentleman. As a consequence Paul was in total fury.

'There is a plot,' he said as I entered the room. 'Have you heard anything about it, Figaro?

I bowed.

'Not a word, Your Highness! Not a word!

'Are you lying? If you are lying I will find out.'

'I am your loyal servant. You can rely on me!'

But Paul was already looking further afield. Not for a moment did he seem to suspect I had any knowledge of whatever was afoot.

'It's Alexander,' he thundered. The boy is an idiot. But this is the last time he makes an idiot of me.'

'Alexander?' I said, shocked that Paul knew even this much.

'Of course. He wants to be Emperor. He always did. His Grandmother wanted him to be Emperor. He can't wait. He wants it now. But he's not getting it.'

'Surely not Alexander?' I pleaded.

Paul's response was to take his cane and beat me across the shoulders. I was forced to stoop onto my knees and shield my head with my elbow as the blows continued. More by accident than intention one of the strokes caught me fair and square on the nose and made it bleed.

At the sight of the blood rushing down to the carpets, Paul's tantrum changed. He lifted me to my feet and placed a handkerchief over the injured part:

'Look what you made me do,' he said. 'Why could you not have been the one that brought the news to me?'

'But what news?' I said, mumbling through the handkerchief.

'The plot, you fool. There is a plot. But never mind. I will nip it in the bud. I will see to it. They will not do to me what they did to my dear father.'

With that he sat down, threw down his offensive cane, and

succumbed to a fit of tears.

'Go. I'm tired of you. I have much work to do. You are not needed anymore today.'

Still clasping the cloth to my face, I beat an ignominious retreat.

THE EMPEROR DID indeed have much work that day and the following days.

He made lists of dozens of suspects whose faces he did not like. Evidence of the actual plot was sketchy. But Paul was capable of imagining its extent well beyond the realms of reality.

As I know now, not many were involved. Certainly not humble guardsmen, porters, cooks, messengers, sentries, nurse maids, gardeners, serving wenches. But he sent out for names from all levels of society. Any on the list were either dismissed from their occupation, flogged, imprisoned or exiled.

Gossipy tales abounded of his behaviour. When some fool accidentally rang the fire alarm bell, Paul ran amok through the palace convinced revolution was imminent.

He drew his sword and threatened some hussars with the words 'Get back you scum!' before demanding that one or two of them be whipped in front of him for starting the confusion.

The biggest victim was Alexander, regarded as the primary culprit. He was given a quantity of humiliating military duties from inspecting the latrines to supervising daily punishment.

Arakcheev, the infamous martinet of Gatchina, was brought over from the main St Petersburg garrison to supervise Alexander. The heir to the throne had to prepare a signed daily report of all his activities every morning which Arakcheev delivered forthwith to the emperor.

The atmosphere in the court grew stifling. A single word amiss in Paul's presence could provoke a storm. His dreams of murder and strangulation were recurring nightly. From such nightmares his most unreasonable behaviour grew like a cancer.

Even certain servants were kicked out from the palace. Only a few were secure. Their qualities were assessed in some unfathomable way by Paul's hunch about them.

'That man does not stand upright,' Paul would mutter while dining. 'I don't trust him. Get rid of him.'

The Head Butler himself was soon dismissed for alleged incompetence yet he had served the palace for thirty years.

I feared constantly for my own position. Once again I sought Pahlen's advice.

WHEN I VISITED Pahlen's house for the second time, General Bennigsen, veteran of many battles and (like Pahlen) of German descent, was there. He found it difficult to talk to me, regarding me as a lower order. His friendship with Platon Zubov had been sufficient for the emperor to remove him from the army. Such treatment, it was said, had embittered him.

'I have heard good things about you,' growled Bennigsen.

'Thank you general,' I replied.

Then abruptly, Bennigsen bowed and departed. It was very disrespectful.

Pahlen's special champagne came out. The liquid flowed generously into the glasses before our conversation even began.

'Could I seek your advice?' he said.

'I came to seek yours,' I replied.

'You need no advice from me,' he said with a little chuckle. 'You are the Emperor's right-hand man. You have seen His Majesty in ways none of us could imagine.'

Yes, I had seen the emperor stalking round his bedchamber naked except for a general's hat. I had seen Paul urinating into a pot while signing death warrants. The man had cried on my shoulder many a time. He had also slapped me across the face and chastised me with his cane.

'But first of all, what was it you wished to ask me?' he said.

'Ask you, sir?'

'Yes, in the matter of advice.'

'Ah yes.' I was brought back to the reason for my visit. 'It's a matter of the deepest confidentiality.'

'Naturally. These things always are.'

Pahlen was known in the court as the 'Professor of Cunning'. The very flatness of his tone was deceptive. His calmness was unnerving.

'I am very anxious about the Emperor's well-being,' I said.

'The Emperor's well-being? *His* well-being seems on the whole to be excellently provided for.'

'Things have got worse lately,' I remarked. 'In so many ways.'

'Give me an example!'

'There are so many things. Sacking the Head Butler for example. A servant of impeccable character.'

'There you have it,' said Pahlen. 'A man of power can do anything he wishes. Who is to stop him?'

I paused to reflect:

'That is it,' I replied. 'Nobody can stop the Emperor. His will is absolute.'

'Then what do we do?'

'Make the best of a bad situation. Try to make things better. A word here, a comment there.'

'Does that work? Do things get better?'

'Not at all. They are getting worse.'

'What if the Emperor abdicated? What if he were persuaded to pass his power to Alexander?'

I paled at the thought. Coming from Pahlen this was strong language.

'Impossible, sir,' I said. 'The Emperor would never agree. He would kill any person who suggested it.'

'Exactly. Therefore that is no solution. None of us wants to end up with our neck in a noose.'

'Perish the thought!' I said.

Pahlen's response was to laugh out loud:

'So you think it's not possible to persuade the Emperor to relinquish the throne?

'Not in a thousand years,' I exclaimed. 'The very idea chills me to the bone.'

'That is the voice of fear,' said Pahlen.

'But it is also,' I added, 'the voice of reason.'

'Quite so. I think you summed up the dilemma perfectly.'

'But what did you want to ask me?' I said. 'I believe there was something you wanted my advice about.'

'That is true.'

Pahlen poured out more champagne:

'Count Kutaissov, I would like you to do a very simple thing for me.'

Simple things were never simple. But I would be pleased to help him.

'If I can assist in any way − that would be my pleasure.'

___

'It is very easy. I would like you, if you wish to win my favour, to put in a word to the Emperor for the Zubov brothers. They are good men. The Emperor needs them. His Majesty disposes of good men and promotes the bad. You could persuade him.'

'I think, sir, you overestimate my powers of persuasion. I can persuade His Majesty to wear this wig or that but in matters of state and policy I cannot meddle.'

'This is not a matter of state. It is a matter of friendship. Count Kutaissov, I admire you. I want you as my friend. Just try your best. A simple word, thrown in at the right moment, could make a world of difference.'

Who could resist such a plea? I was won over. I was also slightly tipsy and feeling comfortable. What harm could a word or two do? I might get beaten with the cane. But worse things happen.

'I will do that for you,' I said. 'You have persuaded me.'

'Thank you, my dear friend,' said Pahlen.

He came and clasped me close to him. As I turned to leave, Pahlen spoke again:

'Dear Count, could you do something else for me? It could be to your advantage.'

'I will be pleased to oblige,' I said.

'Could you call at the house of Olga Zherebtsova? She wishes to speak with you.'

I had never been introduced to the renowned Zherebtsova, sister of the Zubovs, mistress to Charles Whitworth, the British ambassador. She was reputed to be a beautiful woman.

'That would be a pleasure!' I replied.

KEPT MY PROMISE and visited the home of Olga Zherebtsova. A servant opened the door. I was shown in to the drawing room.

Olga Zherebtsova came in almost before I had gathered my wits together.

'Good afternoon, Madame,' I said.

She smiled:

'You wished to see me.'

'So you are Count Kutaissov! My brothers told me about you long ago.'

(I was not sure what sort of tale she might have heard!)

'I have not had the opportunity to get to know your brothers,' I replied. 'But their reputation has spread far and wide.'

'Not always to their advantage,' she said.

'I have only heard good things,' I replied.

'They have been unfairly exiled. Platon was exiled because of his great service to the Empress. Why the others were sent away is beyond me.'

'The Emperor has his ways,' I said. 'I am only a simple servant. I do not understand these matters.'

Once more she laughed out loud:

'Come now, sir! I have heard you are expert in many arts, including politics and healing.'

'I have had modest success in the latter, but no success with politics. I leave such things to one side.'

'Indeed? I understood you are counsellor to the emperor.'

I may have blushed, or perhaps not:

'Not at all, Madame! My influence is in helping the Emperor to choose his wig or adjust his uniform. My life is that of a simple servant.'

'That is not what Count Pahlen told me.'

'Count Pahlen is a good friend. But he does exaggerate.'

'I am most eager to have my brothers pardoned. I want to have them with me again in St Petersburg. Could you help me?'

'I will do whatever is within my powers. But I can promise very little.'

'Thank you.'

She hesitated for a moment before speaking again, as if something else was on her mind:

'I have a friend in Madame Chevalier. She has confided in me on various things.'

'Perhaps she should not have done!' I exclaimed.

'St Petersburg is a small world,' she said, a wry smile round her lips:

'So I am aware!' I replied.

'Do not be angry, Count Kutaissov. I only wish for one thing.'

'What is that?'

'It is the pardon from exile for my brothers. They are talented men. The emperor needs them in his service.'

Zherebtsova stood up. It was time for me to go.

'I think we understand each other,' she said. 'It was a pleasure meeting you.'

I WAITED A DAY or two before mentioning the Zubovs to the emperor. Just because Paul smiled or hummed a tune when I entered his rooms in the morning, did not by itself indicate that my master was in a tolerable state of mind. The weather could change from sunny to stormy and back again within minutes.

Eventually I deemed the moment to be ripe. After the usual early rituals of the bedchamber, washing, shaving, clothing, and wigging the great man, conversation of a more pressing kind sometimes became possible.

So I began:

'Your Majesty, I have been in communication with Count Pahlen.'

'An excellent man, don't you think?'

'A very excellent man. Very trustworthy.'

The emperor stared at me:

'He is the kind of character we need. He tells me he has sniffed out the plot and the plotters. He is going to supply me with a list. But only when he is ready to arrest the culprits.'

Such information was unknown to me. At one time I thought I knew everything that was going on. Nowadays I seemed to be trailing behind.

Nevertheless, I continued:

'Sire, Count Pahlen is very eager to recruit the Zubov brothers to your service.'

'The Zubovs? Does that include Platon Zubov?'

I cleared my throat nervously:

'Yes. Sire, I believe it does.'

'And what do you think, Figaro?'

I plunged in:

'I believe Count Pahlen's judgement to be fair.'

The emperor paused. I thought for a moment he was on the verge of either forgetting what I had just said or was still thinking about Platon Zubov, whom he loathed.

'Well in that case bring them back from exile. We'll find some suitable minor positions for them in the court. It will give them an income.'

'I think Count Pahlen would also favour an appointment for General Bennigsen.'

This proved to be too far. Paul reached for his cane and waved it at me, like a schoolmaster threatening a naughty pupil:

'We have given out sufficient favours for one day. Bennigsen is not to be on the list. I distrust him. Understood?'

The cane waved in front of my nose. I nodded. The emperor laughed:

'Figaro,' he said with apparent affection, 'sometimes you are such a fool!'

I SENT A LETTER to Pahlen announcing the Zubovs had been reprieved but nothing was available for Bennigsen.

He wrote back expressing his thanks. He made no mention of Bennigsen's response. (I learned later the general received the news with contempt and fury. But I had done my best.)

The annulment of the Zubovs' exile was officially signed and sealed on 1 November 1800. At the same time various disgraced army officers as well as a number of officials previously banished were granted a sudden amnesty.

This was achieved by Pahlen's intercession with the emperor, a request granted (according to court gossip) partly due to my own endorsement of the man.

The amnesty created problems as the previous administrative posts of exiles had been filled. As a result the city seethed with the discontent of talented but destitute men with too much time on their hands and no income.

A T THAT TIME I became responsible for moving the court from the Winter Palace to the Mikhailovsky Palace, the building inspired by a soldier's vision of the archangel Michael. We began this work in the middle of winter.

When I was looking round the fortress, empty of furniture, with a hundred workmen still completing the plastering, masonry, and woodwork after four years work, its atmosphere was that of a desolate prison. Fortified by a huge moat, over which four drawbridges were constructed, the rooms were cavernous and cold.

Immense walls glistened with frozen moisture, a damp miasma filled every room. The banging of hammers and rough distant voices echoed like ghosts through vast corridors. No quantity of fur coats and layers of thick underwear could dispel the chill which soaked one to the bone.

'This palace, sir, needs another few months to settle down,' said the chief builder. 'Lets the plaster dry. Takes time.'

Paul was not persuaded to delay, his head full of images of treason and his father's murder. To him the Mikhailovsky was security. Only there would he feel safe.

As for me, working in that hideous building made me choke for days. I spat out a mass of vile green phlegm and my lungs ached when I breathed.

The workers too became ill. The chorus of our coughing resounded against the bare walls like barking dogs in a deserted monastery.

THE SPIDER'S WEB

The spider's touch, how exquisitely fine!
Feels at each thread, and lives along the line.

An Essay on Man,
ALEXANDER POPE

A DAY OR TWO after Christmas Olga Zherebtsova put on a soirée at her home. The emperor, following recurrent rumours of plots, had banned gatherings of more than a dozen people several months earlier. A curfew after ten at night was imposed for the festive season. But he was hardly likely to interfere with Zherebtsova's little party when Pahlen was present along with some respectable burghers of the city.

Three of the Zubovs were there, getting drunk in the process, boasting of their return from exile. Nicholai Zubov, a giant of a man, loomed over his brothers. His voice and manners were coarser than his siblings. Yet he was the first, having supposedly been well prepared by Pahlen, to thank me for assistance in bringing the brothers back to civilisation.

'I have done very little,' I said with false modesty.

'Pahlen tells me differently,' replied Nicholai, squeezing my hand, his bad breath uncomfortably close.

Prince Platon Zubov, the most handsome of the trio, the favoured lover of the emperor's mother, had been dispatched from court immediately after Paul's accession. His soft complexion and sly, brown eyes made me uneasy. He was the dominant brother of the three for they seemed to defer to him.

Valerian Zubov, quietly sinister, a former soldier reputed to have killed many men in battle before being wounded, walked with painful gait on a wooden peg-leg.

The brothers clustered round, patting me on the back,

congratulating me for having brought about their freedom.

Embarrassed at their exaggeration, feeling incriminated as if in the release of criminals, I caught a glimpse of Pahlen from across the room. Next to him was General Bennigsen with a truly Teutonic scowl across his gnarled features.

I was attracting too much attention. I prefer to work below the surface like a mole, not revealing my motives, or actions. Seeing the sober Pahlen in company with the drunken, swaggering Zubovs was not to my liking.

Fortunately Olga Zherebtsova rescued me from both the Zubovs and Pahlen. She wanted me to meet some of the ladies of her acquaintance. Very pretty they were too. But, just as our conversation was beginning to flow, Madame Chevalier entered, late but unrepentant, on the arm of her husband.

Chevalier immediately became the focus of all eyes and ears. Everybody wanted to get close to the most popular actress in Russia. Strange too how the Zubovs moved to the front of the pack.

The noise in the room increased as Madame Chevalier became the centre of adoration. Her laughter cut through the swirl of excited chatter like a sabre. She was a goddess entertaining her devoted acolytes.

On the periphery of her circle I watched her with longing in my heart, mindful of the multitude of afternoon embraces we had shared in the house I rented for her. Now she hardly seemed like a lover, more like a distant star, unreachable but lovely.

But even her aura was suddenly eclipsed. A servant came through the doorway in haste and announced in a shrill anxious voice, 'His Royal Highness, Prince Alexander!'

And there he was, the heir himself, accompanied by his aides, a guard or two, and Arakcheev, ugly as ever despite his best army attire complete with medals.

We all lined up as if by instinct. Alexander, with Zherebtsova by his side as hostess, moved quickly from one guest to another. He stayed slightly longer with Pahlen and welcomed back the Zubovs with great warmth.

Madame Chevalier elegantly received a kiss on her gloved hand as if she was the princess and Alexander the commoner. Monsieur Chevalier bowed low and blushed crimson with surprise.

When Alexander came face to face with me he smiled benevolently and shook my hand:

'Ah, Count Kutaissov. How wonderful to see you among friends. I had not expected to find you here.'

'Your Highness,' I replied, 'I am a friend of Madame Zherebtsova.'

'So I heard,' said the Prince. 'You have many friends, Count Kutaissov. We rely on your allegiance.'

I had no idea what allegiance he was talking about. But royalty often conversed in vague riddles. It was what passed for conversation as far as they were concerned.

As the wine and champagne flowed on into the night, the small band struck up. Couples danced round as pretty as a picture, notably Madame Chevalier with Prince Alexander, Count Pahlen with Zherebtsova, and Platon and Nicholas Zubov with two elegant courtesans, friends of our hostess no doubt.

I waited for an opportunity to dance with Madame Chevalier. But she clung to Alexander like a leech with occasional glances in my direction.

After half an hour of this I thanked Olga Zherebtsova for the evening's hospitality and departed into the night.

N THE MORNING the emperor immediately noticed my sleepy demeanour, especially as I failed to stifle a yawn as we proceeded through the routines of washing and dressing.

'What has my Figaro been doing?' he asked, though not in a serious tone, more like addressing a naughty schoolboy. 'Perhaps a visit to a certain actress?'

'Unfortunately not, Sire,' I replied. 'I attended a soirée at the house of Madame Zherebtsova last night.'

'A *soirée*?' mimicked Paul, twisting the word vilely to imitate my poor French accent. 'Nothing less, nothing more, than a *soirée*?'

'A tedious affair!'

'Tedious? Who was at this *soirée*? Anyone of interest? Did you dance?'

'I did not dance, Your Majesty. I am not good at dancing.'

'You answered my second question. Not my first!'

'I am slightly bemused this morning. I did not pay due attention to the first question. I apologise.'

'Let me ask again. Who was at the *soirée*?'

There was no point in lying. Paul probably knew already exactly who was there.

'Well, Sire, your son honoured us with a short visit?'

'Did he indeed? And what other grand persons *honoured us*?'

'Count von der Pahlen was there, and Madame Chevalier.'

'Do go on.'

'And Prince Platon Zubov and his brothers.'

'And General Bennigsen?'

'Yes indeed, Sire.'

The emperor went pale with either fear or anger. The tipping point was being reached. Any moment now he might strike me.

'I smell a plot there.'

I answered hastily:

'Not at all, Your Majesty. It was most cordial. As I said Count Pahlen was there. He is an honest man.'

'So you tell me. But nowadays I suspect my own shadow of treason. I think of my poor father. One cannot be too careful.'

'I remain vigilant, Sire, at all times.'

'Yes, Figaro, I admire your vigilance. But certain things are going on you know nothing about. That worries me.'

'I hope not,' I replied.

The emperor changed direction, asking instead about the move to the Mikhailovsky Palace and how plans were progressing. With this I could be optimistic. Things were working out very well, ahead of schedule and smoothly. Apparently satisfied, Paul became thoughtful. He handed me a list of names, twenty-six in all, army officers.

'What do you think of that?'

'A long list, Sire. But you have the advantage. I have scarcely heard of any of these names before.'

He laughed before replying:

'You see Figaro, you don't know everything that goes on. These are to be exiled immediately and stripped of their rank and privileges.'

'What have they done? On what evidence.'

'Evidence is not necessary. Why should it be? News has reached my ears that their behaviour is incompetent and possibly seditious.'

'Very good, Sire. I admire your judgement.'

'That is more like it, Figaro. We need help in doing our duty, not impediments.'

Ah, if only he had asked my advice! I would have been against this. And I was correct. Sending the officers away raised a storm among all the wrong people.

Even Count Pahlen raised his voice when he heard of it. The whole army seethed with anxiety and resentment. Nobody felt safe anymore.

The earthquake, though I was not fully aware of it at the time, was just beginning.

I ARRANGED TO MEET Madame Chevalier one afternoon at the house I rented for her. She was in a pleasant mood, dressed in one of her fine silk gowns, purring like a cat with the cream.

My passion was a tidal wave of feeling. I truly loved her. Our amours that day were the best, our kisses prolonged for hours. The rapture went on and on, infinite, a drug to lure you in. My skin tingled, my body was refreshed, my mind at peace.

But after the embraces other matters troubled me. First, came the problem of her frequent 'engagements' with her husband.

'How is your husband?' I asked.

'He is fine. In good spirits.'

'You were with him at the soirée.'

'He wanted to come. I couldn't refuse him.'

'You never danced with me,' I said.

'That was Prince Alexander's fault. He came for me time after time. I could hardly send him away.'

Her argument had a kind of logic, The big question still hung in the air like rancid smoke:

'Has Alexander been here to see you?'

'Only twice. Only short visits.'

My soul twisted in torment. As if she had struck with stabbing blows to the heart and stomach. The business with her husband was bad enough. Visits by the prince were sickening.

'Did Alexander say anything?' I said.

'Well of course he spoke to me. He always does.'

'What did he say?'

'The usual pillow talk. Nothing of great consequence.'

'Did he mention the Zubovs?'

'No. He mentioned Count Pahlen. The Prince is fond of him.'

'Fond?'

'Yes. As if he's a kind of friend.'

'Did he say anything else?'

'Why do you want to know?'

'Just curiosity!'

She laughed as if acting a part on a stage:

'You seem foolishly jealous for no reason. You see me whenever you want. I give you everything. What more do you need?'

'I want you. I can't stand the thought of you in another's arms. It disgusts me.'

'All that means nothing. I don't love the others as I love you.'

'I don't know what to believe,' I said. 'I know what I would like. I can't have it.'

'But you do have it!' she insisted. 'You have my love. That's worth everything, isn't it?'

'I suppose so. It's not enough!'

We took to kissing again, leaving words alone. My heart burned with jealousy, my body with desire.

———

FTERWARDS MADAME CHEVALIER'S words about Alexander and Pahlen chimed in my head like bells.

Something was wrong. Alexander had been named about Paul's abdication and then punished for it by excessive military duties.

The only resolution I could come to was that Alexander must be weak in the head, just like Paul. Catherine had never wanted Paul on the throne. She preferred Alexander. Perhaps Alexander himself was only slightly less mad than his father.

Somewhere there was an answer to every question.

HE BEST COURSE of action was to talk to Pahlen again. I met with him two days later. Before I had even sat down in his drawing room he poured out two glasses of champagne:

'It is good to see you,' he said. 'I hope you enjoyed the soirée. Many interesting people there.'

We sat facing each other:

'Sir,' I began, 'I am in the dark about urgent matters. Perhaps you could resolve my doubts.'

'Doubts?' he echoed. 'You are not a man associated with doubt?'

'You flatter me!' I exclaimed. 'I have so many doubts I can't see the wood for the trees.'

'That's not like you. Not you at all.'

'It is about the rumours.'

'Rumours?'

'Yes. The Emperor's abdication. I don't know what to think.'

'Has His Majesty never mentioned such a thing?'

'Certainly not. It would be the last thing he would ever do.'

'Well, that may be true. But things can happen.'

We paused like fencers, as if mopping our brows, waiting for the next round:

'Some things cannot happen. The Emperor's abdication is one of them,' I said.

Pahlen put down his glass, staring straight at me:

'Count Kutaissov, I thought you were on my side!'

I was startled:

'Sir, I am always on your side. That is why I have praised you to His Majesty.'

'I am grateful for that. But consider this. Paul the First is not in a fit state.'

'Why not? What has changed?'

'Everything. All the time. We have Napoleon in Europe, running around, hurting everybody. Soon he may be our deadliest enemy. What then with the Emperor?'

'Napoleon? What has he got to do with abdication? The Emperor adores Napoleon. He would never go to war with him.'

'I usually admire your judgement. But you have little understanding of foreign policy.'

'Sir, that is true,' I said. 'My understanding is limited.'

Pahlen took up his glass again, relishing the champagne, offering to replenish my half-empty glass. I accepted. A smile played round his mouth:

'My dear friend, all that is in the offing is a suggestion His Majesty should relinquish the throne in favour of Alexander.'

'He would never accept that.'

'Not necessarily,' said Pahlen. 'Prince Alexander could persuade him. All we need is somebody such as yourself on our side. It need not be difficult.'

I sipped the drink, a mixture of the sweet and the sour:

———

'Sir, I could never mention abdication to the Emperor. If I said anything I wouldn't live to see my next birthday.'

Pahlen put down his glass before holding up his hands in a despairing gesture.

'All right, please yourself. You often do. Do you deny the Emperor is of unsound mind?'

This was not an appropriate topic for discussion. I knew Paul was mad. I saw it every day in his eyes, his moods, his dreams, his talk. But this could not be admitted to a third party.

'Sir, the Emperor is weighed down by affairs of state. Any man might become…distracted. Other times His Majesty appears less 'distracted' than some of his advisers.'

Pahlen downed the contents of his glass:

'Thank you, Count Kutaissov. You have stated your position with discretion. Many disagree. Prince Alexander strongly disagrees. You have your side of the bargain. I advise you to keep to it. When the time comes you will not so easily run with the hounds and hunt with the hares.'

With that he stood up. I knew he was deeply offended.

'Sir, I apologise!' I said hoping to redeem the situation.

'Not at all. We'll talk another time. When you've had an opportunity to think about what has been said.'

I shook hands and looked him in the eye. I saw something I had not seen before. Pahlen, my friend, was now my enemy.

I would have to tread more carefully.

THE DUTIES OF moving the court from the Winter Palace to the Mikhailovsky occupied me throughout January. Day after day carts rolled through the streets loaded with every item an emperor possesses, each listed and audited piece by piece.

Paul's mood during these weeks of waiting swung like a pendulum:

'Figaro, tell me how everything is getting on,' he asked most mornings.

I reassured him:

'Your Majesty, as *smooth* as clockwork.'

It pleased him if the answer was always the same. Eventually he mimicked me even as I pronounced the words.

As THE DAYS passed one of the emperor's favourite repetitions was to exclaim, 'I do not feel safe here!'

Yet outside the palace his guards were patrolling with more than usual vigilance. Often in the early hours before dawn, dressed in his nightclothes, the emperor stalked the corridors making sure the sentries were in position, prepared for anything.

'We can never be too sure,' he would say.

God help any soldier who wandered from his appointed place. Seeing the emperor wandering the passageways was more frightening for the men than any enemy they might encounter.

Colonel Sablukov commanded these special guardians. Belonging to his Imperial Horse Guards had been considered something of an honour. But when a couple of soldiers were buttonholed by Paul on one of his nocturnal wanderings and flogged that very night for minor uniform infringements, much of the regiment's enthusiasm evaporated.

Such happenings were only to be expected with everybody's nerves on edge. Until the emperor was finally installed in the

Mikhailovsky any sense of security was impossible.

The situation was made worse when Madame Chevalier and her company of actors took it upon themselves at the theatre to stage a play by Shakespeare. I had hardly heard of Shakespeare and knew nothing of England where the man came from.

What I did know was that one of his plays, apparently about the death of Julius Caesar, had been banned on political grounds a few years before. One would think at this stressful time to put on another such drama would be inadvisable.

But an application was made and permission granted. The play, called *Hamlet* (translated into Russian as *Gamlet*), contained more questionable material such as the killing of a king, a prince in waiting for the throne, and contentious matters including ghosts, murders, and the suicide of Gamlet's lover.

The prospect of seeing my beloved Madame Chevalier on stage at her finest was some consolation for the inappropriateness of the plot.

The emperor, accompanied by the empress and Anna Lopukhina, was eager to attend. I was allowed to stand in the rear of the royal box during the performance.

The theatre was crowded. Pahlen and Bennigsen were there with the Zubov brothers (all three of them). I think they had already been at the champagne. Their loud laughter from time to time made many of the audience stare at them in indignation.

I cannot say I enjoyed the play though Madame Chevalier acted superbly in the role of Queen of Denmark. Her husband took the part of the wicked king who murdered his brother and married the widow. Gamlet himself, a mere stripling of a youth, forgot his lines occasionally, causing nastier elements in the crowd to hiss and mock.

The scene which pleased me most came when the father of

Gamlet's lover hid himself behind a tapestry. Gamlet ran him through with his sword shouting, 'How now! A rat?'

A mighty cheer came from many of the spectators, changing to disappointment when it was revealed that the evil king had not died but in his place the foolish old dispenser of platitudes, Polonius.

Paul had begun the evening in a congenial mood. He liked the music before the play began but became distinctly restless as the plot slowly moved on. Before long the emperor became agitated. From the side I saw his face twitch with tension.

What probably finished him off was a strange masque in the play where the king sleeping in the orchard had poison poured into his ear. Paul stayed on for a little while longer. But with the death of Polonius, he stood up (causing the whole audience to rise to its feet) and walked out.

The empress, Lopukhina, and myself, duly followed like obedient lapdogs.

From the floor of the theatre came a mixed uproar of booing and applauding. Certain people left their seats and rushed to the foyer.

Paul made his way to the royal carriage through a forest of genuflecting subjects, his chin inclined upwards, eyes staring firmly ahead.

CANNOT STAND PLAYS that show kings being killed!' said Paul the next morning. 'It provokes treason. It cannot be allowed.'

The emperor's dreams were not about poison or daggers but death by strangulation. Often he stroked his throat thoughtfully just as some men scratch their heads while thinking.

'It's only a play,' I retorted. 'A shadow on a stage, here for an evening, then forgotten.'

'There you are wrong, Figaro,' he replied. 'You have not forgotten what you saw. Neither have I.'

Yes, in a strange manner that play did hang in the mind. Ghosts on the ramparts, clanking armour, the voices of the dead, a poor mad prince driven crazy by his mother's seeming adultery, and so on. I had never seen anything like it.

'But it is make-believe,' I said. 'A little dream.'

'But dreams are terrible. They drive us mad. You are fortunate you do not suffer from them. I have endured nightmares since my father's murder.'

He put his face in his hands, exhaling deep sighs like a man with toothache. He would not be comforted. But I tried my best:

'Your Majesty, please do not despair. In a few days we move to the Mikhailovsky Palace.'

Slowly he stood up, his face a mask of suffering. I had never seen him quite like this.

'Today I will visit Lopukhina,' he blurted out. 'She is the answer. Everybody is betraying me. But Lopukhina is always the same. What a damnation that she took a husband. Though I don't mind as long as she's happy.'

The emperor could have squashed Prince Gagarin with his little finger. He chose not to. For his lover's sake. To keep her happy. A strange happiness. I changed the subject:

'If you will excuse me, Sire, I must attend to my duties at the Mikhailovsky. There is still much to do.'

'How is the work proceeding?'

'Like clockwork, Your Majesty.'

'Thank you, Figaro. I do believe you are my best friend in all the world.'

I bowed from the waist:

'That is my only ambition, Sire.'

It was a happy day when the Mikhailovsky was at last ready for its residents.

In previous weeks hundreds of workers had swarmed through the fortress, covering floors and walls with beautiful things, arranging furniture in patterns similar to those of the Winter Palace, preparing banqueting hall and kitchens, stabling horses and carriages, and lighting a thousand candles.

Unfortunately the Mikhailovsky, whatever its gaudy embellishments, remained true to its own nature. More a mausoleum than a home, its four drawbridges and barricaded doors felt akin to a prison.

However much adornment we lavished on walls and floors, a pervading dampness, a chill never to be dissipated, hung in the air. Fires were lit throughout. But frequently chimneys were blocked, choking smoke billowed back into the rooms.

The sweeps sent apprentices, boys of nine and ten, to dowse the fires and clear orifices. The boys returned covered in filth, coughing up soot and dust. They went up naked, white as polished statues, and came down shivering, black as devils. It was not a good omen.

To welcome those to be incarcerated in this monstrosity, we set out red carpets outside and in. Despite every setback it was a moment of joy when the emperor and empress, with Lopukhina bringing up the rear alongside Alexander and Constantine, processed from their carriages, entering the giant portals of the castle for the first time.

Lackeys showed the royal personages to their rooms after a grand conducted tour. It was my task to attend to the emperor.

Paul was in an ebullient mood. He ordered, forthwith, that the drawbridges, all of them, should be lifted up and the outside doors appropriately barricaded.

'There you are, Figaro,' he announced, 'I'm now as safe as houses.'

It was true that inside the castle, whatever the inconveniences of the design, one felt securely imprisoned. The outside world conveniently ceased to exist when all the fortifications had been established for the night.

A rat could not have entered without being detected. Just to preclude that very event, a number of cats had been enlisted in the royal service to keep down those rodents which had already taken up residence. But of course human rats are a different species and can find their way in more easily.

Colonel Sablukov's Horse Guards were extravagantly deployed inside and outside the building. The soldiers were delighted to be there, swaggering around saluting and presenting arms with a new zeal, their status enhanced by the imposition of responsibility for the emperor's safety.

Pahlen arrived to make himself acquainted with the appearance and lay-out of the Mikhailovsky. I gave him a conducted tour despite a sense of his coldness towards me. He asked many questions about the castle and reminded me twice how he was personally entrusted with the emperor's security:

'His Majesty will be very safe here then!' I said, with a slight tinge of ridicule.

'Yes, indeed, Count Kutaissov. At this time we need the best men round us.'

'Sablukov's men are among the best and the most loyal,' I said.

'Yes, I am glad you pointed that out to me.'

Pahlen was given the passwords and permission to visit the emperor at any time of day or night. Was there anything wrong with that?

Nothing at all! Except it was Pahlen who had harped on and brought to my attention the necessity of Paul's abdication. Was that now forgotten?

THE EMPEROR AND his family remained immured in the Mikhailovsky. Paul never left the fortress, convinced this was the way to keep out of danger.

I had been commanded to move into a suite of rooms on the same floor as the emperor. His bedchamber was accessible along the corridor by a secret door. The furnishings provided were not up to the standard I previously enjoyed at the Winter Palace.

Being separated from Natasha I endured the Spartan hostility of the place better than if she had accompanied me. But my duties as Paul's *confidant* had always remained well isolated from my role as a husband.

The two lives of husband and courtier had never mixed easily. Never would I have tried to bring these parallel existences together. Thus Natasha's defection made things considerably easier for me at the Mikhailovsky.

After my destitute younger years, hardships such as cold

walls and freezing beds could be endured. Aristocrats, with the exception of the emperor himself, pampered throughout their existence, found the place intolerable.

The fortress's monastic enclosure, its rancid odours and clammy chill, made occasional escape from its confines very desirable. For such excursions it was preferable to return before the drawbridges were sealed for the night or things could become difficult.

After the laxity of their previous posting, modified by the emperor's own perambulations round the building at night to check up on them, the guards were now on full alert and sharp as mustard. They would have been delighted to accost in the dark St Petersburg winter, any straggler wandering across the perimeter. If you forgot the password you could be shot on sight. Best not to take chances.

But it seemed necessary a few times to get out from this monstrous captivity. In the early afternoon, once or twice, I therefore went to see Madame Chevalier, making appointments with her suitably in advance to avoid any other of her visitors.

As I have commented previously, Chevalier, despite her deceptions and theatrical affectations, was by nature shockingly honest. Without a modicum of shyness she told me the details of her relationship to Monsieur Chevalier. This was intended to reassure me.

She related tales of the brevity of their amorous encounters and the blandness of their partnership in comparison with the lengthy conflagrations of our own passionate hours. Such talk merely inflamed my jealousy.

Added to these stories came brief mention of Alexander's engagements with her, which enraged me even more. But these too, she insisted, were but mere nothings in the scale of things.

'Does the Grand Duke Alexander ever refer to the Emperor's possible abdication?' I dared to enquire.

'All the time!' she replied. 'It seems he will soon be Emperor himself.'

'Does he know you and I are lovers?' I asked.

'Of course not. How could he?'

I did not wish to accuse her of lying. But Alexander surely knew everything about me. He had his spies I expected, just as I did.

Her skin was pure and white, smoother than the finest silk. I loved to run my fingers down her back, massaging her gently. She adored the sensation, purring and moaning contentedly. But such ecstasy served only to remind me that other men caressed her. Madame Chevalier would never be mine in a hundred years.

In a sense I had already lost her, when she married her husband, let alone when Alexander decided she should be his casual mistress.

My love for her possessed me like a forest fire or a volcano. But it was no good. Jealousy for this lovely woman burned in my heart more scorching than acid or flames.

That night I wrote her a letter bringing our sad drama to its close. I could have written it in my own blood so painful was the parting.

Like a ship leaving the shore burdened with cargo, my heart sighed with sorrow.

The leaving was inevitable. If I had stayed I would have died with desire for something I could never have.

THINGS TOOK A turn for the worse when Rostopchin was exiled to his estates. Pahlen replaced him as President of the Foreign Council and Postmaster with authority to open letters.

I did not at the time consider this the end of the world. Due to the emperor's twisting and turning it was possible Rostopchin might be recalled in days or Pahlen sent to join him.

Being promoted to high office or being exiled were two sides of the same coin. Nothing to do with merit, sin, guilt, deeds, or behaviour. Paul's whims could veer left or right depending on the time of day.

In the streets terror was unleashed as the Secret Chancery cracked down on the rank and file of the populace. The number of arrests could not be estimated as such events were not listed. Talk drifted back of beatings and tortures. The executioners were kept busy.

Dozens of subjects, taken by night, were never seen again. The thugs of the Chancery infiltrated churches and markets. A word out of place from a simple man could seal his death warrant.

Neither was the weather on the side of humanity. Icy fogs creeping in from the river alternated with sleet and freezing rain. The January snowfalls lost their crisp whiteness. The short hours of daylight added a curtain of gloom.

Even in the Mikhailovsky the misery could not be avoided. In some rooms an invasion of fat slugs caused panic among the ladies in waiting.

The empress changed her bedroom because of the abundance of fungus, growing like flowers on the satin-panelled walls.

THE EMPEROR CHANGED his routine now that he was installed in the Mikhailovsky. I was required to be in attendance at 5 AM every morning for ablutions, dressing, and other tasks such as disposing of contents of chamber pots and the provision of freshly laundered shirts, bedding, and underwear. There was much to do.

At 7 o'clock Pahlen entered for daily orders and discussion of outstanding business. Paul often insisted I should remain in the room while this was going on, much to Pahlen's annoyance.

The emperor was obsessed most days with whatever rumours were circulating about this plot or that. According to him there may have been more than one plot on his life in the planning. Neither he nor I could ever arrive at the truth of the matter, rumours being no more substantial than wisps of air. Behind the smoke was fire. But where?

During one memorable session the emperor turned on Pahlen like a snake ready to strike:

'What, Count Pahlen, were you doing during the 1762 disturbance?'

Pahlen, normally serene, went white. Both he and I knew the emperor was referring to his father's murder. That brutal event had taken place nearly forty years previously. The question seemed insane.

Pahlen paused as if trying to remember:

'Well?' said Paul. 'Don't stand there stuttering. What's your answer?'

He was going red in the face while Pahlen was growing paler. But Pahlen's reply sounded convincing:

'Your Majesty, I was seventeen years old at the time!'

'Really?' said Paul, whose grasp of mathematics was always imperfect.

'Indeed, Sire, my rank was that of an ensign in the Horse Guards. We were never given anything important to do.'

Pahlen bowed and began to back out of the room. I stood there awkwardly, not sure of what might happen. The emperor flew into one of his familiar rages, grabbing his cane and striking the dressing table, scattering whatever was on it:

'There are those who want what happened in 1762 to be repeated in 1801. Is that true?'

I expected Pahlen to deny any such thing. But his answer was truly shocking:

'Absolutely true, Your Majesty. Such people do exist. I am one of them.'

His voice as calm as a field of flowers, he continued:

'My duty is to protect the Emperor's sacred personage. I joined the conspiracy from its beginning. The matter is in hand. I am gathering evidence together.'

Paul threw down the cane.

'Names, names, names! You must give us names!'

His voice was more of a croak than a shriek. He intended to shout but words stuck in his throat:

'Sire, that's the beauty of it! The list will be presented to Your Majesty. All will be revealed.'

'When, Pahlen, when? For God's sake when?'

'Soon, Your Majesty. Very soon.'

Paul sat down on his dressing room chair, his anger changed to musing of an unhealthy kind:

'1762…1762…They murdered him in 1762.'

'But, Sire, please believe me,' said Pahlen. 'There is no similarity between now and 1762. You love the Russian people. Your father despised them. He was never crowned. You are God's anointed one. The army distrusted your father. Today your soldiers are loyal. You have been considerate to the peasants and the clergy. You have set a religious example. Your father did none of these things. It is not possible to compare 1762 with today. Things are different.'

It was a long speech. Too long. Its unpredictability won the day. I became convinced. He knew nothing of 1762. He was somewhere else. Was this the truth? It could be so.

When Paul spoke again his voice whimpered rather than ranted, like a child wishing to know where the toys were kept:

'Tell me, Count Pahlen, if you are so sure then why are people plotting against me?'

A good question. We waited for the answer. The riddle was posed. Could it be solved?

Pahlen cleared his throat. Yes, he *was* nervous.

'Sire, some people would not be satisfied if they woke up and found themselves in Paradise.'

Paul laughed. He seemed amused by such a weak reply, so feeble it worked like a charm.

'All right!' he said sharply. 'Bring that list as soon as possible.'

Pahlen bowed low and departed.

The emperor turned to me for comfort, an infant adrift in a cruel world:

'Figaro, there's a good man for you. Don't you agree?'

I am ashamed to say I replied, 'One of the best, Sire, the very best!'

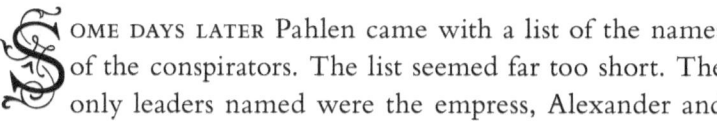

OME DAYS LATER Pahlen came with a list of the names of the conspirators. The list seemed far too short. The only leaders named were the empress, Alexander and

Constantine. They intended to ask the emperor to abdicate – that was all there was to it.

Paul went purple in the face:

'Count Pahlen, we must mount a counter-coup!' he announced. 'Immediately!'

'Excellent Sire,' exclaimed Pahlen. 'Leave everything in my hands!'

After he left Paul became surprisingly cheerful:

'Soon, Figaro, we shall live without fear like brothers,' he said, and clapped me on the back to show his anxiety had been soothed. 'I shall summon Rostopchin from exile and Arakcheev from Gatchina. They'll put a stop to this nonsense.'

Without further ado, the emperor sat down at his desk wrote two letters, and sealed them with the imperial stamp.

'Take these letters straight to Pahlen,' he commanded with a Napoleonic flourish. 'He's the Postmaster. Tell him these are urgent. He has the power to see things are done quickly.'

I carried out his orders. Pahlen was in his office.

'The Emperor wishes you to send two letters as quickly as possible,' I explained.

Pahlen took them from me, glancing at the addresses.

'Good,' he said, in his calm voice. 'Rostopchin's estates and Arakcheev at Gatchina. We can send this in the next day or two. I'll dispatch special riders.'

'The Emperor will be pleased,' I replied.

The trouble was that four mornings later Pahlen was back in front of Paul waving the letters. He had opened them within his authority as Postmaster, read them, and now enquired whether these were genuine communications or clever forgeries. The emperor, more confused than ever, hardly knew what to say.

'Surely Count Kutaissov delivered these letters to you by hand.'

'He did indeed. But we cannot be too careful. It is my duty to check everything. Besides they have only been in my possession a few days.'

'Well, deliver them now. We can wait no longer.'

Pahlen bowed and retreated. The emperor turned angrily towards me:

'When I ask you to carry out a simple task, it is imperative you do so at once!'

'Your Majesty,' I began, 'these were delivered as requested. Pahlen must have neglected to deal with them.'

'More probable is you let things slip for a day or two. You are like that sometimes. Never mind. It isn't too late. Whoever's fault it may be, the matter is now closed.'

To be rebuked like a common servant filled me with rage.

PART EIGHT

IN THE VALLEY OF
THE SHADOW

'What am I frightened of?'
'Of me,' answered the voice of Death. 'I am here!'

Memoirs of a Madman,
TOLSTOY

YOU WILL HAVE guessed. Pahlen was the betrayer, the very Judas. I stumbled like a blind man. The clues were there. I never saw them till it was too late. The emperor, poor mad fool, depended on me to sniff out the plot. I failed.

Alexander failed too. He never realised what folly would be unleashed.

On 11 March the emperor was in a good mood. A banquet was arranged with twenty guests. The one-eyed General Kutuzov attended, guest of honour. They all ate and drank too much.

After the meal, Paul spent time with his children chasing them up and down the corridors pretending to be a lion. Their laughter was heard round the building, echoing like bells.

I observed previously that this was the duty evening for Alexander's Semyonovsky Guards. They were not as smart as Colonel Sablukov's Imperial Horse Guards. But the latter had to have one night a week for manly revelling. Nothing unusual about that.

One or two Horse Guards patrolled the immediate vicinity of the emperor's apartments. But Pahlen was granted admission to Paul's presence. He suggested the guards could possibly be 'Jacobins', the worst kind of traitor in the emperor's opinion, and should be dismissed for the night.

Paul, eager it seems to cut his own throat, sent them away. Also on Pahlen's advice, he locked the door to the empress's room, 'just, you understand, as a further precaution'.

The emperor retired early that night, donning his drawers, a white linen waistcoat, and a nightcap, his customary attire for the bedchamber as I knew only too well.

He hung his sword on the end of the bed, along with his cane and ornamental gold sash.

AT THE WINTER Palace, as I heard later, special celebrations were being enjoyed. In the apartments of a certain General Talytzin, a gang of well-connected individuals were drinking as much as they could get down their throats.

These included the Zubov brothers, several army officers, some ruffians, and a few princes and senators. Bennigsen was there but did not drink any alcohol. Before midnight Count Pahlen, fresh from his duties with the emperor, joined the company.

'Let's drink a toast to the new Emperor,' he shouted. They all joined in with riotous hurrahs and much back slapping.

Pahlen then divided his bunch of criminals into two groups. Platon Zubov and Bennigsen would enter the Mikhailovsky through a postern-gate at the back of the building. Their mission was to arrest the emperor in his bedchamber.

The second group, with Pahlen at the head of them, were to surround the palace and capture Paul if he tried to escape.

Like so many clowns, some of the first group lost their way in the dark. Which meant that only twelve conspirators managed to cross the drawbridge.

Bennigsen led the way, closely followed by Platon Zubov and his giant of a brother, Nicholai. A junior adjutant, Argamakov, an insignificant runt of a man until this treacherous moment, guided them through the labyrinth of corridors.

Such was their drunkenness it was rumoured that the louts sang loudly as they approached the emperor's bedchamber. They drew their swords. Argamakov supplied them with candles to grope their way into history.

CERTAIN ELEMENTS OF this tragic saga will not appear in history books. Some truth, as well as blatant falsehoods, will die when I do. The conspirators, the victors, will write their own story of the encounter, twisting it whichever way they intend.

The truth is Paul had already slept. Until a strange dream roused him in a feverish sweat. He ran through the secret door of his bedchamber to my lodging and banged on the door.

'Figaro, I am troubled,' he shouted.

I should have brought him into my room. He would have been safe. But propriety required that I must escort him back to his own quarters.

'I am with you, Sire!' I said.

'I had a dream. My father appeared. It was a warning!'

This premonition often disturbed his nights. He had never before sought my assistance in the hours of darkness.

Paul usually unburdened himself in the morning, the story spilling out of his mouth faster than he could tell it.

My presence had often soothed the storm in the dawn light. But not during this night. The emperor wept like a child on my shoulder. I put my arm round him:

'Figaro, you have been a fine servant,' he said. 'When I am gone, you must put in a good word for me.'

We heard voices down the corridor. Paul shivered, the tassel of his nightcap shaking back and forth.

'Hide, Figaro. They are coming.'

He pushed me behind the tapestry. It was hide and seek, a game I did not resist. The emperor doused the candles and positioned himself behind the screen used when performing his bodily functions.

The noise grew louder. The door opened. A procession of flickering candles advanced. One might have thought it was a parade of monks engaged in chanting.

I heard Bennigsen's voice:

'He's not here. But the nest is still warm.'

I recognised another voice, that of Platon Zubov. Behind him stormed a number of drunken men. The moon broke from behind a cloud, luminously flooding the end of the room, lighting up the screen.

'I can see his damned feet,' shouted Bennigsen. 'Voilá!'

Confused shouting erupted. They all seemed to be yelling together, ranting meaningless abuse and shouting 'Arrest him, arrest him!'

Paul's thin and whining voice rose above the tumult:

'Arrest?' he said. 'Did someone say arrest?'

Platon Zubov delivered his own judgement, telling Paul he no longer remained emperor but was safe if he did not resist. Paul shouted a few words. Some ruffian (I believe it was Nikolai Zubov) slapped him round the face. More riff-raff came into the room, pushing, jostling, moving towards Paul. I heard the screen crash to the floor as they knocked it over. In the melee

Paul fell screaming to the floor.

The horde of hooligans fell on their prey like wolves on a stag, with the sounds of hitting and kicking, and groaning from the fallen emperor. At this point, though I did not see it, one of the Zubovs snatched the heavy snuffbox from the desk and smashed it into the victim's face.

Somebody else grasped the emperor's hair, banging his head against the floor. Others seized the gold sash from the bed and twisted it round the man's neck.

Gurgles merging with screams came from the imperial throat. Even as their prey moved into silence, they continued to beat him with feet and fists. Their task completed I heard a dragging sound as they pulled the body along by the sash, its arms splayed like a puppet.

Bennigsen shrieked a command. Someone, perhaps Bennigsen himself, threw the lifeless remains onto the bed with a loud thump. Another decided to light the candles in the room to illuminate the grisly scene.

They left, quieter than when they entered, slamming the door behind them. I heard chattering in the corridor outside, some laughing, another singing, then quiet.

I crept like a mouse from my hiding place behind the tapestry to stare at the emperor's ruined face, his left eye displaced from its socket, the infamous pug-nose broken by the force of the blow.

The front of the skull was disfigured, the tongue stuck out from the mouth like a hideous mask. The gold sash, of which its owner had been so proud, was wrapped tightly round the windpipe.

Fearful for my life, I returned to my chambers through the

secret door, gathered a few possessions together and put on my fur coat and hat.

I knew the Mikhailovsky as if I had built it. I eluded any guards and stray groups of conspirators quite easily.

Breathless, I hurried out into the bitter night.

I HAD CHOICES. I could perhaps take refuge with Madame Chevalier. But she had cleaved to Alexander. She knew more than was good for either of us.

So I turned back to Natasha. Running, stumbling, sliding, and tripping through the frozen streets, I eventually reached her house, chilled to the bone.

I pounded the door and pulled the bell a dozen times. I thought she might be away from home. Natasha took ages to come down. I began shouting. It was like waking the dead.

Finally a candle or two were lit in the upper window. She came down the stairs. I heard her footsteps.

'Who is it?' she shouted, from behind the barricade. 'At this time of night?'

'It is your husband! Kutaissov! Kutaissov! Let me in?'

Slowly the door opened. Just a crack at first. Natasha had a pistol in her hand. Muffled in my sumptuous best coat, hat askew, my face wrinkled with cold, I was an unfamiliar guest to be welcomed in the darkest hours.

'Natasha, it's me! Your husband!'

She looked up and down the street, the pistol cocked and raised.

'Well come in then,' she said, 'before you freeze to death!'

Just as I entered, the children came down the stairs. They rushed to hug me, Tatyana, as ever, being especially fond. Natasha sent them back to bed. They retreated slowly, waving as they went.

I took off my coat and hat in the hallway. We went through to the drawing room where the lamps were lit.

Natasha laid down the pistol. She poured out some vodka to bring life to my veins. I gulped back the precious liquid as if it were medicine for the soul.

The remnants of a fire still glowed. Natasha threw a few sticks onto the embers. As the wood was consumed with small flames, I warmed my hands, images of horror dancing among the shadows.

'The Emperor is no longer with us,' I said, my face still as cold as a corpse.

'The Emperor is dead?' said Natasha in a shocked voice.

'Dead and gone!' I said.

'How did he die?'

'I don't know. I can't tell you. It's too terrible.'

'But the Emperor *is* dead?'

'Dead for ever. It's all over.'

Natasha sat by the fire, staring into it, just as I was.

The death of a monarch is strangely shocking. The world shakes at its foundations. No solid ground remains. All is quicksand and uncertain. Especially in Russia.

I decided to spare her details of the emperor's death. Witnesses, or those with knowledge of witnesses, are dangerous to themselves and others.

'Are you involved?' she asked.

'Of course not!' I replied.

'They might think you had a part in it.'

'It would be a lie. Many lies are being told tonight. More will be told tomorrow.'

'Will they arrest you?' she said.

'I have my enemies.'

'But do you have friends?'

'I shall find out,' I said.

'If you are not involved, why should they arrest you?'

'These people don't need a reason. If they want to they will arrest me.'

Natasha was no fool. She saw the signs. She knew I was up to my neck in all this.

I never told her. Everything I had seen that night was locked till now in the private vaults of my memory.

NATASHA WAS A generous wife. In the middle of trouble she did not hold a grudge. That night she allowed me to sleep in her bed. Chastely, like brother and sister, we embraced, our bodies warm together. I slept a little until dreams of the emperor's broken face chased me into consciousness.

For several days Natasha and I lived as in our early days of marriage. I romped with the children, though they were getting too grown-up for much frivolity. They quite enjoyed discussing serious things such as my relationship with the emperor, personages of the court, etc.

I indulged and obliged them where possible. Often it was necessary to hold one's tongue and not spill the beans or answer their questions fully.

After four days the knock on the door came. Or rather

a series of hammer blows characteristic of a certain type of government official delivered at nine o'clock in the morning. That the call had not come at the crack of dawn was perhaps a propitious sign.

It was none other than Peter Obolyaninov, head of the secret committee, a pig of a man, with bloated cheeks and huge stomach, oozing a sense of importance. (I found out later he had been briefly arrested following Paul's demise but was deemed loyal, as indeed he was.)

Obolyaninov was outwardly courteous as such men sometimes are. He addressed me appropriately as 'Count Kutaissov' and shook my hand in a friendly manner.

His two companions were less prepossessing, more like well-muscled monkeys released from captivity.

'Your presence is required at the palace, Sir,' said Obolyaninov, after the polite formalities were concluded. Natasha was weeping into her handkerchief, the youngsters cried openly as if this was to be our final meeting.

In the carriage with my three companions I tried to find out what was happening. Their discourse was guarded.

'I take it,' said Obolyaninov, 'that you heard about the Emperor.'

'I did indeed. I am deeply sad.'

'I gather you were on leave from the palace at the time of his death.'

'Yes,' I replied. 'I did take some leave. But it was not official. There was illness in the family.'

'Illness?' Obolyaninov's eyebrows moved slightly. 'Your wife looked very well to me.'

'Ah, it was only a childhood ailment the boy suffered. I was originally a barber by profession. We were trained to deal with simple illnesses.'

'Yes, I have heard of your healing powers.'

One could never be sure whether such a comment was sarcasm or praise.

I let it go without comment for at that moment we were arriving outside Obolyaninov's headquarters.

INTERROGATION FOLLOWED OVER the next two hours. I was taken down endless steps into a cellar with clanging iron doors which obscured every sound of the outside world. One could have screamed to death in there in perfect privacy.

I sat on a steel chair opposite Obolyaninov's desk. He sat behind his desk. Behind me stood the two apes, their backs to the door, as still as statues.

'You were on leave from the Emperor's service when he died?' said Obolyaninov in his opening gambit.

'Yes. for a few days.'

'Yet you were seen in the Mikhailovsky Palace that day before the Emperor passed away?'

'That is true.'

'Were you not on duty during that night when he died?'

I paused. One never knew how much these people had been informed:

'I should have been. The message concerning my son's illness came to me in the evening.'

'Who brought the message?'

'The message was passed to me. I don't know who delivered it to the Mikhailovsky.'

'Perhaps we can find out.'

Obolyaninov hesitated. The apes shifted about behind me.

'Do these men have to stand in this way?' I said, pointing over my shoulder with my thumb. 'It is not polite.'

Obolyaninov laughed:

'Polite? That is not usually how their presence is described.'

'Am I to be considered under arrest?' I asked.

'Under arrest?' The man stopped as if to ponder a difficult philosophical question. 'These days we are all of us, one way or another, under arrest.'

'So I *am* under arrest?'

'For what crime would you say? Corruption, fraud, bribery, larceny, fiddling the accounts of the palace? I dare say we might find something along those lines if we put our minds to it.'

'I was the Emperor's Master of the Royal Household. I had no need to augment my income in that way.'

'I know what your position was in the court. Everybody knew. But not many people liked it. You have made many enemies.'

'I served His Majesty faithfully,' I replied.

'Indeed you did. Like a faithful dog. You carried out his every command. No one denies that.'

'Then why I am under arrest?'

'I never said you were. Unless you feel I should arrest you for some reason known to yourself.'

'I know of no such reason.'

'Well, it is a pity you were 'on leave' when your master died. Strange, isn't it, that on the very night our Emperor dies, you were absent from the palace?'

'I was called away. On urgent business. I was not to know the Emperor would die that night.'

'Of course not. Yet if you had been in attendance you might have been able to assist His Majesty. In view of your "medical expertise" you might even have been able to save his life.'

I could not see where this labyrinth was leading. Obolyaninov's art was to confuse his victims till they hardly knew what they were saying or why they had said it.

'Sir,' I replied, 'I do not know how the Emperor died. Or what disease has been diagnosed. I doubt if my presence in the bedchamber could have ensured his survival.'

Obolyaninov looked surprised:

'Count Kutaissov, have you not heard? The Emperor died of apoplexy. Simple apoplexy. I am not a doctor, and neither, sir, strictly speaking, are you. Yet we can agree that apoplexy is a common enough cause of death, can we not?'

The magnitude of the lie spread through the land appalled me. Obolyaninov surely knew the emperor had been murdered. Alexander knew, Bennigsen and the Zubovs knew. So did the ruffians who laid their brutal hands on his defenceless self.

But if the official verdict was apoplexy, there would be no arrests, no criminal charges, no trials, no verdicts of guilty. Obolyaninov was a dog barking up an empty tree. It was bluster, show, mere charade. The authorities were hiding the truth by a huge falsehood. Alexander was the new emperor, but his very assumption of the title was patricide.

The situation was volatile. In such an atmosphere a man could be swept away like a twig before an avalanche.

Whatever was happening with my so-called 'arrest', I was in the clear. Nothing could be laid at my door. Any appearance in court would risk the reputations and lives of all the conspirators.

I waited for what Obolyaninov really wanted to tell me. But first I cleared the air.

'Sir, you are telling me I am not under arrest!'

'Of course you are not. Why should you be?'

'I know of no reason why I should be in this room talking to you.'

'I am sorry to have to go through these procedures. But I have good news for you.'

'Good news? With our dear Emperor not yet buried? Have you no respect?'

Obolyaninov blinked a little, the tables having been turned:

'I apologise, my dear Count, for the phrase 'Good news'. Every cloud has a silver lining. That is said with respect to yourself and our nation.'

'Silver lining?'

'Indeed. The Emperor, now passed on (God rest his soul) has bequeathed to you in his will a small estate one hundred leagues from St Petersburg.'

'A small estate?' I whimpered, my voice failing me.

'Yes, and a stipend each year for the rest of your life.'

'That is generous. But what if I would like to continue working at court?'

Obolyaninov almost cut me off in mid-sentence:

'That is not possible. Emperor Alexander has no need of your services. You will leave St Petersburg after the funeral.'

He shook hands with me, bowed slightly, and dismissed his two disciples who slouched from the room, perhaps disappointed not to pay a different kind of attention to their visitor, banging the door noisily behind them, leaving the two of us in that awesome silence.

'I think I know where you were on that night,' said Obolyaninov when his companions had departed. 'But I have it on good authority you were nowhere to be found. That's good enough. You are a fortunate man, Kutaissov. Things could have been very different.'

BOLYANINOV ARRANGED FOR a carriage to take me back to Natasha.

During that short journey I was overcome by weeping. My master's tortured face would be my companion for some time to come.

PAUL'S OPEN COFFIN lay in state for a few days. Hundreds walked past his corpse, sobbing as if they had lost a friend. I joined the file, curious to see what he looked like.

The embalmers had done their work. He lay there in his best general's uniform pinned with many medals, the damaged eye and nose miraculously restored.

Looking at him you might really believe that natural apoplexy and not deliberate murder had carried him away.

The funeral was a strange affair. Alexander maintained a dignified military appearance. By his side was Pahlen, fawning and cringing. The other killers, Bennigsen and the Zubov brothers were in attendance, furtive smiles on their faces. I recognised one or two other conspirators.

At the burial, as is the custom, mourners threw coins into the grave, followed by symbolic fistfuls of dirt. Once religious ceremonies were completed and the former emperor laid to rest, Pahlen, now Alexander's Prime Minister, came up to talk:

'Count Kutaissov, I hear you are going into retirement. I wish you well.'

'Such is the rumour,' I replied.

'You are a fortunate man,' said Pahlen, in a phrase too reminiscent of Obolyaninov. 'Some will not be so lucky in the future.'

'At least I have clean hands,' I murmured.

'I don't know what you mean. You should be careful what you say.'

'We all need to be careful,' I said. 'Who knows what is round the corner for any of us?'

'The Emperor has much work to repair the damage of previous years. You must respect that.'

'I am sure, sir, you will assist His Majesty in every way.'

'Thank you for your confidence in me. I shall try my best.'

I did not shake his hand. His snake-like fingers were best left untouched.

P AHLEN DID NOT last long in the emperor's favour. By the middle of June he was in trouble. Dowager Empress Maria Feodorovna, Paul's grieving widow, set up an icon in her chapel. The text engraved on it, from the Book of Kings, read, *Had Zimri peace, who slew his master?* (Zimri, a soldier, murdered his King and reigned for seven days.)

Courtly tongues wagged. Pahlen wanted the icon removed. The dowager empress went to Gatchina, vowing never to enter St Petersburg while Pahlen was there. Pahlen resigned and moved to his estate in Courland. He never came back.

Panin, involved in the planning of the conspiracy from the first, was a hundred leagues away when the deed was done. He returned triumphantly to St Petersburg in his role as Vice-Chancellor, pleading innocence, worming his way, so they said, into the affections of the dowager empress.

But it could not endure. His guilt was soon out in the open. He departed in disgrace, forbidden to enter St Petersburg, living the rest of his wretched days on his estate at Dugino.

The curse of guilt spread like the plague. General Talytzin, in whose house the conspirators drank themselves into folly, died in May, Valerian Zubov passed into eternity two years later, Nicholai Zubov met his end soon after that.

Bennigsen, crafty fox that he was, lasted longer than any of them, being destined for military glory. His luck finally ran out in 1807 when Napoleon slaughtered 20,000 of General Bennigsen's soldiers at the battle of Friedland.

SOMEHOW, ONCE OBOLYANINOV had finished with me, I became forgotten as far as St Petersburg was concerned. This was a blessed condition in which to find oneself. My deceased emperor's Last Will and Testament provided me with a handsome estate, an annual stipend, and a generous endowment of several thousand roubles. Added to the amount I had accumulated, this made me a wealthy man.

I persuaded Natasha to forgive my previous wayward steps and to come with me to our new residence. It was not easy but even rich women admire security and prosperity.

We have hopes of marrying off Tatyana to a certain aristocrat whose land is no more than ten leagues from here. He has shown interest as any healthy man might in such a filly. She finds him attractive, a feature not always present in marriage.

Boris talks about becoming a soldier. I try hard to dissuade him. If he insists I could buy him a commission at Gatchina. Whatever he decides it will not (I think) be connected with the profession of barber.

I am reasonably content with my wealth, my livestock, fine horses, and a host of serfs to till my soil. I shall live here till I die.

M y testimony is written, with only a few slight untruths here and there. My health is not good. I have strange chest pains when I walk too far or too fast, my eyes cannot see as well as when I was a few years younger.

No matter. Life is stranger than death. Old age brings on memories of one's early life and occasional attacks of conscience which I never had before.

I see myself as a swimmer in rivers of corruption. Unlike poor Abdullah, I did not drown but floated among adverse currents to reach the far shore.

I cannot be blamed for surviving, especially in those unfortunate, tragic circumstances thrust upon me. I might have done better to remain a village barber. But that was not to be.

History may afford me a footnote or two, probably not of a pleasant kind.

Acknowledgements

Cover images from collection of
The State Hermitage Museum, St. Petersburg:

Patersson, Benjamin. *View of St. Michael's Castle from Connetable Square.* Russia, 1801. Inv. no. ERR-3332

Portrait of Paul I. Russia, late 18ᵀᴴ century. Inv. no. ERZh-583

Portrait of Count Ivan Kutaissov. Russia, late 18ᵀᴴ – early 19ᵀᴴ century. Inv. no. ERZh-295

I would like to express my gratitude for editorial advice generously provided by Chris Dell in England and Charles Postlewate of Texas.

I would also like to thank my wife, Sue, for her patience and wise assistance during the writing of the novel.

The author acknowledges his debt in the writing of this novel to the following historical publications:

K. Waliszewski, *Paul the First of Russia, The Son of Catherine the Great* (London: William Heinemann, 1913, re-published Miami: Hardpress, 2013)

E.M. Almedingen, *So Dark a Stream, A Study of the Emperor Paul I of Russia, 1754–1801* (London; Hutchinson, 1959)

Hugh Ragsdale, *Tsar Paul and the Question of Madness* (Westport, Connecticut: Greenwod Press, 1988)

Roderick E. McGrew, *Paul I of Russia, 1754–1801*
(Clarendon Press, Oxford, 1992)

Simon Sebag Montefiore, *The Romanovs 1613–1918*
(London: Weidenfeld and Nicolson, 2016)

Also by Graham Wade

BIOGRAPHICAL STUDIES

Profile of Federico Mompou (Naxos ebook, 2011)

Profile of Joaquín Turina (Naxos ebook, 2011)

Profile of Manuel de Falla (Naxos ebook, 2011)

Nombres Propios de la Guitarra: Julian Bream
(Córdoba Lecture, IMAE Gran Teatro &
Ayuntamiento de Córdoba, 2009)

The Art of Julian Bream (Ashley Mark, 2008)

Portrait of Rodrigo, His Life, His Music
(Naxos, 2008, with 86 page booklet by Graham Wade)

Francisco Tárrega (1852–1909)
(Stanley Yates & Graham Wade, Mel Bay, DVD, 2008)

Joaquín Rodrigo – A Life in Music (GRM Publications, 2006)

Gina Bachauer – A Pianist's Odyssey (GRM Publications, 1999)

John Mills, Concert Guitarist – A Celebration
(GRM Publications, 1997)

A New Look at Segovia, His Life, His Music, Vols 1 & 2
(with Gerard Garno, Mel Bay, 1996)

Maestro Segovia (Robson, 1986)

Segovia – a Celebration of the Man and his Music
(Allison & Busby, 1983)

CLASSICAL GUITAR PUBLICATIONS

Traditions of the Classical Guitar
(All World Classics, re-print from 1980 edition, 2012)

Classical Guitar – A Complete History (ed. John Morrish,
thirteen essays by Graham Wade, Balafon, 2002)

Distant Sarabandes – The Solo Guitar Music of Joaquín Rodrigo
(GRM Publications, 2nd Edition 2001)

A Concise History of the Classic Guitar (Mel Bay, 2001)

Guitar Teaching and Learning – Interpretation and Style
(University of Reading, 1998)

The Guitarist's Guide to Associated Board Examinations
(Graham Wade and Brian Jeffery, GRM Publications
& Tecla Editions, 1997)

The Guitarist's Guide to J.S. Bach (Wise Owl Music, 1985)

Joaquín Rodrigo – Concierto de Aranjuez (Mayflower Press, 1985)

Your Book of the Guitar (Faber 1980)

Graham Wade/ICS Guitar Course, Vols I & II
(International Correspondence Schools, 1972 & 1975)

GENERAL MUSIC PUBLICATIONS

A Concise Guide to Understanding Music (Mel Bay, 2003)

The Shape of Music (Allison & Busby, 1983)

NOVELS

The Emperor's Barber (The Choir Press, 2017)

The Fibonacci Confessions
(GRM Publications 2010, The Choir Press, re-published 2017)

POEMS

Aranjuez and Other Poems (In Remembrance of Joaquín Rodrigo)
(GRM Publications, 2016)

Goats in the Trees (and other Moroccan Poems),
(GRM Publications, 2015)

Daniel and the Lions (A performance poem for young people)
(GRM Publications, 2015)

Mother and Other Poems (GRM Publications, 2001)

Frog and Other Poems (GRM Publications, 2001)

War Baby and Other Poems (GRM Publications, 2000)

In Whim or Design (Denstone College, 1969)

TRANSLATIONS

Heitor Villa-Lobos and the Guitar, Turibio Santos (Translated and edited by Victoria Forde & Graham Wade, Wise Owl, 1985)

EDITIONS: EDITED BY ELIZABETH AND GRAHAM WADE, MEL BAY PAPERBACK SERIES

A Concise History of the Electric Guitar, Adrian Ingram
(Mel Bay, 2001)

A Concise Guide to Musical Terms, John Robert Brown
(Mel Bay, 2002)

A Concise History of Jazz, John Robert Brown (Mel Bay, 2004)

A Concise History of Rock, Paul Fowles (Mel Bay, 2009)

A Concise History of 20th Century Music, Graham Hearn
(Mel Bay, 2010)

A Concise Guide to Orchestral Music, 1700 to the Present Day,
David Fligg (Mel Bay, 2010)

Reviews and Comments

A New Look at Segovia, His Life, His Music, Volumes 1 & 2 (with Gerard Garno)

The most remarkable piece of classical guitar scholarship we are ever likely to see.
BRENDAN MCCORMACK,
INTERNATIONAL GUITAR FESTIVAL OF GREAT BRITAIN

Segovia – A Celebration of the Man and His Music

Graham Wade has spent a generous amount of time putting together this book in praise of 'my first' 90 years. My gratitude corresponds faithfully to his noble intention and the arduous work accomplished...I hope that this lively and affectionate book will be received with the appreciation and success it merits.
ANDRÉS SEGOVIA

Traditions of the Classical Guitar

Graham Wade has shown his love of the guitar from the first page to the last – true love and understanding.
ANDRÉS SEGOVIA

The most important recent publication of the last few years...The first stylistic critique of guitar music from the beginning through all the centuries.
JÜRGEN LIBBERT, NEUE MUSIKZEITSCHRIFT

Gina Bachauer – A Pianist's Odyssey

I treasure every page of this fascinating biography, a beautiful testimony of love and admiration of both the human being as well as the artist who has left us with so much to enrich our lives.
IRENE, PRINCESS OF GREECE

This book provides an excellent record of a unique life.
SIR EDWARD HEATH

I know of no biography of any pianist – not even the greatest in the world – whose life, both musical and personal, has been chronicled in such illuminating detail. No music lover in the world could fail to enjoy every page of this vivid story. JOAN CHISSELL

The Art of Julian Bream

Graham Wade is the ideal writer to undertake the task of writing a detailed book about the musical achievements of our most celebrated guitarist...This book is surely indispensable to anyone who values the work of Julian Bream...It comes off successfully, even triumphantly, and will be the definitive book on Julian Bream for a long time to come.

COLIN COOPER, CLASSICAL GUITAR

This eminently readable and quite fascinating book, superbly and generously illustrated, is most enthusiastically recommended.

ROBERT MATTHEW-WALKER,
INTERNATIONAL RECORD REVIEW

Joaquín Rodrigo – A Life in Music
(Travelling to Aranjuez 1901-1939)

My family and I believe that this is the book which needed to be written and that it will generate an enormous interest in both the music and the life of Joaquín Rodrigo. CECILIA RODRIGO,
MARQUESA DE LOS JARDINES DE ARANJUEZ

Author Graham Wade has become the composer's Boswell...Rodrigo's fascinating life story comes shining through...the Rodrigo lover's jackpot.
PHILIP CLARK, BOOK OF THE MONTH, CLASSIC FM MAGAZINE

This first biography of Rodrigo in English is further testament to Graham Wade's seemingly inexhaustible energies...a terrific tale...a revelatory read. ANDREW GREEN, CLASSICAL MUSIC

Enter the tireless author, teacher and guitarist, Graham Wade, to tell a story of even more tireless determination to succeed. And the music in all its unfamiliar range is the heart of Wade's mammoth undertaking, the first in English.   ROBERT MAYCOCK, BBC MUSIC

The Shape of Music

I know of no book like this on the subject of music: and apart from the wealth of information which it contains, it is every bit as absorbing as a work of popular general literature on any subject.
                                                              MALCOLM WILLIAMSON,
                                                    MASTER OF THE QUEEN'S MUSIC

Mother and Other Poems

Graham Wade's best are his tragic poems, which is rare for most incitements to pity by modern verse-writers are mere sentimentality...His poems have the true pathos of the soul.   KATHLEEN RAINE

The Fibonacci Confessions

It reads as if it could be a movie, fast, moving, exotic, lots of adventure – I really enjoyed everything I read, particularly the tenth letter, through the wilderness with Guillaume, and the sixth letter too in Egypt. Congratulations!
                                                        PROFESSOR BRIAN SWANN
                        (DEPARTMENT OF LITERATURE, COOPER UNION, NEW YORK)

This is an excellent book I would recommend to anyone. I was particularly struck by the form of your presentation of a twisting and turning story in letter form to re-create the life of Leonardo not only in his own words, but those of others closely involved in the plot as well... I envy you in completing every writer's dream!
                                      CHARLES POSTELWATE (GRANBURY, TEXAS)

A huge achievement. Impressively written. – stylish, assured, beautifully structured, not a word out of place. Very satisfying (and easy) to read. Triumphant prose. Wholly convincing in its exotic period flavour, elegant and sharply detailed. Poetic and sensuous.

Many congratulations on what is undoubtedly a stupendous achievement – it must be very fulfilling for you that the novel is born, after a gestation of fifteen years.

My abiding memory is that I have very much enjoyed the rich panorama, wonderfully detailed and evoked, of so many aspects of life in the 12TH/13TH Century, the unfolding excitement of the mathematical quest, the voyages, and the company of the enigmatic hero!

JOHN CARRINGTON (TAUNTON, DEVON)

Marvellous book. I congratulate you. You are obviously a master of the language. What impressed me was your ability to capture a style that seems of the period and yet you didn't revert to tricks in trying to imitate the language of the twelfth century. You did a wonderful job. It was fascinating.

PATRICK READ (SAN FRANCISCO)

I want to congratulate you for your fantastic research and for your fantasy. I didn't know that on top of guitarist, scholar, writer, and more, you are also a mathematician! CECILIA RODRIGO (MADRID)

This is an amazing book. You are drawn in and the characters are clearly visible. The writing is sumptuous and engulfs you in a richly embroidered Renaissance cloak. BRIAN JERVIS (GERMANY)